Margaret Bacon was brought up in the Yorkshire Dales, and educated at The Mount School, York and at Oxford. She taught history before her marriage to a Civil Engineer whose profession entailed much travel and frequent moves of house. Her first book, *Journey to Guyana*, was an account of two years spent in South America. Her subsequent books, including one children's novel, have all been fiction. She has two daughters and is now settled in Wiltshire.

Also by Margaret Bacon

Fiction

Going Down
The Episode
The Unentitled
Kitty
The Package
Snow in Winter
The Kingdom of the Rose
The Chain
The Serpent's Tooth

Non-Fiction

Journey to Guyana

For Children

A Packetful of Trouble

Other Women

Margaret Bacon

HEADLINE
REVIEW

First published in 1994
by HEADLINE BOOK PUBLISHING

First published in paperback in 1994
by HEADLINE BOOK PUBLISHING

A HEADLINE REVIEW paperback

10 9 8 7 6 5 4 3 2 1

ISBN 0 7472 4532 0

Printed and bound in Great Britain by
Cox & Wyman Ltd, Reading, Berks

HEADLINE BOOK PUBLISHING
A division of Hodder Headline PLC
338 Euston Road
London NW1 3BH

Other Women

Chapter One

Bill Anderson propped the *Daily News* ('*the English Daily with the largest circulation in Sri Lanka*') against the marmalade jar and read the report on the death of Grover Blackford. It was brief, briefer than Bill had expected, but then maybe, he reflected, the loss of one life seemed a small thing nowadays; on the same page was a report of six men being blown up in an ambushed lorry and another of fifteen people, mainly women and children, killed or injured when a train overturned on a railway line which was being repaired after a recent dynamite attack.

It was with evident relief that the paper reported that at least in Grover's case there was no suspicion of foul play: he had been on an expedition with his wife and three friends when he had fallen to his death. Moreover there was no question of the safety arrangements being inadequate. Most emphatically people must not be deterred from climbing the famous fortified rock of Sigiriya, one of the most fascinating places on this beautiful island which had so much to offer foreign tourists. Mr Blackford's death was very sad and inexplicable but it was undoubtedly accidental. It was nonetheless a great tragedy and the paper offered its condolences to everyone concerned, most especially to his widow, Mrs Corinne Blackford, and to his host, Mr Bill Anderson, a British engineer working here in Sri Lanka, and his friends, Mr and Mrs Matthew Portman, a headmaster and his wife, also visitors from England.

The episode was closed. Bill Anderson smiled and read the report for a second time, still smiling. It was all very satisfactory. He shook his head as he remembered the man, then put the paper aside and concentrated on his coffee. It was eight o'clock

1

and he had already been working out on the site for two hours. He was ready for his breakfast.

In Trillington, Surrey, Grover's widow cut out the report in *The Times* and filed it away. Bereavement had brought out the methodical in Corinne; she positively relished tidying away the last of her husband. She had two more letters of condolence to answer, but when she got them off, plus yet another letter to the solicitors, who never seemed to settle anything in a week if they could possibly do it in a month, she would book up her cruise and turn her mind to the jollier aspects of widowhood. She also was smiling.

In the headmaster's house at Masham School, near Oxford, Matthew Portman read the same report as he finished his breakfast. He did not read it out to his wife, who was sitting opposite to him, but left it folded back so that she could not fail to see it.

'I must be off, Becky,' he said. 'I want to see Parker before assembly. I'll leave the paper for you.'

He handed it to her, kissed her and left. He too was smiling.

Becky took the paper and went upstairs. She lay down on the unmade bed and read the account of Grover's death. She wept.

Chapter Two

'Don't go on a cruise, Mum,' Priscilla had said. 'Honestly, just because you're a widow now it doesn't mean that you've got to spend your holidays sitting around with a lot of old biddies in deck-chairs, looking at the sea. It's so *boring*.'

'They let you off sometimes to look at places.'

'Herded about and you've got no choice. Why don't you go somewhere *interesting*? Why not India or China or Egypt? I've got all my maps and things and—'

'If you think I'm tramping around the world with a pack on my back—'

'Of course not. You're far too old. But you're not old enough for a cruise. You're at an awkward age really,' she added judiciously, looking her mother up and down.

'What do you suggest, then?' Corinne asked, suddenly realising she was enjoying this reversal of roles, this being mothered by her daughter.

'Well, you can afford to stay in a proper hotel and not sleep rough, but still do your own thing. We stayed a week in a super houseboat in north India. Really luxurious. I mean it had a proper bed and everything. It cost about four pounds a day including food. We thought it was expensive, but for you it would be all right. And there was a proper loo, you know it *flushed*, and a shower. It was funny really because when you flushed the loo it went straight out into the lake and when you had a shower it came back over you.'

'Thank you, darling, but—'

Priscilla shook her head. 'Actually, I've just thought, it's no good. The weather was lovely in August, but it would be far too cold up there now. It would have to be southern India. Or maybe Egypt. Oh Mum, I've got it.'

Her face lit up. 'Listen,' she said, 'just think, if you go to Egypt you could sail down the Nile. That way you'd be getting your cruise, wouldn't you, only far more interesting than the sea. You can go to Luxor and Aswan and you could see the temples at Abu Simbel. I missed seeing them because it cost too much to fly and there wasn't enough time to cycle.'

'Would *you* like to come too? I mean if I postponed the holiday till the Easter vac?'

'No.' Her daughter was firm. 'We've agreed you're going away the minute I go back to college. And not less than three weeks mind, preferably a month. And you'll leave the keys with the agent and forget all about the bloody sale.'

'Well, I'd—'

'Right, that's settled. I'll go and hunt out the maps and guide books and we'll work out a route and then we'll go to the travel agent's and ask them to arrange all the flights and stuff. Let's have some more coffee before we start.'

She jumped up from the kitchen table, where they had been sitting over breakfast, and began noisily gathering up mugs, milk and coffee, rattling biscuits in tins, filling the kettle with much splashing. Then she stood by it, willing it to boil, and surveyed her mother critically.

'We can't have you turning into an old widow-woman wrapped in a shawl on board ship just because of what happened at Sigiriya, Mum,' she said. 'I mean you're still *young*-looking. Couldn't you make a start by getting rid of that boring little grey suit you've been living in recently? There's an amazing 1950s dress in the Oxfam shop for two pounds. You'd look stunning in it. It's not as if you'd gone grey and all your teeth had fallen out.'

'All right, you've made your point. You don't like the idea of the widow's cruise,' she had punned.

The little joke had fallen flat.

'The *crews*,' Priscilla had repeated, horrified. 'Mum, you're not thinking of getting off with sailors, are you? I mean do

4

widows miss sex all that much? And so soon?'

'Priscilla, really! I meant the other sort of cruise and I simply will not have you talking to me like that.'

'Oh, I see. Sorry. All the same, I shall worry about you. I mean, you've led a pretty sheltered life. I bet you've never even stayed at a hotel on your own, have you?'

She had tried to think of a time and couldn't. So instead she said again, 'I don't think you should talk like that. It's really no way for a girl to speak to her mother.'

Priscilla had laughed, of course. 'It's all right to make implications the other way round, isn't it, Mother dear? I notice that whenever some boring old government pamphlet about Aids comes through the letter box you just can't wait to thrust it in front of me.'

'Only because I'm concerned for you, darling. I don't want you taking any risks.'

'Well, I'm concerned for you, too. You're the only mother I've got. So I'll give you back one of your precious pamphlets before you go.'

And she had plonked the overflowing mug of coffee down on the table, spilling some in the process and said, 'Now drink that up and then we'll get down to organising this Egyptian holiday of yours.'

So really, Corinne reflected, it was entirely due to Priscilla that she was sitting here now, flying low over the desert, astonished by its variety. She had expected it to be endless sand, flat and boring, but there were hills in it and ridges like yellow snowdrifts with wide plains of sand between them, sometimes rippled like the seashore, sometimes rough and pock-marked, sometimes swept smooth as if polished by the wind.

It was evening. As she sat gazing out of the window, the sun was setting, throwing the shadow of the aeroplane on to the slope of a sandstone hill on her left so that another plane, dark and blurred at the edges, a tiny replica of their own, seemed to fly just ahead of them, leading them into Cairo, like a guide beckoning the way.

She still couldn't get over how easy it had been to arrange the holiday. It had not been thus when Grover was alive. He had always raised difficulties: it would either be too hot or too cold, or it would be out of season and deserted, or it would be in season and dreadfully crowded, or it wasn't the sort of place people went to nowadays, or it was too popular and full of hoi polloi with whom he dreaded to be confused. She had got into the habit when she combed through the travel brochures of thinking up arguments in advance to forestall the objections which Grover would undoubtedly raise. When they got there, wherever it was, they always quarrelled. The only advantage was that she had always been glad to get home.

All the same, she'd been a bit scared about coming alone. 'How about coming with me?' she'd asked her friend Paula, 'I can afford to pay for you, too. Don't be silly about the money.'

'It's not that. I can't leave Charles and Ian for so long. I mean, Ian's got A levels, you know.'

She knew it was nonsense; Paula's husband and son could perfectly well manage on their own. It was the money really. A pity, because she'd got lots of it now and would have liked to spend it on her friend. Grover had always been better at making money than using it; it was time she redressed the balance.

Her thoughts were interrupted by a crackling sound, followed by an announcement in Egyptian, and then in something resembling English which ended with 'Please to prepare for destruction', but couldn't have been since there was no reaction from any of the passengers. Then they flew low and touched down with a little bump followed by a tremendous roaring sound, as if a great battle of wills was being fought out on the runway between the forces of velocity and restraint, and they finally juddered to a halt.

The heat seemed to leap at her when she got off the plane, although it was already evening. The atmosphere in the airport buildings was stifling: she waited, hot and sticky, for her luggage, queued for an hour at immigration, and then again to change money. 'Is hot like summer,' the taxi driver told her.

'Today is high in nineties. Tomorrow is cooler on forecast. No problems.'

She was so relieved to hear this, she realised later, she gave him the equivalent of five pounds as a tip.

She had intended to have a meal. 'Buffet bar open all night,' the receptionist told her, smiling invitingly and indicating the dining room as she handed her the key to her room. But she was too tired. Perhaps, she thought miserably as she stood at last in her bedroom, the whole holiday was a mistake. Suddenly she felt very weary, very alone, very far from home.

She wandered across the room, touching things. Behind the curtain was a balcony. She pushed the door open and stepped outside, then stood still, amazed. Well, yes, she should have guessed; she was, after all, twenty-four floors up, but all the same the view was incredible. Below her lay the Nile, hardly moving, wide and serene in the moonlight, crossed by bridges whose traffic was reduced, at this distance, to lines of light which streaked the road with gold and orange. And over it hung a brilliant moon. The air up here was warm and gentle, almost tangible in its velvety smoothness. She felt she could lean against it.

In better spirits now she went back into the room and began to feel hungry. There was a refrigerator in one corner, 'room bar', they called it. She battled with the handle, discovered she had a key for it, and opened it up. She took out a packet of crisps and a bottle of lemonade. Two thoughts came to her as she lay on the bed. First that it was good not to have to worry about Grover emptying the fridge of all the hard liquor it contained, and then that she was really going to enjoy this holiday. This is better, she thought as she jabbed at the plastic bag with her nail file to get at the potato crisps. Certainly better than that place where she and Grover had spent their last boring holiday, tedium interrupted by rows, on some Greek island whose name escaped her, where Grover had spent most of his waking hours drinking vodka with an American businessman whom he referred to as the only other civilised chap on the island.

The crisps made her thirsty. She finished the lemonade and sought the refrigerator again, bringing out a carton of orange juice and a Mars bar. As she bit into it, it struck her that this was the kind of diet that Priscilla always lived on abroad: crisps and biscuits and bottles of fizz.

How she'd worried about her the first time she'd gone off backpacking. Sick with anxiety she'd been, not much reassured by airmail letters which revealed that Priscilla had strayed into the Sinai unaware that there was any trouble there, vaguely surprised at the number of abandoned houses. Apart from that, she always knew that Priscilla would edit out of her letters any information that she regarded as too alarming or just unsuitable for mothers.

She remembered the joy with which she had said to herself, 'She'll be home tomorrow, this time tomorrow she'll be home.' She had been preparing for a dinner party; Grover had invited two visiting American vice-chairmen of the company, plus their wives. She knew how edgy he would be; already he had spent hours tasting a great variety of wines, fussing on about the ice and putting the glasses in the refrigerator to cool, so there was no room in it for the puddings she'd cooked in advance. Serve him bloody right if she put his blessed claret in the fridge too, she had thought as she finished laying the dining-room table, rubbing up the best silver as she set each place, carrying the water-lilied napkins gently over from where she had created them on the sideboard, checking the salt cellars, all the usual bits and pieces. In the kitchen she had the canapés arranged on trays and the little ramekins of chocolate soufflé and wobbly crème caramels, ready to put into the fridge when Grover took the glasses out.

It wasn't yet five o'clock. She was pleased with herself for being in such good time; ample time to get ready before Grover came home at seven.

She heard the back door rattle, she heard footsteps in the hall. Surely he wasn't back early? No, she'd have heard the car. A burglar? She made herself go and look, then she stared in disbelief.

'Hello, Mum.'

Pack on back, skinny in her faded jeans and grubby T-shirt, face brown except where patches of pink showed through the peeling skin, hair wild, grinning all over, there stood Priscilla.

'Oh, darling, you're safely home.'

They rushed at each other. She feels thinner, Corinne had thought, clutching her tight, and taller, half a head taller than me now.

'You've grown, you great thing, you,' she said, hugging her. 'Oh, how lovely you're back early. You should have rung. I'd have met you somewhere.'

'I thought I'd give you a surprise.'

'You have.'

'Got a lift. Is there a cup of tea going? Oh, this is civilised.'

She heaved a great sigh as she dumped her pack on the kitchen floor and sank on to a chair.

'You're thinner,' Corinne said, filling the kettle.

'Couldn't afford to eat much, and got the trots most of the time. Gippy tummy, everyone gets it. Actually I think I've got amoebic dysentery,' she added, helping herself to a canapé.

'Those are for tonight,' her mother said, moving them away, but not before Priscilla had grabbed another one as the tray passed by. 'I'll get you something else.'

'Don't bother. I like these. Can I have one of those puds?'

'No. I'll get you some biscuits. Or how about a sandwich?'

'Mm, yes please.'

'Sorry there's no white bread,' Corinne remarked, busy now with cold ham and a carving knife. 'Only wholemeal.'

'That's all right, I like brown.'

'You *what*? You've always said you couldn't bear it.'

'Only because you said it was good for me. I liked it really.'

'You mean you've grown up now?' Corinne said, laughing as she put the sandwich in front of her. 'There are some letters for you. I was going to put them in your room.'

'Yes, that's right. I've grown up,' Priscilla confirmed, biting into the sandwich and looking at the mail. 'Mostly postcards. Gosh, my friends do get around, don't they? Peter's in Bolivia, Richard's in Russia, Ali's in China. I can't make out where Sara is. I'll read them later. What's this brown envelope then? Oh, exam results. I've got a First in political theory, would you believe?'

'Clever girl,' Corinne said, getting up and kissing her. 'Well done.'

'You won't expect me to get a First in the Finals now, will you?' Priscilla inquired anxiously.

'Of course not. I don't mind what you get as long as you do your best.'

'Dear old Mum. You see, the trouble is that your brain cells start dying from the age of seven, so I'll have a lot fewer in two years' time than I've got now. You do understand that, don't you?'

She looked around the kitchen suddenly and asked, 'Hey, who's all this posh nosh for? Is someone coming to supper?'

'Colleagues of your father's.'

'Oh, gawd.'

'Here's your tea,' Corinne said, putting the mug down on the table. 'And just leave those puddings alone,' she added, beginning to move them towards the sanctuary of the refrigerator. 'You're very brown, aren't you?'

'It's mostly dirt,' Priscilla told her, heaving the pack up on to the kitchen table and beginning to untie the cords.

'Not in here, *please*,' Corinne had begged. 'Not all over the cooking.'

'It's all right, I just want to get your present out. It's wrapped up in my clothes and things,' Priscilla explained, pulling out what seemed to be pieces of grey rag. 'Ah, here we are, safe inside the towel.'

'*Towel*? That's a towel?'

'Well, I did wash it. Twice. In the sea. It's hard to get a lather in salt water, that's the trouble.'

10

She pulled out a further tangle of garments; sand and grit trickled on to the table and thence to the floor.

'Priscilla. Please. Just take it all outside. OK? On to the lawn, or into the garage, but not in here. We'll see to it tomorrow.'

'All right, but I've got something else for you. Let me find it, then I promise I'll dump the rest.'

There was a clatter as sand-filled seashells and a few pebbles spilled out of the rucksack and more grit showered on to the floor. A few small stones followed.

'Bits of Abydos temple,' Priscilla explained. 'An Australian guy gave them to me. You shouldn't really take the antiquities but he said they were just lying around getting trodden on. Just think, four thousand years old! Oh, it was all *amazing* and so beautiful, you can't imagine. Look, it's here, in this bra, I remember now.'

From what looked like a piece of grey string with two circles of paler grey cloth, she extracted the necklace.

'Scarabs,' she said, 'very holy in Egypt.'

'It's lovely, darling. What's it made of?'

'Some green stuff they have there,' Priscilla told her, reaching up to put it round her mother's neck. 'Oh, the catch has broken. I'm afraid things aren't always very well made in the bazaar. Now where is your other present?'

She had the entire contents of the pack strewn around the kitchen table and floor before triumphantly saying, 'Ah, here it is, right at the bottom. I remember I put it there to pad my back where the frame digs in. Sorry it's a bit creased,' she added, pulling out a long yellow garment, soiled and crushed.

'It's a galabia and it could do with ironing,' she remarked. 'Shall I do it? You could wear it tonight?'

'No, thanks, darling, we'll see to it tomorrow. Now just dump all this lot in the garage, will you? *Now.* I'll bring you another cup of tea in the bath.'

She tried to lift the pack for her, when everything was replaced, but could not get it off the floor.

'It's heavy, Mum, leave it,' Priscilla said, swinging it up easily

11

on to her back and striding out, scrunching the grit and pebbles, the shells and sand underfoot as she went.

'Can I use your shower?' she asked when she came back in. 'It's better than the one in the bathroom.'

'No, sorry, I'll be in there. And actually you'd do better to soak in the bath. Get some of the dirt off.'

'Come and talk to me while I soak?'

'No time. Now just *go*.'

Priscilla laughed, and she heard her singing all the way upstairs as she herself set to with brush and dustpan to repair the ravaged kitchen. It was nearly half-past six.

'Hey, that's a nice dress you've got hanging up in your bedroom,' Priscilla called down. 'Is it new?'

'Yes, darling, got it specially for tonight.'

'Can I borrow it?'

'No.'

'I don't mean now. Just some time.'

'Still *no*.'

'Meanie.'

'Get into the bath before I come and beat you up,' Corinne shouted.

All the same, her heart was light with relief. She hadn't realised how worried she'd been, how heavy had been the weight of anxiety until it was lifted.

Grover looked at his daughter with disapproval. 'I thought you weren't coming back until tomorrow,' he said.

'Well, you see, I met this chap—'

Corinne, counting the plates, only half listened to the convoluted explanation which Grover interrupted with, 'Never mind all that. We agreed, as I understood it, that you'd ring from London tomorrow and we would meet you at the local station.'

'I wanted to give you a surprise,' Priscilla said, 'I thought you'd be pleased.'

Corinne ached for her. She had noticed the sudden trembling

12

of her lip, even if Grover hadn't. All the same, she understood what he felt. It mattered to him very much what the Americans thought. He wanted to impress them with his house and his garden, his car, his wife and his life-style. Part of her shared these concerns. But Priscilla's pain at not being welcomed home was of a different order of things.

Not that Priscilla let it show; she stared defiantly back at her father, returning hard look with hard look.

'Well, I expect you're tired and want to get off to bed,' he said.

'I'm not tired. I'm hungry,' Priscilla said. 'And I've had a bath so I don't smell and I'm quite fit to be in the company of others, so you needn't worry about offending your precious guests.'

'I've laid a place for you,' Corinne said quietly. 'Now just go upstairs and get dressed.'

'Well, we'll say no more about it,' Grover conceded. 'But next time just show a bit more consideration for your mother and don't come home without warning. You've been very thoughtless.'

'Oh, I have, have I?' Priscilla suddenly rounded on him. 'You're so bloody quick to condemn everybody else, aren't you? Why don't you take a critical look at yourself sometime?'

And she flung out of the kitchen, slamming the door behind her.

Grover made as if to follow.

'Leave it,' Corinne said. 'She's hurt and tired and hungry.'

'She'd better watch that tongue of hers this evening, that's all I can say.'

'If anyone has the knack of bringing out the worst in her, it's you. You never learn. Now for God's sake let me go up and put my dress on or I'll still be in my dressing gown when they arrive.'

Grover sighed, a man sorely tried by his womenfolk. 'That's all it would need,' he said. 'I work round the clock and come home to two females wandering round the house

13

in their dressing gowns, nothing ready—'

'Everything is ready.'

'And where are the glasses I specifically asked you to leave in the refrigerator?'

'I took them out to make room for the puddings. They're perfectly cool enough on the marble slab in the utility.'

'Then I'll go and shave. You'd better get ready too.'

'I *am* ready underneath,' she said. 'I've only got to put my dress on.'

She was half into the dress when she heard a roar from the bathroom.

'Just look!' Grover was flushed with fury.

Priscilla's dirty underwear, jeans and T-shirt were spread around the floor, something grey was soaking in the basin, and her father's bath towel, a big white one, was smeared with brown and grey stains and hanging over the side of the bath.

'I'll get you another towel,' Corinne said. 'And I'll soon clear this lot up.'

'She should be made to do it herself.'

'Not now,' Corinne said. How soon she had slipped back into the role of peacemaker.

'When I think that our guests might have come in here and found this slum—'

'I'd have checked first,' Corinne told him.

In the event, the guests were late, the chauffeur having lost the way due to an unacknowledged mistake in Grover's directions. It gave him time for three vodkas before they arrived. Corinne sat sipping a sherry and wishing he'd stop fidgeting, stop moving little dishes about, stop drumming his fingers on the arm of his chair.

It was a relief to them both when the doorbell rang. Grover had rushed to open it and greet his guests with his usual curious mixture of overbearing solicitude and suspicion, as if defying them to find fault.

They were quite ordinary friendly people, Corinne observed,

and wondered what he had made so much fuss about. The senior man, Garfold Benfetter, was a bit pompous maybe, talking in polysyllables with long pauses between sentences, as if he considered they might need time to catch up with his weighty thoughts. If there's any trouble with Priscilla, Corinne thought, it'll be because of that one; she placed her daughter alongside her, ready to intervene if necessary. But Priscilla had behaved exemplarily, helping to clear, bringing in courses, listening intelligently, saying not too much. All was going well; Grover would be soothed, she thought.

'Is it rum and vanilla that's in this chocolate mousse?' Mrs Hambling asked.

'Yes, that's all.'

'It's truly delicious.'

'As I was explaining,' Garfold Benfetter droned on, 'we envisage that the corporations will have joint control of overseas enterprises. Power-wise it will be a condominium.'

Then, turning to Priscilla, he repeated the word, pronouncing each syllable carefully, and said, 'For the sake of this young lady here, who is, perhaps, unacquainted with modern business terminology, I should explain that condominium means joint sovereignty, a sharing of power.'

Corinne thought of that First in political theory and glanced apprehensively at her daughter. Too late. Priscilla was gazing at Garfold Benfetter, wide-eyed. 'Really?' she sighed. 'And I always thought that it was a teeny, weeny contraceptive.'

There was silence, then all three women began to talk at once, Corinne dominating with, 'Just help me clear, Priscilla, then we'll bring in the cheese.'

In the kitchen, 'What possessed you?' she hissed. 'That was unforgivably rude.'

'Well, he is rather a pompous old fart, Mum.'

'And don't use words like that.'

'Oh, all right. God, that Stilton stinks. I can tell you, Egyptian drains don't pong half as badly as our dairy produce.'

'That's enough. Here, take these biscuits in, will you?'

'Your mother tells me you're a great little traveller,' Mrs Benfetter said kindly to Priscilla. 'I think it's just marvellous the way you kids get around nowadays. More than we ever got the chance to, isn't that so, Corinne? Wouldn't you say, Mildred?'

'Maybe we just didn't have the dough,' Mrs Hambling suggested.

'Oh, we all earn it,' Priscilla said, 'before we go. Some people earn their keep as they travel, but then often they forget to come back.'

'And how did you earn it?'

'Well, I stayed up at college at the end of term and worked as a cleaner.'

'Humph,' humphed Grover from the end of the table.

'What does that mean?' Priscilla inquired with extreme politeness.

Please God don't let them start, Corinne prayed.

'Just that when I consider the state in which you leave the bathroom and your bedroom I am amazed that any right-thinking person can employ you to clean anything.'

'Ah, but you don't *pay* her to clean at home,' Mrs Benfetter pointed out.

Bless you, thought Corinne.

'That's right,' Priscilla agreed. 'Then in the afternoon I painted pictures and sold them to the tourists and in the evening I worked in a bar and a restaurant.'

'That's great. Is that what all the English stoodents do?'

Priscilla shrugged. 'Oh, they do what they can. Some of the blokes take tourists out in punts on the river.'

'Like gondoliers? Isn't that just marvellous?'

'Well, they don't sing at them. They pretend they're university guides and make up any old rubbish.'

'Like what?'

'Well, like this. One guy I know pointed to a bush growing on the bank and he said, "That's the most famous tree in the whole of England. On that tree lived all the silk worms that

16

were made into Lady Diana's wedding dress." '

'And is that true?'

'Lord, no.'

'But they believed it.'

'He said American tourists will believe any old crap,' Priscilla informed her.

'Last year,' Corinne cut in wildly, 'Priscilla went to India.'

'Did you? Gee, that must have been fascinating.'

Maybe they hadn't heard. 'Saw the Taj Mahal, didn't you, darling?' Corinne babbled on, 'but found the crowds a bit too pressing, so many people always and—'

'Tell me,' Garfold Benfetter interrupted, 'how did you find the local population? Were they hostile to Westerners?'

'Oh, no, quite the reverse. When they weren't squeezing your tits they were pinching your bum.'

'Coffee, let's have coffee,' Corinne said, but it came out in a kind of squeal. 'Shall we go into the drawing room? We'll let you go now, Priscilla, you must be tired out.'

Priscilla yawned hugely. 'Yes,' she said, 'I *am*. I think I'll go up now. Goodnight.'

They all said goodnight and she left them. Corinne, her eyes still averted from Grover, sighed with relief.

'She's a lovely girl,' Mrs Benfetter said. 'She's so *natural*.'

'Yeah, that's what I like about her so much,' Mildred Hambling agreed.

'Well, about all the kids nowadays, they're so uninhibited. I mean, when we were their age we were so, well, inhibited, wouldn't you say so, Corinne?'

'Nobody could call Priscilla inhibited,' Corinne conceded.

Grover kept himself under control until they had gone, but only just. No sooner had the car door slammed behind them than he burst out, 'You'll have to do something about her, Corinne.'

She took a deep breath. 'What sort of a something?' she asked.

'I don't know. You're her mother. If she'd been a boy I'd have seen to her upbringing. But she's a girl and therefore your responsibility. That's always been understood.'

Corinne, who hadn't understood that there had been any such agreement, said, 'They seemed to like her, actually, just as she is. Mrs Benfetter told me she thought she was really cute.'

'That was very kind of her. God knows what they really thought. Anyway, I don't happen to enjoy being shown up like that before the Mrs Benfetters of this world.'

He was so mixed up in his views of the Americans he worked with, she thought, half despising them, half admiring. Worse still, he despised them for a certain directness, a simplicity which she liked, and he admired them for the ruthless materialism which she feared.

'Well, forget it for now,' she said. 'I'm just going to put the food away and go to bed. I'm too tired to do the dishes tonight.'

'I'll have a nightcap,' Grover said, emptying the remains of a bottle of vodka into a glass and following her into the kitchen.

Everything was cleared, wiped and immaculate. Priscilla had done all the washing up.

'Oh, bless her,' Corinne exclaimed, but Grover failed to say Amen.

Corinne blessed her daughter again now as she went and stood for a moment on her balcony, gazing out over Cairo, savouring the very air of the place. She was going to enjoy this holiday, she said to herself with sudden conviction, and she owed it entirely to her daughter.

In fact, she reflected as she went into her luxury bathroom and bent over the tub to turn on the taps, Priscilla had been a great support since Grover died. Water gushed out of the shower above her head and soaked her. She swore mildly as she struggled with knobs and gadgetry and finally managed to divert the flow into the bath.

Yes, she thought as she stood rubbing her hair on a towel, Priscilla had really grown up since her father died, helping and supporting in all sorts of ways. A real prop, she'd been.

She'd been nice about Grover too. 'He was a good father

really,' she had told her mother. 'I mean he always bought anything I needed when you told him to. And he's left you jolly well off.'

It wasn't heartless. He had always seen things in material terms; it was natural and fitting that it was in material terms that his daughter should judge him.

Chapter Three

'If you do nothing else in your one day in Cairo,' Priscilla had told her, 'just go to the museum. Forget the pyramids and sphinx and all that rot, just get yourself to the museum. The things there are quite out of this world, Mum, and not just the Tutankhamen treasures either.'

Corinne wasn't a great one for museums actually, but true to her new-found respect for her daughter's judgement, she climbed up the museum steps the next morning and entered the world of the First Dynasty. Dates always confused her, especially this business of counting backwards. 'Fourth millennium,' she said to herself, reading the guide book. 'That's three hundred years BC. That's amazing.' She walked on, stopped, looked again at the book. 'No, it isn't, it's three *thousand* BC.' She used her fingers to do some calculations. 'That's longer before Christ than we've had since,' she told herself, awestruck.

A crowd of people had entered the museum with her, but they were soon lost, dispersed in the vastness of the building. She wandered about, entranced by the incredible age of all the works around her. Yet there was a freshness about some of them, a feeling of here and now. Look at this woman hard at work crushing grain, kneeling to her task. And this man ploughing. Oh, and this woman cradling her child. Touched by the gentleness of her expression, Corinne stood in front of her and marvelled. How did they do it? Could that tender smile, a smile she had often seen on the faces of her women friends at home as they looked at their children, really have been carved out of cold, hard stone thousands of years ago, chipped out of granite that was already ancient even then?

She walked through the dim galleries in a daze. She wasn't given to contemplation, didn't have much sense of history, so it assailed her unexpectedly, this overwhelming feeling of awe. She began to understand Priscilla's enthusiasm, her impatience with Grover's preoccupation with ephemeral things. Maybe when she rounded on him sometimes with, 'Oh, what does it *matter*?' she had been bursting with frustration because her different perspective made him seem utterly incomprehensible. Maybe she had this sense too, that was growing in Corinne now, that everything that mattered was timeless.

She found herself standing in front of a hymn, written on papyrus, to Amen-re 1580 BC. So the need to worship, like the need to love, is timeless, she thought as she read the translation.

> Thou art the one maker of all things that are,
> The only maker of what has been.
> Who maketh herbage to nourish cattle
> Who sustaineth the fishes of the river
> And the birds of heaven.
> We adore thy will for thou didst make us;
> We bless thee because thou didst form us;
> We praise thee because thou hast cared for us.

She remembered singing similarly as a child. And no doubt Grover had, too, once he had become a pillar of the church. She smiled as she remembered. Poor Grover, the more he worshipped the mighty dollar, the more he seemed to need to bend his knee in public to the unmoneyed Son of Man, whom he would have thought of little consequence if he had met him at a party.

Did they do the same, she wondered as she moved among the statues of gods gilded by royal craftsmen? Did they make God in their own image, as Grover had done? For somehow he had contrived to make of that broken man, skewered and twisted on the cross, a respectable establishment figure like himself.

These thoughts were interrupted by a sudden urgent need for a lavatory. A vista of endless stone corridors, halls and galleries opening off, and a distant stairway lay ahead. She turned to ask a guide, but as she approached he sank to his knees and began to pray. Nonplussed, she made for the stairs. By lucky chance she found what she was seeking; a smiling lady beckoned her in, opened a lavatory door, wiped the seat and the pan, while she herself hopped impatiently up and down. Last of all the smiling lady delicately tore off a ration of two pieces of toilet paper and handed them to her like royalty bestowing medals. Blessedly she had a packet of tissues in her bag.

Afterwards, the woman turned on the taps for her, filled the basin, put the soap into her hands. She even refused to allow Corinne to pull out the plug. Smiling she offered a towel, simultaneously leading her to a hand-drying machine. It was then that Corinne realised that the smallest note in her bag was the equivalent of ten pounds. She hovered, hoping that the woman would be distracted but, still smiling, she had positioned herself strategically by the door.

'I'll get change,' Corinne told her in sign language.

It took her half an hour to go back to the entrance, leave the museum, find the shop that sold postcards, calculate how many to buy to make sure of getting small change, and find her way back through the galleries and up the stairs. The woman looked at her with surprise, with real pleasure. It was more than the money, her expression said, you took trouble for me. A message, an understanding, seemed to pass between them, without words.

It was a tiny thing, she knew, but it mattered to her. Grover would have told her not to be silly, all that fuss for the sake of about twenty pence, for goodness' sake. And she would have accepted his judgement that it was silly and not gone back and consequently felt badly about it. No more. She could assert her own priorities now.

She should have done so before, she told herself. Easy to

say, now that he was dead. When he'd been there, there had been something so massively powerful about his intolerance that there was no way she could have said to him, 'All right, it seems silly to you, but you must just accept that it matters to me.'

It was just as well, she realised, glancing at her watch, that she'd come upstairs; the treasures from Tutankhamen's tomb were up here and there were only two hours left until the museum closed. She'd give the rest of the ground floor a miss. Besides, she was beginning to flag.

The tiredness vanished at the sight of the treasures. She had imagined necklaces and brooches laid out in showcases; she was quite unprepared for the glittering array which filled these rooms, for the life-size statues, the gilded chariots and chests of beaten gold. All the necessities of life were there; everything this king could possibly want in the afterlife had been thought of, from the royal boat to a humble walking stick. There was even a board game to help to while away eternity. His royal innards were there too, wrapped in bandages, ready for the day when he would need them again and take them back into his mummified body.

She found herself standing in front of the throne, entranced. It wasn't the beauty of the gold and silver and precious stones, but the scene on the back panel which took her breath away, a simple picture of the young king and his bride. He was sitting down, relaxed, and she was bending towards him, touching him on his shoulder, handing him a little vase.

It was amazingly lifelike. Again the sense of timelessness assailed her; it could have been a young couple now, she thought as she sat down on a bench to look at them. Oh, yes, it was any young man and his wife, proud of each other, proud to be what they were to each other. She remembered that feeling, she remembered the first time she had heard Grover refer to her as his *wife*, on the second day of their honeymoon. And he had taken a picture of her standing under a tree and on the back he had written simply, 'My wife'. She had loved that monosyllable; it had seemed the most wonderful thing in the world to be called a *wife*. How the young would mock nowadays, she thought; nobody knew now if a couple was married or not, and didn't care either. But when she was young, it had been special, there had been married couples and The Rest. She had felt as if she had joined a sisterhood, belonged with the married ones. It had meant something and she had treasured it.

More fool her, she thought now. In the end, what had it meant, the little word *wife*? It hadn't meant helpmeet, companion, lover. Slowly, with the passing of the years, it took on a mildly pejorative sound: *the wife*, the one left at home, the appendage. It was a role bestowed on her by him and it had diminished her; her confidence grew less as his increased. He had promised to care for her, but it was she who did all the caring. What did he give in return? He had worked hard, yes, but he would have done that anyway. If only there had been the promised cherishing, the promised caring, let alone worshipping, the word *wife* might have kept its magic. But men have other priorities and work spreads and dominates, work which in Grover's case included absences abroad, expense-account dinners, meetings which were interesting but not really essential. How do you assert the claims of that little word *wife* against all that? Grover derived all his sense of importance from his work, she came to realise; he would have been as nothing without it. And the further he worked his way up in the business world, the more powerful he became, the weaker she seemed by comparison.

She had been ill-prepared to cope with him from the start really. She had moved straight from being a dependent daughter to being a dependent wife. Oh, there had been a brief spell in a job, but it was really only a time-filler. Her father's idea of educating a daughter had been to send her to a rather silly little private school conveniently situated near home, then to a genteel secretarial college where flower arranging and French conversation were optional extras he was glad to pay for, as he had told his friends. Nothing was too good for his daughter, he used to say. He was proud of her. He liked Grover, thought he was a man who would make his way in the world. He had been delighted to give her away in holy matrimony to such a man. His paternal duty done, he handed her over, inexperienced, untaught and vulnerable, to Grover Blackford.

So she had ceased to be a daughter and become a wife and, shortly afterwards, a mother. I was never anybody in my own right, she thought suddenly now, I always existed in relation to somebody else. But Grover wasn't defined by the fact that he was my husband or Priscilla's father. Not a bit. He just happened to be those things as well as himself. That's why he had been able to dominate, that was why she hadn't resisted better. That was why he had been able to hurt her, for she had had no weapons in those early years, apart from a kind of childish nagging. Then the final blow: not even to be special among women. That was the point at which she had realised that her love of the word *wife* had been mistaken.

The ridiculous thing was that it had all come out by mistake. They had been driving back from London after a dinner party, or rather she had been driving, Grover being well aware that he was over the limit. They had intended to stay the night in town, but the girl whom they had left in charge of the four-year-old Priscilla had said that she had to be at work by nine o'clock the next morning, so it had seemed simpler to go straight back home.

There was a surprising amount of traffic about still, and Grover was a bad passenger, irritable and edgy, constantly pointing out hazards that she had already seen. She hadn't enjoyed the dinner party much either; the head of Grover's section, a fat American in his late middle-age, was showing off his latest wife, a former model, baby-faced and sulky, with long fair hair tied back and wearing something bright blue with splits here and there designed to reveal the maximum amount of flesh. The other husbands paid homage to her obvious charms with ogling eyes and fatuous remarks, which their wives bore with varying degrees of strain on their faces.

'Very nice girl, Stella,' Grover remarked as she drove. 'There's a car parked by the lights.'

'I've seen it, thank you. Yes, she seemed friendly enough.'

'Lucky chap, old Leary.'

'Well named, too.'

'That remark is unworthy of you, Corinne. He is an excellent businessman and must be worth at least a billion dollars. Could buy the rest of us out.'

'Yes. Stella said she thought of him not so much as a husband as a hedge against inflation.'

'Oh, did she say that?' Grover had asked, deflated.

She had meant him to be. But it was true all the same. After the meal Stella had led the women into her bedroom, kicked off her shoes and lain down on the vast bed. The bedroom was palatial, hung with flounces and ornaments, carpeted with what felt like tufted angora, so deep that you lost your feet in it. Two bathrooms led off the bedroom, one with a sunken bath, all modern, and the other Victorian, mahogany-seated and gold-tapped. Stella encouraged them to prowl around and admire. 'Don't be jealous,' she said suddenly. 'There's not much to be jealous of really.'

Surprised by this unexpected frankness, they stopped admiring her surroundings and looked at her instead. It was then that she made the remark about not thinking of Leary as a husband, and she seemed suddenly childish and nicer; the other wives began to feel protective towards this girl, so pathetic did she now seem.

'But didn't you want a proper husband?' one of them asked. 'I mean, a girl like you of twenty-one—' for during dinner much stress had been laid on her age.

'I've had one "proper" husband, thank you,' Stella said. 'I married him when I was eighteen and much good did it do me. I stuck him a year. We had no money and two abortions. Not that I've ever had anything, mind. Not even married parents. And now I've got all this,' she said, indicating the vast room. 'And an impotent old man for a husband. Well, you can't have everything, can you?'

'I suppose you could always have a boyfriend?' someone suggested.

Stella shook her head. 'Not worth the risk,' she said. 'He could turn nasty, Leary could. He's got a very spiteful side to him.'

She went and sat in front of a dressing table the size of a small boat, and examined her profile from all angles in its triple mirror, then, scowling, began delicately to probe, with a scarlet fingernail, a minute pimple lurking in the fold of her left nostril.

'He tried sobe dreatment last year,' she said, speaking adenoidally as she pressed her finger against her nose. 'He'd read aboud dis doctor who dreated impodent men wid injections dey gabe demselves.'

'That's nice,' Corinne had put in, embarrassed.

Stella released the blemished nostril. 'Not really,' she said. 'He couldn't manage the needle either.'

They sat, the four wives on the bed, powdering noses, combing hair, all resentment gone now, eager to help.

'Perhaps he could get a nurse or doctor to inject him?' someone suggested.

'Yes, he must be rich enough to employ a whole army of medics to assist in his sex life.'

'Not much fun for Stella though.'

'Oh, I don't care either way,' Stella said. 'I'd sooner have scrambled eggs any time.'

Corinne had repeated this conversation with some relish to Grover as they drove.

'There's a pedestrian crossing coming up,' he said. 'Better change down.'

'I have seen the pedestrian crossing,' she told him sharply. 'And the elderly couple waiting to cross it. I hadn't actually planned to mow them down. It isn't the season for culling old age pensioners.'

'All right. I just thought you might not have noticed.'

'If I hadn't noticed it, that would mean I'm no more fit to drive than you are.'

'I'm perfectly fit to drive. It's just that I don't want some officious bobby, with nothing better to do, to come breathalysing me and taking away my licence.'

'It might have been simpler to drink less in the first place.'

'You can raise your lights now we're out of the built-up area.'

Corinne, who had been just about to do so, changed her mind and left them dipped.

'Ever thought of joining the firm's scheme for drying out executives?' she asked instead.

'I am not in need of drying out, Corinne, as you well know. Besides, when Jameson went away to be dried out he came back teetotal but addicted to smoking. Everyone knows that nicotine is more dangerous to a man's health than alcohol.'

'But less dangerous to other people's lives,' Corinne pointed out.

A car was coming towards them. Instinctively she moved the dipper, forgetting that the lights were already dipped, thereby dazzling the oncoming driver, who retaliated by turning his headlights full into her face. She swerved, but quickly regained control.

'For God's sake, Corinne,' Grover began.

She slowed down. 'Do you want to drive?' she asked, angry with herself as much as with him.

'No, but do try to be more careful.'

They drove in silence for a while. They were well into the country now. The road was familiar. Grover dozed off, began to snore. Corinne relaxed. She enjoyed night driving, liked the way the car followed its own beam of light into the darkness, round the corners. You could go faster, knowing there were no oncoming lights.

Grover woke with a start. 'It's still limited to sixty you know,' he said, 'even if there aren't any signs.'

She tensed immediately. 'Oh, go back to sleep,' she told him.

'I wasn't sleeping.'

'Then why were you snoring like a pig?'

'There's no need to be abusive. A man can't help snoring.'

'Especially if he's too fat. Thin men don't snore. I noticed you didn't worry much about your diet this evening.'

He sighed. 'Must you nag so?'

'It's for your own good. When the doctor gave you that diet, you asked me to help you keep to it, if you remember.'

'It's better to be overweight than anorexic.'

It was hopeless trying to argue with Grover.

'Well, all I can say is I'm fed up with thinking up slimming dishes for you,' she said. 'Messing about with steamed fish and braised chicken and grilled lean steak and salads.'

They were approaching a side road on the left. A van was waiting there, giving way to them. A car was approaching.

'And then the minute you're out of the house,' Corinne went on, 'you stuff yourself with expense account food, with goodness knows what in the way of rich sauces and cream and pastries and—'

'Look out,' Grover yelled. 'There's something coming out of that turning.'

Thinking he had seen something she had missed, she swerved violently over to the right and would have hit the oncoming car if its driver had not pulled off the road, bounded along the grass verge for a few yards, and then got himself back on to the road. Evidently he was so startled that it took him a few seconds to recover. Then he blasted his horn and shook his fist in the driving mirror before disappearing round the next corner.

Shaken, Corinne pulled into the side of the road and stopped.

'What did you yell like that for?' she demanded furiously. 'There was nothing there.'

'I thought you hadn't seen the van. I just caught sight of it and thought I'd better warn you.'

'If I hadn't seen the damned van, I shouldn't be fit to have a driving licence,' she said. 'I saw it way back, waiting for us to

30

pass. You nearly caused a very bad accident.' Suddenly her temper snapped. 'You're a menace,' she said. 'And stupid with it. How would you feel if you were driving and I pointed out every sign, every traffic signal, every car, every crossing? You'd go mad. And don't forget you took your test three times to my one. And anyway your reactions are slower than mine and you're much more aggressive about overtaking, or rather not letting other people overtake you.'

Grover was sitting speechless, which encouraged her to rage on.

'Don't you stop to think how distracting it is? How can anyone concentrate with you nagging and fussing away the whole time? You can bloody well drive yourself now. I've had enough. You've been foul the whole evening, slobbering away over that pathetic little Stella, swilling wine and overeating. God knows what you're like when you're abroad. And don't think I don't have a pretty shrewd idea of what you get up to there either. It would hardly be in character to spend your nights alone in your luxury hotels, would it?'

The odd thing was that she hadn't meant it. She was still thinking of boozing companions, but she saw his expression change, read plainly in his eyes what he thought she had guessed. The anger left her, something awful was happening inside her. Oh no, please no, not that. She took a grip on herself.

'Well?' she said quietly.

'How did you know?' he asked.

Since she hadn't known, that was impossible to answer.

'I've no intention of telling you,' she said. 'Wives always find out in the end.'

'Have you known for long?'

That was difficult too.

'Quite a while,' she said, hedging her bets. 'Maybe not the first few times,' she risked.

From his silence she knew that she'd guessed right.

'What do you intend to do about it?' he asked.

He was subdued. For once she had the upper hand. She chose

the way of dignity. She said in as queenly a manner as she could, 'We will discuss it in the morning. Now it is neither the time nor the place. And you will kindly refrain from making any more comments on my driving.'

Then she turned on the ignition and put the car into gear. Unfortunately it was the wrong gear and the car shot backwards into a tree.

Somehow in the days that followed, Grover contrived to make it seem that the wrong that he had done her had paled into insignificance in comparison with the damage she had done to his expensive car.

Somewhere in the distance a bell rang; it was telling them that the museum would close in fifteen minutes. She could still sit for a while looking at this young couple, the young king gazing fondly at his wife, and she could let herself remember that Grover had looked at her tenderly once, a million years or so ago. This couple was more real to her now than that dead love. Did the young king betray his wife? He had a locket of her hair buried with him in his tomb. Unless, of course, it was someone else's hair. Did this young queen suffer the pangs that she herself had suffered, the torment of sexual jealousy, the outrage, the disbelief? She could still remember the pain of it, the way her imagination tortured her if she gave it half a chance, which gradually she schooled herself not to do. But at first, before she toughened, it ran riot as she grieved for what he had destroyed. Because it wasn't just the present he had damaged, and the future; he had cast a shadow over the past, besmirched their early happiness, turned off the light. He had widowed his bride with his infidelity. That was the time she had felt truly bereft. His death now was only an official notification that she had lost the status of being his wife.

Now he had once more bestowed a status on her. He had made her his widow.

She thought about the word: *widow*. Maybe it should replace the word *housewife* on her passport? She smiled at the idea as she began to reflect on her widowhood. There would be no more false promises now; dead husbands don't let you down, not if they're well insured, anyway. No more jealousy, no more uncertainty, no more resentment, no more rows with a man who was impossible to argue with. It occurred to her now, with something akin to compassion, that perhaps poor Grover's brain had been educated beyond its capacity, and he therefore could use false arguments and ploys denied to the truly intelligent. On the other hand, being shrewd but not wise had given him strength, so maybe she needn't feel compassion. Rather it was her younger self who should be pitied, for she had been under-educated and could not cope with him; her mind had seen the falsity of his arguments, but she had lacked the means to counter them on his own terms.

She could see it all more clearly now, she realised as she got up and made for the stairs. Already she was beginning to wonder at the way she had let him get away with it, let him convince her that all his silly prejudices and whims actually mattered. How he had fussed on about trivia; as if the world would come to an end if the wine glasses were too warm or the plates too cool or she forgot to include his cummerbund when she packed his evening clothes. She smiled now as she remembered the self-righteous indignation with which he had pointed out that the junior members of staff couldn't be expected to dress correctly on these occasions if the seniors didn't set a perfect example. Worse still was the time she forgot to pack the suspenders that kept his evening socks from wrinkling round his fat ankles. But she hadn't laughed then. These were her wifely responsibilities, these were the rules she had been made to live by. They were not to be derided. And what of him? He had been a law unto himself. If asked, he would have said he had fulfilled his duties as a caring husband and father by providing for her and Priscilla. As for any lapses, like breaking a solemn vow, well they were but peccadilloes. How she hated that smug, convenient, foreign-sounding word so fashionable among politicians and businessmen. How typical of them that they had turned it into almost a word of praise.

She was free of all that now, she realised, as she left the cool of the museum and stepped out into the sunlight. She could do as she liked, free of his criticisms and of judgements based on values different from her own, but which she had somehow been persuaded to accept, uncomfortable though they had made her feel, ill-at-ease with herself. Even that tiny incident of getting money for the woman in the cloakroom had been an intimation of it; for she had been free to act according to her own lights, not his. Oh yes, Corinne thought as she walked out into the street, it was a far, far better thing to be Grover's widow than his wife.

Chapter Four

There were only eight English-speaking passengers who boarded the *Floating Pyramid* at Luxor. Corinne recognised some of them from the flight to Cairo. They were pale now and chastened by the early morning start, worried about not being allowed into the cabins until midday, anxious about the way their luggage was left unguarded on pavements and quays.

'It's all safe, no worry,' their guide, Mohamet, told them. 'You are in land of no theft. Relax and enjoy yourselves. Soon you will unpack and have lunch and then I will take you to the beautiful temple of Karnak. Ah, now he says you can go to your cabins.'

It was the first time, Corinne realised, that she had unpacked on holiday alone since she was married. Not only holidays, for she had travelled with Grover on business trips too when work required the presence of the wives. 'The Wives' had ladies' lunches arranged for them and outings organised. Indeed, if she had half a day on her own, which she longed for, Grover would ask anxiously what she intended to do with herself. How did he think she managed at home on her own when he was away, she used to wonder, if she couldn't cope with half a day alone in a strange city? No, in his eyes she was on these occasions an official wife and needed a minder.

Well, she didn't have a minder now, thank goodness, she thought as she viewed all the cupboards in her neat little cabin and realised she had them all to herself. And tonight she wouldn't need to stuff cotton wool in her ears to keep out the sound of his snoring, nor be woken in the small hours as he crashed about looking for the loo. She finished unpacking and lay on her bed luxuriating in being on her own, conscious of the space around her which she alone occupied. This is my space, she thought childishly, all mine. Nobody can impinge on it. I am free in it for always. The last time she had felt like this was the day she left school. A bit scared too, to be honest.

On her way to the dining room she explored the boat. There wasn't a great deal of it: two long corridors, one above the other, each with cabins on both sides. Hers was on the lower deck, where the gangplank and the little shop were. Above were the upper deck cabins and dining room, and above that a sun deck, which she didn't, for the moment, explore, knowing it would be grillingly hot. Altogether it was a compact and practical little vessel, like some small floating hotel, comfortable and unpretentious, two star, maybe, and not aspiring to more.

The English party had a table to themselves, a little Anglo-Saxon group in the centre of the dining room, surrounded by tables of French and Italian passengers.

'Like a little oasis in the sea, aren't we?' a grey-haired lady remarked as they sat down.

'Desert,' her husband corrected.

They were called Paste and came from Yorkshire where he was a builder. All this he explained to them, adding, 'I'm Charlie and she – ' indicating his wife who was struggling with spaghetti Bolognese – 'is called Patsy. Funny thing, names. I mean her parents were called Brown and they couldn't know when they christened her Patsy that she would marry someone called Paste. Otherwise they'd maybe have called her something different, mightn't they, Patsy?'

His wife nodded; a rope of spaghetti escaped from her mouth and rejoined the pile on her plate. She put down her fork. 'It's all right for Italians,' she said.

At the other end of the table sat Mrs Fortescue. Corinne sat to one side of her, opposite a Mr Anderson and a younger man called Cliff whom she took to be his son.

If Charlie Paste dominated the conversation at one end of the table, Mrs Fortescue held court at the other.

'I hope you don't mind my sitting at the head of the table,' she said graciously to Corinne. 'I do it instinctively, having chaired so many committees in my time. But now I'm having a break in order to give younger women a chance.'

She was tall, with white hair tinted blue, heavily made up and hard of eye. She was hard of hearing too, Corinne eventually realised.

'Where is your cabin?' she asked Corinne.

'On the lower deck, right at the end, on the left-hand side.'

'Of course, I'm on the *superior* deck. I find it important to have plenty of air.'

'Well, they're all air-conditioned.'

'And then I had a word with my nephew in the admiralty and he spoke to the captain who arranged for me to be on the port side, so I shan't have all the noise of the harbour at night. I shall look out over the water.'

'It doesn't seem very noisy.'

'I'm wintering in Cyprus with friends, actually,' Mrs Fortescue went on, 'and it was they who suggested that I might like to have a little break on the Nile for a week.'

Understandably, Corinne thought. If you were wintering with me I'd be pretty keen to pack you off somewhere for a week. She wondered if they were expected to sit in the same place at every meal. She'd much rather be down there with the Pastes, who struck her as being fun, and not at all the sort of people Grover would have approved of.

Mohamet appeared when they had reached the fruit course.

'Here is my plan for you,' he said. 'This afternoon I take you to the beautiful temple of Karnak. Ready please at half-past one for there is much to see. Tomorrow we start early for the Valley of the Kings, because it is very hot and many people come to it. We cross the Nile in another boat and then go by small coach.'

'What time is early?' the man next to Mrs Paste asked. Corinne hadn't caught his name, but had heard the woman next to him called Kate and assumed she was his wife.

Mohamet hesitated. 'You will be called at half-past five,' he said. 'Ah, I know you do not like that, but you will like it when you are already at the Valley of the Kings at eight o'clock before the sun burns.'

'He's very good, isn't he, the guide?' she who was called Kate remarked. 'Such good English, too.'

'And well informed,' the woman sitting next to her agreed. 'Somebody said he has a degree.'

'That's all very well,' Charlie Paste cut in, 'but we've got to watch it. You can overdo the sightseeing. We had friends, me and Patsy, came out the year before last. You remember, Gladys and Bert?'

Patsy, struggling with an orange the segments of which could not be persuaded from its skin, nodded.

'Bert said it was like a bloody floating university, their cruise was. Mind you, it was known for it, stuffed full of archaeologists and historians and that sort of thing. Non-stop hard work, he said. Every time they lowered the gangplank some professor came dancing up it and began to lecture at them.'

'But we do want to learn,' Kate pointed out.

'Oh, yes, don't get me wrong. Very fascinating the history of Egypt is. I've read it up a bit before we came, I can tell you. But all things in moderation. It's a holiday as well. But there are eight of us and only one of him, so no doubt we can make our views known.'

Corinne began to feel sorry for Mohamet. But she needn't have done, she realised as he shepherded them round the temples at Karnak that afternoon. He had been doing this for several years and was clearly unperturbed by the vagaries of his charges. He'd be a match for Charlie Paste, she reckoned.

Besides, they were all, including Charlie, overawed by the sheer size of the place and everything in it. They stood under massive doorways, dwarfed by pillars. They looked up at colossal statues whose knees were way up above their heads. They peered at the ninety-foot-high obelisk which sliced like an arrow into the fierce blue of the sky.

'Queen Hatshetsut ordered it to be cut out of a single piece of pink granite at the quarry at Aswan,' Mohamet told them. 'Then it was floated seventy miles down the river to this place.'

'It must have taken a lifetime,' Charlie said.

'No, the order was completed in seven months. Within that time it was erected here. As you can see, it is free of any support. It keeps its place only by its own weight and the fine grinding of the stone on its base.'

Charlie, Mohamet and Kate's husband then set about discussing how it had been erected. Patsy Paste kept well clear, believing that, since it wasn't properly planted into the ground, it might well get pushed over. Never mind that it had been there a few thousand years, she said, there's always a first time.

'Now I will show you the biggest hall of any temple in the world,' Mohamet told them. 'In area it is fifty thousand feet—'

'You could get twelve houses on that if you had planning permission,' Charlie interrupted. 'A site like this would cost quarter of a million where I come from. Prohibitive, the cost of building land is in England.'

The massive columns towered up into the clear blue sky and the afternoon sun blazed down where once the roof had been. Corinne sought the shadow of the pillars and even so cowered beneath the shade of the big coolie hat which Priscilla had brought back from India for her, as she tried to concentrate on what Mohamet was saying about the hieroglyphics which covered the walls. Afterwards he left them free to wander about; she would gladly have stayed in the relative cool of the colonnades, but Charlie insisted that the whole party should stand by the obelisk and have a group photograph taken.

'Oh, come away from that thing, do,' his wife exclaimed in sudden rebellion. 'It's not properly fixed.'

'You will see another obelisk soon at Luxor temple,' Mohamet said, trying to soothe her. 'Perhaps you will be more accustomed by then.'

'I think we must tell him,' Charlie said that evening to

Corinne who was sitting next to him, 'that one temple per day is enough, don't you agree?'

'But they were both lovely, weren't they?'

'I'm not saying I didn't enjoy it,' he told her. 'I can enjoy a temple with the best of them, but we like a bit of time to ourselves in the cabin in the afternoon, Patsy and me. I mean it's not much of a holiday if you can't have a bit of a lie-down with your own wife in your own cabin without some lecturer knocking on your port-hole.'

Corinne listened to him entranced, her pleasure increased by the knowledge that Grover would have thought him quite dreadful.

Mohamet came over to their table.

'The captain is going to welcome you,' he told them, nodding towards the end of the dining room, where a tiny little man had appeared.

'He's never in charge of the boat, is he?' Charlie asked, aghast. 'I mean how can he manage the steering, a little fellow like that?'

'No, he is in charge of the running of the boat. It is a kind of courtesy title.'

'Well, that's a relief. What's he on about?'

'He is introducing the crew, Nubians, to you. He is talking now to the French and Italian passengers, but next it will be to you. He is saying that afterwards the crew will entertain you with Nubian dances in national costume.'

'I hope they don't choose the sailors for their dancing prowess,' Charlie remarked heavily. 'I'd not like to think we was in the hands of a lot of ballet dancers if we was shipwrecked.'

'Sailing on the Nile is hardly dangerous at all,' Mohamet reassured him. 'You need have no fears.'

The crew was subdued, self-conscious even, as they began their dance, a somewhat repetitive affair in which they shuffled backwards and forwards, wriggling their hips and twisting their shoulders in time to the beating of the drum. Then they moved steadily forward, obviously intent on getting the passengers to join in. Corinne regretted sitting so near to the front, hating the idea of making an exhibition of herself even among these friendly amateurs who were trying so hard to please. A tall Nubian advanced towards her and she suddenly thought, if I refuse he won't realise it's because I'm middle-aged and rather shy and anyway out of practice. He'll think it's because I'm stand-offish, even racist. So she thought to hell with it and kicked off her shoes and joined in the shuffling and wriggling. Soon nearly everybody was on the floor, not dancing with anyone in particular, just bopping about, as Priscilla would have called it, in a friendly kind of way.

This is a bit different, she thought, shuffling and swaying, from the office dances of the past. She remembered the hours of sitting at their tables trying to communicate above the noise of the music, which seemed to be louder each year, the women's voices inaudible, however hard they strained, so that they gave up and just listened to the men, whose larynxes seemed better equipped to cope with twentieth-century official entertainment. Grover was meticulous about dancing with each of the wives, in turn. It was one of his rules. 'I always do the round of the table,' he would say in the voice of one who knows he has done his duty. 'The wives appreciate that.'

Corinne wondered sometimes if they did. He had a curious dancing movement, Grover had, thudding up and down vertically, rather than gliding horizontally like most people. It wouldn't have mattered in this sort of bopping, but the office functions leaned heavily on the waltz and other traditional ballroom dances. He was inclined to come down heavily on his partners' feet which, given his size and weight, caused pain. At least she had no cause to be jealous on the official occasions; a pillar of respectability, Grover was, at the office. He became a father-figure to his juniors as the years went by, a real family man with silver-framed photograph of his wife and daughter on his desk to prove it.

She slept well that night, exhausted after the long, hot day.

She awoke to what she thought was the buzzing of a mosquito but actually was a kind of humming instrument being sounded along the corridors to wake them up. Dawn was breaking. She looked out across the water. Wide and placid it lay, as if waiting for the sun to rouse it.

She was hungry, got up quickly, and went to the dining room. Only Mrs Fortescue was already installed. She tapped the chair next to her. 'You may sit here next to me,' she said.

Corinne sat.

'I cannot understand it,' Mrs Fortescue said. 'Someone appears to have turned the boat round in the night. Yesterday my cabin was facing out across the water, and this morning I looked out and I was opposite the bank.'

'Yes, you're right. I'm facing out now. I hadn't thought.'

'There were locals walking along the path. I shall complain.'

'Morning both,' Charlie appeared. 'Bright and early, are we? Well, so long as they don't make a habit of it.'

Mrs Fortescue looked at him as if restraining her contempt for lower mortals and did not reply.

He sat down heavily next to Corinne, his wife on the far side. 'Cheese for breakfast? Well, I never. I suppose there aren't any cornflakes?' he asked the waiter, who was pouring out coffee.

'No corn. We have rice.'

'Ah yes, then, I'll have Rice Krispies.'

He returned with a bowl of fried rice, which Charlie rejected in favour of a roll. The others drifted in, but it was early and the conversation desultory.

Mohamet met them on the ferry boat and took them across the river and was instantly assailed by Mrs Fortescue.

'Somebody turned the boat round in the night,' she accused.

'Excuse?'

'The boat. It was turned round in the night so that my cabin would be on the wrong side.'

'Ah yes. At night it always lies with the water current.'

'But the whole point of asking for a portside cabin was to

have the benefit of not being close to the harbour.'

'It won't matter. There is no noise from the bank.'

'There were natives on the footpath. I had to keep my curtains drawn. In all modesty I had to keep my curtains drawn.'

Silly old bat, Corinne thought, and then realised that she was beginning to speak the language of her daughter. Funny to think that Grover would probably have considered Mrs Fortescue the nearest thing to a lady on the boat, the other civilised one.

'Here the ancient Egyptians buried their dead kings,' Mohamet declaimed as they stood in a vast and desolate landscape, already grilled by the sun even at eight o'clock in the morning. 'Here, deep in these cliffs, they built their tombs so that they could sleep for ever, safe from robbers and undisturbed by the eyes of the curious.'

But it hadn't worked out like that, Corinne thought. Over the centuries the robbers had found their way in and now the curious were queuing up to have a look. From France and Italy, Holland and Belgium, Germany and England they came, organised in little groups, waiting their turn to see the tombs of the mighty Egyptian dead.

Once inside the tomb, Corinne forgot everything. The pictures which covered the walls and ceilings were as bright and fresh as if they were painted yesterday. And so real. This dead Pharoah being judged, for example: you could see that he was really anxious. Thousands of years ago the artist had given him that worried look and he had it still.

'He is answering detailed questions,' Mohamet was explaining, 'about whether he has sinned by stealing and murdering, blaspheming and committing adultery. If he has, he will be damned for ever, but if not then he will sail away to eternal bliss.'

'He'd be a fool not to deny everything,' Charlie pointed out. 'I mean, he had a lot at stake. Eternity's a long time, eternity is.'

'Look, you see there? They are weighing his heart against a

feather and if his heart is light enough to balance the feather then he is innocent and will have eternal life.'

'Quite right,' Charlie said. 'There'd have to be some way of checking up on him.'

In a trance, Corinne walked slowly down the tunnel which led to the tomb. It seemed to her like a magic cave whose walls were covered in paintings so vivid that she felt that if she reached out she could touch living flesh. Here were the women weeping for their dead lord, the tears still trembling on their cheeks, as if on the very point of falling. And this embalmer, busy for seventy days preparing the body, how tired he looked as he bent to his task, but how serene were the goddesses bearing the sun through the day and the moon through the hours of the night. The wicked were horribly in evidence, too: decapitated, hanging upside down, manacled in chains.

'They are paying for their sins,' Mohamet told them as they stood in the great tomb itself. 'Look on the walls and ceilings and on the sarcophagus: the judgement, the resurrection, the damned.'

'It's just like us,' Charlie exclaimed. 'However did they know?'

Corinne smiled vaguely, moved by the painting, not wanting to be distracted. How light this feather was: tawny-brown and fragile, and looking, even after all these years, as if had just fallen from a bird flying overhead. It twirled down, light enough to be taken up by their faintest breath and blown away. How did anyone paint like that, then or now?

It drew them together, the wonder of it. Even Kate's husband, whom Corinne had labelled as toffee-nosed, said, 'Marvellous, marvellous,' in awestruck tones, as if humbled by the perfection of this ancient art, or perhaps by the faith of these people who invested every skill, as well as all their material wealth, in the afterlife, so total was their belief in it.

They saw many tombs after that, tombs of queens and kings, of princes and nobles. And as they walked between them, the sun beat down on their heads and reflected up into their faces, as if the rock had absorbed the heat of ages and was throwing it back at them now. No air stirred. And Priscilla cycled in this, Corinne realised, and in August too. It would have killed me, she thought, a little in awe now of her rebellious daughter.

She had fallen behind the others, partly because she couldn't hurry, but also because she wanted to walk alone, still lost in the wonder of the paintings, remembering the freshness of them, the clarity of their colours. She saw again in her mind's eye the tears which had rested on the cheeks of the mourning woman as if at that moment they might quiver and fall. She felt again the lightness of that feather and the weight of the sarcophagus as the men strained at the ropes which pulled it. If she looked long enough, would she ever understand the secret of how it was done?

She remembered thinking the same thing years ago; as a schoolgirl she used to spend a lot of time in art galleries. She'd always liked looking at pictures better than reading books. She had worked it out that you had to be clever to understand books, whereas pictures came to you direct, bypassing the brain which, she had always assumed, was in her case rather small. Anyway, art had been the only subject that she'd been any good at when she'd been at school. Her teacher had thought she might go in for it. But her father had reacted to the idea of art school as if she had suggested enrolling in a brothel, so nothing had come of it. It had been stupid of her, she thought now, not to put up more of a fight. Priscilla would have done.

Back on board the boat, she was restless, unsettled by the paintings. When the others went to their cabins after lunch, she made her way up to the top deck, found a corner of shade at the far end, and gazed at the countryside as it slipped by, for they had set sail now and were moving gently upstream towards Aswan. The river-bank was fringed with strips of flat land, cultivated where the silt had laid down soil, tilled in furrows, the ridges topped with little screens of reeds to shade the vegetables from the sun.

Corinne found herself looking at it all with an assessing eye, trying to see how it could be shaped into a picture. The ridiculous thing was that she didn't really want to; she just wanted to sit and enjoy the scenery. She needn't feel obliged to do anything about it, she thought irritably. Besides, she told herself, it was absurd even to try at her age when she didn't have the skill. Then suddenly she jumped up and went to her cabin, returning with pencils and sketch-pad. Priscilla had insisted on lending her paints and brushes and sketching things. 'You know I get the drawing bit from you, Mum,' she had said. 'You ought to take it up again.'

It was as if something that had been building up in her since she first arrived in Egypt couldn't be held down any longer. It had begun that first day when she stood in the museum, bewildered by the way that such ancient art could move her. And in the tombs she had felt it even more strongly, the wonder of the way these painters spoke so clearly to her across the centuries. They had set down what they had seen and the truth of it had lasted for ever. Could it really be as simple as that? Whatever it was, she needed somehow or other to be a part of it now.

She began sketching scene after scene on the bank, frantically covering the pages, hardly thinking what she was doing, engrossed in the detail, in problems such as how to show the most imperceptible ripple of water behind a drifting felucca, or convey that protective look of the reeds as they leant over the tender green plants. From the bank to the paper her eyes moved, backwards and forwards, oblivious of everything else. Sugar-cane was being cut here, where the strip of land widened, and carried in bundles so huge that they hid the men beneath. How do you show that the cane is a burden and that a man is carrying it, even though you can't even see him?

In the fields that had already been harvested, flames flickered yellow and orange where the stubble had been set alight. Tongues of fire darted unpredictably across the fields like fireflies, while the air between them shimmered in the heat and thin wisps of smoke twisted and curled as they rose into the darkening sky.

For the light was fading now; the setting sun had cast the river-bank into shadow. Beyond it the sand had turned almost purple under the strange evening sky. It was rippled like the sea, this stretch of desert: yes, that was it, it looked at once fluid and rock-like, as if caught on the turn and abruptly frozen, she thought as she tried to sketch this petrified ocean of sand.

Then even that became too dark, and only the tops of the mountains were still lit by the western sun. Range after range, they seemed to stride along parallel to the river; huge exotic shapes, jagged and geometric, some like pyramids, some like massive statues lying on their backs, some like temples, so that she could hardly believe, as she tried to draw them, that they were natural formations, so much did they resemble the works of man which she had seen at Karnak and Luxor. Yes, she thought, as she sat back at last, suddenly weary, you could really believe that they were wrought by the same hand.

Now it was too dark to draw, but still she stayed, mesmerised by the beauty of the evening, the softness of the air, the gentle gliding of the boat, which slipped between the banks so smoothly that it seemed as if the land was moving and they were stationary upon the water.

She felt strangely relaxed, as if drained by the frantic efforts she had been making to try to find the skill to set down what she saw. The restlessness had left her, she was content to lie back, feel the air soft against her face; grateful to be allowed to sit here and enjoy the peace of the evening. Grover would have carted her off to the bar to sit in some stuffy, smoke-filled room making conversation. 'Time for a drink,' he would have said, and she would have obeyed like a child at school, because it was on the timetable.

'Getting too dark to sketch, isn't it?' a voice said. She jumped and turned. She had thought she was alone up here.

'Oh, hello.'

It was Kate's husband.

'I'm sorry if I startled you,' he said, sitting down alongside her. 'I've been drawing too. I thought you'd seen me. But it's too dark now. I like that one – or do you hate people to look at your work? I loathe it myself, when they do, so perhaps—'

'No, I don't mind. I'm not good enough to mind,' she said.

She let him look at the pad; he turned it to catch the last of the light. 'But they're good,' he said. 'I like the one with the village. We passed it back there on the east bank, didn't we?'

'Did we? Well, it was that side,' she said, pointing.

'You've caught it, the way the women looked up from their washing. And the children, too, they're very good.'

'Thank you. Can I see yours?'

'Oh, mine aren't of people. I can't do figures at all. I've been sketching the temples we saw yesterday. I did a few quick sketches there and I've got some postcards and so on.'

Looking at them, she was taken aback. 'But they're professional,' she said. 'Even I can see that.'

He smiled. 'Well, I'm an architect,' he said, 'so I'm used to drawings, but I'm afraid I'm hopeless with anything other than buildings. I might have a go at this landscape though. Have you noticed how architectural it is?'

'Yes, the shapes of the mountains – I was noticing as we sailed.'

'It makes you realise, doesn't it, why they built as they did? The pyramids and temples and those colossal statues, they just had to build like that or they'd have been outclassed by nature's works all around them.'

'I hadn't thought of that.'

'I have a theory,' he said, 'that people have always built in scale to their surroundings. You know, the English built small churches in their little valleys and—'

'But nowadays,' she interrupted, 'don't architects just plonk things down off the drawing-board regardless? Oh, I'm sorry. I mean I'm sure *you* don't,' she added, floundering.

'That's all right,' he said. 'Architects are in the doghouse nowadays, we all realise that.'

'Does your wife draw?' she asked to change the conversation.

'My wife?'

'Yes, I mean . . .'

She'd assumed that Kate was his wife. Maybe just a girlfriend. You never knew nowadays.

'I'm on my own,' he said. 'In the other single cabin, next to Mrs Fortescue.'

'Oh, on the wrong side, but on the superior level,' she said, laughing to get away from the subject of Kate.

'What a fuss she makes. And anyway, it makes no difference at all which deck you're on, and there's no noise from the shore, and we're hardly in our cabins anyway. Actually, I thought she was your mother at first when I saw you sitting together.'

'No! I just got landed with her at meal-times.'

'I kept clear, I'm afraid. Who did you think my wife was? Which one?'

'Kate. At least I think she's called Kate, the one you were sitting next to?'

'There's Kate and Karen and they work together in London in an office. I'm not actually quite sure which way round the names are.'

'I'm sorry I married you off to one of them.'

'Don't be sorry. We're all guessing about each other, aren't we? I know you're called Corinne Blackford and, in case you don't know, my name's Bernard Coates and I live in London. I think I've just about sorted everyone else out now.'

'Tell me. There's Mr and Mrs Paste – they're easy. And Mrs Fortescue, and the father and son—'

'Wrong. He's called Mr Anderson and the younger chap is Cliff something, but not Anderson, no relation. But they are together.'

'Thanks. That's saved me another embarrassing mistake.'

'I tell you I wasn't embarrassed. I did have a wife once, but she preferred somebody else so she left me two years ago.'

'I'm sorry.'

'Not your fault,' he said lightly. 'And you?'

'I'm a widow,' she said. It was the first time she had heard herself say the word. 'My wife', Grover had said all those years ago. 'His widow', she was saying now.

'Well, that's all of us sorted out. We're a mixed bag, aren't we?'

'Pretty varied. I like that. It's fun. And Mohamet keeps us all well under control, doesn't he? Rounds us up, puts us on boats and buses.'

'Gets Charlie round the temples . . .'

'But even he won't turn the boat round again for Mrs Fortescue.'

They laughed and talked and that evening sat next to each other at supper.

Patsy was missing.

'The curse of Tutankhamen,' Charlie said. 'Gippy tummy. She's got it both ends.'

Kate offered tablets, Karen offered cream crackers and they all offered sympathy.

'Very kind of you,' Charlie said, 'but we've brought our own medicaments and I don't think she's in any state to touch confectionery. Thanks all the same.'

The next day Karen was missing, the following day it was Kate's turn, but by then Patsy was back.

'Ten little nigger boys,' Charlie said at lunch-time. 'You'll see, it'll be all of you in turn. I'm all right. Nothing upsets my stomach. What's this we're eating now, anyway?'

It was hard to analyse; lumps of brown meat in a reddish-brown sauce, interspersed with chunks of some fibrous root vegetable.

'Lancashire hot-pot, maybe,' Charlie said. 'Or the local equivalent.' He was good at finding equivalents of things at home. 'They could be slag-heaps,' he said that afternoon, catching sight of sandbanks against the skyline as they sailed towards Edfu to see the temple. 'Only yellow, of course.'

'I think,' Corinne remarked at supper that night, 'that Edfu was the most beautiful temple we've seen.'

'Well, that's as maybe,' Charlie said. 'But one temple gets to be very like another.'

'Oh, no, Charlie,' she demurred. 'They're all of different periods. Edfu was—'

'Oh, I grant you they had their Pharoahs and their Rameseses and their Pot-thingummies, but the whole point is that they didn't change their ways in all that time. Not for thousands of years they didn't. And once they got the hang of their sign-writing, they just kept on doing it. I mean, every time you look at a wall, it's covered in birds or fishes or some of them cartouches. Not a spare inch anywhere. Show the ancient Egyptians a bit of flat granite or sandstone and they had to set about it, scribble, scribble, scribble, chip, chip, chip.'

'But, Charlie, think of the craftsmanship, and of the height they were working at, and the carving is so precise and—'

'I don't deny it. I'm just saying that, when you've seen one linear yard of hieroglyphics, you've seen the lot.'

'But,' Kate put in, 'it's only because we don't understand it that it all looks the same. I mean, our newspaper columns would look pretty well the same to someone who couldn't read. Some of those hieroglyphics were calendars, some describe mummification—'

'Ah, now, I've read a bit about how they mummified people,' Charlie interrupted. 'Now that really is very interesting. They took their brains out to start off with, pulled them with a hook down through their nostrils. Must have come out like string.'

'They couldn't have,' Patsy objected. 'Their eyes would have got in the way.'

'Well, maybe their brains was differently located in them days. You have to allow for evolution. Near their jaw, their brain might have been.'

'I doubt it, Charlie, I really do,' Patsy said. 'It might have got bitten.'

'I'm only making a suggestion. I just meant that everything in their heads might have been differently arranged from what we are.'

'It looked in the drawings as if they only had one eye,' Patsy conceded.

'Well, they're sideways on, that's why. They only knew how to draw in profile. That's why they look as if they've only got one breast.'

'They did, didn't they, only have one breast? The women, I mean.'

'No, that was the Amazons, Patsy. Mind you, same sort of thing, river-dwellers.'

The next day they saw mummified crocodiles behind a grille in Komombo temple.

'It would be difficult to get a crocodile's brain down its nostrils,' Patsy pointed out. 'Think of the distance.'

'Possibly crocodiles don't have much brain,' Charlie said.

He took the subject up again on the way back. 'Many people think,' he said, 'that it was just people that got mummified, but that's not the case. I read all about it in this book. They'd mummify anything, the Egyptians would. Crocs, rams, even rodents and birds, it was all the same to them. You name it, the Egyptians mummified it.'

He sighed and then said, 'I'll tell you something else. I'm fed up to here with temples. It'll make a really nice change to see the quarry and the dam at Aswan tomorrow. That's more the sort of thing that appeals to me: something useful. I mean you couldn't call a temple *functional*, could you?'

'It is entirely due to this dam,' Mohamet told them, addressing them from the front of the little bus as they drove out of Aswan town, 'that we have no fear of drought. Think how fortunate we are compared to other African states, suffering such bad times now without rain. We have enough water in the Lake Nasser to keep us for four years in supply. We are very grateful for this and compare our fortunate lot with those other starving countries. You may get down now and inspect the high dam.'

She strolled with Bernard across the road and gazed out over the dam at the lake beyond.

'I can hardly believe we're actually standing here,' he said. 'What a parochial view we took of all this at the time of Suez.'

She was puzzled, not sure what he was on about.

'How old are you?' he asked.

'Forty-two,' she said, surprised.

'I'm sorry, I didn't mean to be rude. I was just thinking of the past. I'm forty-five, and that three years makes such a difference when you're still children. I mean, I was old enough to understand something of what was going on. I had a much older cousin in the sixth-form at school, and I remember how he and his friends used to talk about what they would do if they were called upon to fight in an unjust war. So you see, my generation cared a lot about it.'

Taken aback because she had thought he was much younger than she was, Corinne didn't reply. Then she made herself think about what he had said.

'Yes, it's true. I wasn't concerned. But my husband – my *late* husband,' she corrected herself with some satisfaction, 'spoke of it sometimes. He was very much in favour of it. He said we should have bombed the living daylights out of them. I can't remember why.'

Bernard didn't reply at first, then said, 'Well, there was a lot of rabble-rousing in the press. Eden was neurotic and wanted to play Churchill. Funny how all second-rate people seem to want to pretend they're Churchill. He never needed to be anyone except himself. So Nasser had to be cast as Hitler, which was nonsense. He was just a very nationalistic, patriotic leader, obsessed with this scheme to save his country by giving it a reliable water-supply instead of depending on the chance flooding of the Nile. Time has shown how right he was.'

They looked at the upper end of the lake which reached three hundred miles to the south.

'I think they're remarkably unembittered towards us,' he went on. 'I don't think I'd be so charitable if they'd bombed us.'

'Did we bomb them?'

'Yes, without warning. In fact they trusted us so much that they even guided the planes in.'

Grover would probably have thought that rather clever of us, Corinne reflected; he was always on about the surprise element.

'Shall we go and look at it more closely?'

'No, you go. I'll stay here. It's nice sitting in the shade.'

He laughed. 'All right,' he said, and left her.

Frankly, to Corinne, it was just a lot of concrete and water. She settled herself more comfortably, pulled her coolie hat forward to shade more of her face, and gazed out over the lake. So he was forty-five, that really was surprising. He looked younger. Much, much younger than Grover. Weight makes a lot of difference. And he had one of those faces that stays young, thoughtful but unlined, fresh-complexioned. It was a firm face, the features clear-cut. In profile it reminded her of somebody. She tried to think who it was. No, it was a picture. That was it. When she was at school, the art teacher used to talk to them about her favourite paintings and show them slides. One of them was this Doge by Bellini. He was older than Bernard, but had the same kind of clear-cut look. A face of integrity, the art mistress had said. The sort of face you could trust.

Trust. They'd have had different views about that, Grover and Bernard. They probably wouldn't have liked each other much. Of course, Grover didn't trust anyone ever. He was deeply suspicious of the world. It suddenly occurred to her that perhaps that was because he was untrustworthy himself. They had had a fearful row about it once. Well, they'd had rows about a lot of things, but this one stuck in her mind because it involved Priscilla's godparents and she was very fond of them both.

She'd been surprised when Grover suggested that Bob and Marion should be Priscilla's godparents. Bob was Grover's boss at the time. He had done a lot for Grover, and she knew that the main reason Grover wanted them as Priscilla's godparents was to strengthen the business bond. She'd really rather have had an old school-friend, but she'd agreed and in the end had come to like both godparents very much.

Marion was older than she was, had three children already at school, gave her good advice on how to care for the baby, was always reassuring, like an older sister she had been to Corinne, who was an only child.

'You'll be more relaxed with the next one,' she had said. 'It gets easier.'

But they didn't have a next one. It didn't happen; she'd been going to do something about it when Priscilla was four, but then she had found out about Grover and the women abroad and somehow, after that, although they patched things up and he had promised, falsely as it turned out, to mend his ways, she somehow didn't want any more of his children. He hadn't insisted. In fact, he had said it was better to give one child everything than to stint two.

They hadn't seen much of Marion and Bob after Grover had left Crewson's and joined Chemtec Inc., doing she was never quite sure what, except that it involved a lot of what Grover called wheeler-dealing. She was surprised when, years later, he had suddenly suggested she might ask them to dinner. Pleased, too, because she had thought he had outgrown his former boss.

'Of course I'll ask them,' she said. 'I was just surprised. I mean, after all these years.'

'Well, they are Priscilla's godparents, after all.'

'I agree. I was just surprised that you chose now. You haven't mentioned them for ages.'

'Well, she's ten now. Growing up. They might like to see more of her. Besides, we may have business connections soon. Chemtec's got its eyes on Crewson's.'

'Eyes? You mean to take them over?'

'That's the idea.'

'So you'd be working with Bob again?'

'That's right.'

'I'm so glad. Marion will be too.'

'Well, ring her and arrange something for next month. Don't mention the business side, though, it's not quite tied up.'

But by the time they came to supper, everything was tied up.

'Actually,' Marion said to her, 'I think Bob feels rather badly about it. You see, all the staff have been made redundant except him. He'd thought they'd keep on some of his key men.'

'Well, it's not his fault, is it? I mean, they'd keep him on because he's the boss.'

'It's Chemtec's decision, of course, but he's still worried about the men he's worked with for years. He said the atmosphere is quite awful. It was just the research side they wanted really. Asset stripping, you know.'

'Yes, I remember. Grover said something about that.'

'Grover's been marvellous as a go-between. I thought it might have been awkward for him, but not a bit of it.'

Grover was in good form that night. In matters connected with work he could be amazingly relaxed, almost jovial. He and Bob talked shop the whole evening, understandably in the circumstances. He cross-examined Bob about all the changes in the organisation since he had left, obviously keen to catch up.

They stayed late.

'It's been lovely,' Marion said as they left. 'We mustn't leave it so long next time. Why not come one weekend, then Priscilla can come too, lunch and tea one Sunday?'

'I'd love that.'

'By next month the bluebells will be out in the woods. We'll have a walk. Oh, I can't tell you how pleased I am that the men are working together again.'

She was surprised, when she mentioned it to Grover later, that he wasn't more enthusiastic.

'Just leave it for a while,' he said. 'Tell her I'm abroad for a bit. Think up something.'

'Grover, you don't want to go, do you? Is something wrong?'

He hesitated. 'No, nothing's wrong. Everything is a bit fraught at the moment. I'd rather leave it for three or four weeks, that's all.'

'Oh, that's all right. So long as it's not later or we'll miss the bluebells.'

But by the time the bluebells were in flower, Bob had been made redundant.

It was Marion who rang to tell her. She sounded distraught. 'I'm sorry, Corinne,' she said, her voice breaking, 'but it's so unexpected. He went in as usual the day before yesterday, and this new American chap rang to ask him up, so he went and took some papers he thought they'd be discussing, and this man just said he wanted him to leave by lunch-time, clear your desk, he said, and go. And hand in the keys of the car. Yes, he thanked him for what he'd done and told him to clear out.'

'Oh, Marion, how dreadful. Poor Bob.'

'He came home as if, I can't describe it, honestly I thought he'd been mugged, he looked so shattered. I mean, physically shattered. That's what's so awful, the way they did it. I mean, you know Bob, he's a reasonable bloke. If they'd told him earlier and given him time to look about, he'd have kept his self-respect, but to be treated like a criminal – it's just dreadful. We haven't told the children yet. I made him come out with me yesterday, just walk all day, talk and walk in the fresh air. Today he's gone to see somebody who might help.'

'I'm sure Grover will help if he can. He'll be shattered too.'

Marion made no comment.

That evening, when she told him, Grover just said, 'Yes, I know.'

'But why? Couldn't you have stopped it? I mean, they promised to keep him on, they made such a fuss of him.'

'Well, it's like this. We needed all the information we could get out of him, about how his department meshed in with the others. You see, he was in overall control, so the system was really his, worked out over the years. During this month he's provided us with invaluable information.'

'You mean you planned to use him to get this information and then chuck him out when you'd got what you wanted?'

'More or less, yes.'

'But that's dreadful. It's despicable.'

'It's a hard world, Corinne. Tough decisions have to be made in business. You can't let personal considerations enter into it.'

'But you did. You used the fact that he was your friend to trap him. Why didn't you tell him what the plan was, let him stay on until he'd got another job lined up, do the thing decently—'

'And let him put all sorts of useful things in the shredder?'

'He wouldn't have done that. Not Bob. Where's your judgement? You should have known him better than that.'

'Even if I had, my bosses wouldn't.'

'So you didn't say a word in defence of your friend? After all he's done for you in the past?'

'I tell you, Corinne, you simply don't understand. Friendship didn't enter into it.'

'And I tell you it did. He might not have believed them, but he believed you because you were his friend. He trusted you.'

'That was up to him. He didn't have to trust me. I don't trust anyone.'

They had argued half the night, but it was only now, years later, sitting here by the Aswan dam, that she understood. People like Grover, who don't trust anyone, are like that because they know that they themselves are not to be trusted. Why hadn't she understood that at the time? Sometimes it seemed to her, as she looked back at herself as Grover's wife, that she had been incredibly naïve.

Mr Anderson was missing that evening from dinner.

'Patsy isn't quite right either,' Charlie said. 'We'll both be glad to get back to proper food.'

'There's one thing about having a tiny cabin,' Cliff said giggling, 'my friend can sit on the loo and be sick in the basin at the same time. He doesn't have to choose as he would at home.'

'What do you think the real relationship is?' Corinne asked Bernard over coffee.

'I don't know. Cliff's gay, but not Mr Anderson.'

'Besides, there's a Mrs Anderson who stays at home because she prefers Brighton.'

'So he says. Perhaps he says it rather too often.'

'We'll never know. It's been fascinating speculating about everyone. I shall miss Charlie and Patsy. Everyone is flying back to Cairo tomorrow, aren't they? Except me.'

'Are you staying on, too? I'm having a week on Elephant Island.'

'How extraordinary. I thought I'd made a very special arrangement. I reckoned I'd need a rest after all the sightseeing. Wouldn't it be funny if the whole lot of us turned up at the same hotel?'

But the others all flew back to Cairo the next afternoon. Only Corinne and Bernard went by ferry across the river to Elephant Island.

Chapter Five

She woke with a start the next morning. Still only five o'clock. She lay remembering. She'd been dreaming she was in bed with Grover, only it was years ago. Vague, like all dreams, about location, just a feeling that there were cliffs and the sea outside the hotel and that Grover and she were looking out at them through a wide window as they lay in bed, pleasantly relaxed and sexually sated, in the early morning. Then she had awoken, and still had that feeling on her as she lay alone in bed in this hotel in Aswan.

She must have gone to sleep thinking about him, she supposed, and somehow he had merged into the dream. She had been thinking about him a lot on this holiday. She could be more detached about him now that he was dead; when he was still around she was always trying to think in his shadow, couldn't get a clear picture of how things really were.

Now, for the first time, she had been thinking of the early days, the good days. It made sense to treasure them, too. He had been such a love at the beginning. Oh yes, she had been in love with him all right. He was so different from her other boyfriends. She could still remember the shock of it; after their tentative necking, their little dry pecks, Grover had descended on her like, well, like Grover. Wholeheartedly, to put it mildly, single-mindedly, with intense and concentrated passion. Passion arouses passion. They had been good days and even better nights.

She had seemed to matter so terribly much to him. It had been a new sensation for her; she had never felt very important before. She hadn't been highly regarded at school, she had been insignificant in the little job she had done afterwards, she had been treated like a child by both her parents, so it had been an extraordinarily enhancing thing to be so desired as an adult woman, to feel she mattered so much.

And not only her, but everything about her seemed important to him: every detail of what she wore, how she did her hair, even what sort of material her nighties were made of. He was very sensual, sensitive to the feel of things, whether it was skin or fabrics. 'Wear that silky one,' he'd say. 'I like fumbling around under it.' And she'd laugh at him, but really loved to pander to his whims. She couldn't think why these liberated women objected to being regarded as playthings; it was jolly nice being Grover's plaything.

Yet he who was so confident in bed was strangely unsure of himself out of it, terrified of doing the wrong thing. At first she found it endearing, this need of his to do everything in the correct manner, to be socially acceptable. Later it seemed obsessive. But since she wasn't given to analysing people, it hadn't occurred to her to wonder why he was like that; he just was. He was more aggressive and intolerant than she was, too, presumably because he was a man.

She couldn't really understand why he had got so discontented at work. She'd thought they were good days, when he was at Crewson's, using his professional skills, working with Bob. He had seemed happy enough at first, then he seemed to get impatient and restless, critical of his colleagues for no particular reason. He always assumed the worst of anyone, was suspicious of everyone's motives.

'But you enjoy your work,' she had said. 'I mean, you find it's satisfying, don't you?'

Afterwards she had thought that going to Chemtec Inc. had changed him, made him harder, more brutal, but now she thought not. It had only given scope to what was latent in him. If it hadn't been them, it would have been some other big company. He would have found an outlet. For she understood him much better now. It wasn't job satisfaction he had sought. He had that. He needed a special sort of success at work to boost his confidence, to show that he'd made his way in the world. He needed recognisable success and the power that derives from it. He needed the tangible trappings so that people could see them. He needed all this, she realised now, because he was fundamentally weak. How had she failed to understand that, she wondered. He had all the signs of an unsure person: he could never say he was sorry, he was afraid of appearing foolish, 'looking spare', as he called it, and he was critical of everyone because it was his way of boosting his ego. Poor Grover, there was something very pathetic about him, very vulnerable. If she had been more mature, perhaps she would have understood him better, been able to help him, instead of letting it end as it did.

But no, he would only have resented anything she said, been defensive. It would have ended in a row. Besides, she hadn't wanted to put at risk what happiness they did have. For they had been good lovers. The change had come about slowly. It wasn't a lessening of passion: no, not that. It was more that at first she had felt that it was she who was so special to him, she could feel it in his touch as he explored her. But then he seemed to become curiously detached from her, almost as if he were saying, 'Women like this, so I'll try this on her.' It worked, she wasn't pretending it didn't, but there was something impersonal about it. Funny word to choose, she thought, for something so very personal, but that's what it felt like. No longer special to her, somehow. As if he might have read it in a book. She had said as much once, and he said, 'Well, why not? There's always some new trick you can learn.' Besides, responding as she did to some new trick, why should she object? But in calmer moments afterwards, sometimes even at the time, she felt a kind of loneliness, an awareness of being worked on, so that she felt detached from him, appreciative of his efforts, of course, but conscious of the technique behind them. It hadn't been like that at the beginning of their marriage.

Later, after Priscilla was born, and they were both so proud of her and drawn closer together, sharing her, she had tried to talk to him about it. He had looked at her, smiling, knowing, 'You don't like it?' he had teased. 'I wouldn't have guessed.'

'I'm not saying that. It's just that I feel you're thinking of me as a woman—'

'What the hell else should I think of you as?'

'Oh, do try to understand. It was perfectly all right before, there's no need to try to be too clever.'

'I'm not trying to be clever, Corinne. I don't know what you're complaining about.'

'I'm not complaining. I just think it's a bit dangerous to think too much like that. Honestly, I'd rather you just thought of me as the woman you love, not as *a* woman to be roused, just any woman. I think deliberately setting about getting a woman frantic is too calculating. It gets too much like exercising power rather than expressing love.'

She'd been pleased with that sentence. It wasn't like her to put her thoughts so well.

'Yes, that's what I mean,' she had repeated. 'It's as if you enjoyed having power over me.'

'Well, power comes into everything, doesn't it? Love and work and money, the lot. No harm in it. Power's a great aphrodisiac, women like it. A part of them wants to be dominated.'

Increasingly he generalised about women and what they liked. Of course, later on, when she found out about the other women, it all made sense. The techniques he had acquired hadn't all been learned from books.

'It's all over, Corinne,' she reproved herself now. 'Forget it, bury it. Nobody can hurt you like that any more. Get up and look at this new world.'

The view from the balcony was strangely reminiscent of the one in her dream, only this water was the Nile and these cliffs were the sandstone hills of Aswan. Feluccas were tied up, straight-masted, along the shore, while others, their sails already unfurled, drifted across the river like families of swans.

She thought they were the only moving things in this

landscape of blue and green and golden brown. Then she noticed, far below by the riverside, men working two abreast, digging long furrows in the sand. They moved rhythmically, patterning the pale ground with darker lines.

She needed to paint it. She felt it quite suddenly and decisively; she must paint it now, today. She was filled again with the excitement she had felt when she looked at the tomb paintings, marvelling at the lightness of the feather, the weight of the sarcophagus, the tears of the mourning women. She had to try, she needed to try. The pencil drawings had been all right for the gentle evening scenes from the boat, but now she needed to try to catch the brilliant daytime colours of this land. She must start straight after breakfast, not put it off.

She was one of the first in the dining room, which was mainly occupied by dozens of waiters in tunics who lined the walls and stood guard by the tables. She was greeted, ushered in, handed from one waiter to the next, until she was finally seated at a table by the window, a napkin spread on her knee, coffee offered.

In the centre of the room, breakfast was massively displayed on a great oval table, hollow in the middle and tiered like a grandstand. Pyramids of oranges, pinnacled with pineapples, rose up at the back of the top tier, with hands of bananas reaching up to them between piles of limes and bunches of dates. Baskets of rolls of all shapes and sizes nestled below with croissants and biscuits, toast and crunchy bread, crusty loaves and slices of cake studded with fruit. The spaces between them were filled with dishes of butter floating in ice, with little jars of jam and honey and marmalade. Below them, on the next tier, were bowls of figs and fruit salad, bunches of grapes, slices of melon and pawpaw, giving way to silver platters of bacon and mushroom, tomatoes and sausages and tureens of scrambled egg, plates of ham and tongue and cheese. There were jugs of orange juice, mango and lime. The colour and abundance of it all, the deep greens and bright yellows, the different shades of orange, the shiny surface of the water melons, the softness of the lush pawpaw, all of it entranced her. She thought of it as something to paint rather than to eat, and was startled when the chef, tall, smiling, white teeth against dark skin, said, 'Spanish omelette, perhaps?'

She nodded and stood watching as he whipped the yellow liquid until it foamed, then poured it in a golden stream into the pan, where it thickened and slithered about as he coaxed and cajoled it with a wooden spatula. It was as she was carrying it, with the rest of her breakfast, back to the table, that her memory stirred. This was just such a place as Priscilla had described that morning, that Sunday morning after the party for the new Chemtec chairman. Three years ago, it must have been.

They had got back very late, she and Grover, after a more than usually exhausting dinner-dance in honour of the new chairman. She remembered thinking she was getting too old for these jamborees as they sat over a late breakfast, stale-mouthed and headachy. The Sunday papers were spread about, Grover had the financial pages in front of him, she had the political bit, but wasn't reading it, Priscilla was deep in an article on cheap travel in the colour supplement of which she was deeply critical. 'It's so silly,' she said, 'to tell people to plan and book ahead. I mean, when you get there you pick up all sorts of useful tips from other students.'

'Like what?' she had asked, yawning.

'Like where to hire cheap bikes and which fifth-rate boarding houses will let you sleep on their roof for a quid. One of the best things we were told about was this posh hotel where you get a marvellous buffet breakfast for two pounds, which sounds a lot but isn't really because you help yourself to as much as you want. The trick is not to eat anything the day before, so you're really starving and of course save money. Then you just go round and round this great buffet, I mean it's as good as a four-course dinner.'

'Didn't they mind you doing that?' she had asked.

'I don't expect so. I mean it was one of those really grand

places packed with rich tourists who just nibble at things because they're on diets, so really it's quite fair that somebody comes and eats a lot.'

'What did you wear to go into this very respectable hotel?' Grover had asked.

'Wear? Well, what we always wore, of course. What do you think? Shorts and T-shirts and sandals.'

'In a five-star hotel?'

'Yep. Actually we went in filthy and came out clean because they had these amazing loos. All marble and glass and basins and everything. So we took our clothes off and washed them. We sort of dried them under the hand-dryers, but it didn't matter if they were a bit wet because they soon dry on you in that heat anyway. Washed our hair, too. And ourselves, of course. All for free. Then we went back and ate some more and filled our little plastic bags with rolls and fruit and things which lasted us for the rest of the day, so though two pounds sounds a lot, in fact it lasted us for two whole days.'

'You realise you might have been thrown out?'

'So what, we weren't. I mean we didn't exactly wave the stuff about before we put it in the plastic bags. We nicked it quite discreetly.'

'It's the sort of place my colleagues might well go for a working breakfast.'

'Yes, that's right, Dad. It was full of boring-looking men in suits.'

'Priscilla,' Grover said. 'I wish to make it quite clear that I absolutely forbid you to do such a thing ever again.'

'Really,' Priscilla said, chin going up, eyes suddenly defiant. 'Do you? And how do you intend to enforce this new edict?'

'I have no intention of financing you if you go abroad and disgrace your family in this way.'

It had occurred to Corinne at the time that it was a bit much for Grover to pontificate about misbehaving abroad, but she said nothing. Besides, Grover had two sets of rules: one which applied to himself and one for other people.

'But you *don't* finance me,' Priscilla said. 'I *earn* my own money for travelling.'

'I was speaking of your keep at home and your university allowance which I make you and—'

'All right. Go ahead and cut the allowance and I'll apply for a grant as an unsupported student. They probably won't give me one on the grounds that you are too rich, but maybe when it gets out, into the local papers and all that sort of thing, kind people will send me subscriptions out of pity.'

Then she had jumped up and gone out of the room laughing.

There was no doubt about it; Priscilla had always dealt better with Grover than Corinne herself did. He invariably ended up huffing and puffing and doing nothing at all to alter his daughter's ways. If anything he simply blamed her mother for them.

'I can't understand why you let her dress like that,' he had said that morning. 'And that awful accent, almost cockney that she puts on. And must she call us Mum and Dad? It's so common, I mean after all we've spent on her education . . .'

'Her education's been fine and she works very hard. You realise that, don't you, Grover? If she was a layabout and got into debt and went on drugs the way some students do, we'd have something to worry about.'

'She's so thoughtless. You must speak to her about all this ringing up and reversing the charges. If she had to pay for her own calls she'd think twice about ringing home so often.'

'You ought to be glad that she wants to keep in touch with us. For goodness' sake, we're not short of money for the telephone bill.'

'That's not the point. It's the principle of the thing. I often wonder what she does with her allowance. She doesn't spend it on clothes, that's for sure. Must you let her go round looking like a tramp?'

Corinne, who didn't care for the way Priscilla dressed any more that Grover did, always found it hard to defend her on this one. 'Well,' she said, 'there's no point in making a fuss about things that don't really matter. Besides, they all go around looking like that nowadays.'

'Not all of them. I was interviewing young trainee accountants on Friday and all of the young women were very neat and presentable.'

'Did you take anyone on?' she asked, hoping to divert the conversation from Priscilla's clothes.

'A girl and two chaps. They were all very good. The girl was nervous but had excellent reports.'

'Well, I suppose it's a bit scary, being interviewed for your first job.'

'I told her to relax. If she'd been a man I'd have told her to take her jacket off.'

'Since she was a girl, I suppose you told her to take her bra off?' Corinne suggested.

'I shall ignore that as unworthy,' Grover had said grandly. 'We were discussing Priscilla, if you remember. I can see no reason for her to look so scruffy. When I was a student, none of us had much money, but we always looked clean and decent. As for you at her age, you were very neat and tidy. I was proud to be seen with you. I can't imagine any young man being proud to be seen with Priscilla.'

'She doesn't seem to lack for boyfriends,' Corinne pointed out.

But it had been true, what he'd said, all the same. At Priscilla's age she had always been neat in her straight skirts, trim blouses and court shoes. Her hair had always been tidy and her pretty little face always carefully made up. From her first passport, long out of date but never discarded, that face looked out at the world, unformed, eager to please, somehow naked in its prettiness. Priscilla stared out from hers, defiant and challenging, not in the least bothered by what the world thought.

Never having been a student herself, she had at first found Priscilla's casual ways and scruffy clothes hard to understand. She had been hurt, if she was honest, when Priscilla rejected in horror her suggestion of a shopping expedition together to buy her something pretty to wear at Christmas. Above all she had been baffled by the way Priscilla questioned everything. She herself had accepted her father's views as completely as Priscilla had rejected Grover's; she had accepted the decisions made on her behalf, repressed that little flutter of rebellion about going to art school, believed it when her father had said that the people there would not be suitable for her to mix with. It hadn't entered her head to question it, to go there and find out for herself.

No wonder, she realised now, that she had at first found it hard to understand Priscilla's student ways, she who in her wildest dreams would not have thought of venturing on a foreign dig, travelling rough, working in a kibbutz. The height of adventure for her was to go on a two-week package holiday with her parents. For the rest of the year she was quite happy to sit with them in the evenings, watching television or reading her women's magazines; or to go out with a boyfriend now and then to the pictures or for a little gentle necking in the park.

She had never been a person in her own right. Priscilla was very much a person in her own right. Priscilla had never been just a daughter, so she would never be just a wife. Nobody would land her, unprepared, with a Grover for a husband – if they did and he behaved as Grover had done, no doubt she'd boot him out, smartish.

If she herself had been a student like Priscilla, or at least gone away from home and grown up, found out who she was, before she was married, would she have managed better? Would she have been able at least to deal with him on equal terms? He always seemed to speak with higher authority, he who knew about the world, the bigger world outside. If she was suspicious of his goings-on, he was pained that a wife should be so untrusting and unloving. On the other hand, when her suspicions proved well founded, he told her that that was the way things were in the world, and she was unworldly-wise not to realise it. She never seemed able to get at the heart of anything that mattered because he wasn't interested in the truth, only in scoring points.

She reacted childishly, she knew that, but she knew no other way. She had no weapons; he could hurt her in a way she could not hurt him. It was a very unequal fight, made more so by the fact that she didn't want to fight anyway, whereas he relished confrontation. And that particular morning, upset by Priscilla's storming out laughing, she had gone on bickering, even though she knew it was silly and that they were both tired.

'Want a drink?' Grover had interrupted.

'It's not eleven o'clock yet.'

'Never too early for a drink,' Grover said, getting up and going to the refrigerator for bottle and glass.

'I should have thought you had enough alcohol last night to last for the rest of the weekend,' she said.

'Actually, Corinne, if you remember, we had no drinks last night. They served nothing throughout the evening except champagne.'

'There are people, Grover, who classify champagne as alcohol.'

'Well, I never come across them,' he said, pouring out the vodka.

He drank, he relaxed. 'That's better,' he said. 'I needed that after last night. These functions are quite exhausting for me, you know. You just turn up and get entertained, but it's work for me. I can't relax. I'm responsible for keeping the conversation flowing, making sure everyone is enjoying themselves, dancing with all the wives.'

'Yes, I saw you virtuously plodding the boards with each unfortunate lady in turn.'

He put the glass down. 'God, you've got bitchy since I married you,' he said.

'Yes, quite an achievement on your part,' she replied sharply.

But she had felt tears in her eyes all the same. She didn't want to be bitchy, that was the unfairness of it. He took a certain pride in his brutality, but she was humiliated by her own ineffective little attacks. There was something invulnerable about Grover, all sixteen stone of selfishness of him. He was like a tank, armour-plated. Yes, her little barbs bounced off him like arrows off a tank.

They had bickered on and off all day while Priscilla was up in her room, working. The argument was always there, ready to be stirred up at intervals, like a damped-down fire which flares up when you poke it. But in bed that night he had taken her in his arms and said, 'Forget it, Corinne, forget it.' She had tensed against him. The persuasive Grover, the ingratiating Grover had taken over. He wasn't drunk, just fuddled, maudlin. 'Don't sulk,' he said, turning her face towards him. 'Come to Daddy.'

'What made you say that?' she asked, drawing away from him, but she knew already from the way he spoke that he'd said it before, knew that he'd said it to some young woman, to reassure her. She said as much, answering her own question.

He hesitated. 'Yes,' he admitted. 'But not recently. It's quite unimportant.'

'To comfort them? Make them feel safe with you, was it?'

'Perhaps. Some girls have that kind of relationship with their own fathers, you know.'

'And you remind them of it? You don't think that was terrible?'

'It was nothing to do with me. It was between them and their fathers, wasn't it?'

She knew that anything horrible like that had a fascination for him. His tolerance of evil frightened her; such a little gap between tolerance and complicity. It was then for the first time that she realised the harm he was doing her. For the first time it occurred to her that she might improve her life by getting Grover out of it. And that she didn't want him in her bed any more either. Tomorrow she would think about it, she told herself, as, like a bull seal scrambling up on to a somewhat inhospitable shore, he hauled himself up on top of her.

* * *

'May I join you?' Bernard asked.

Corinne, still thinking of Grover, jumped. 'Of course,' she said, recovering herself.

'I'm sorry I startled you. I'll go and help myself to breakfast. Can I get you anything?'

'No, thanks. Well, maybe an orange. I'll come with you.'

They wandered round the buffet together and, when they got back to their table, she told him about Priscilla and the breakfast.

'I hope she put a mark on the door when she left, the way tramps used to, to let the others know it was a good place,' he said, laughing. 'She sounds fun, your daughter.'

'Yes, I'm afraid her father didn't always think so. Nor did I, now and then.'

'I suppose if it's your own child you feel responsible, don't you, so you worry about things you'd find quite funny in other children?'

'Yes, that's it. False pride really. You're afraid people will think you've made a mess of bringing them up. Do you have children?'

'No, my wife didn't want any.' He hesitated, then asked abruptly, 'What are you going to do today?'

'Don't laugh. I'm going to paint.'

'Why should I laugh?'

'You will when you see the paintings I'm likely to produce. I haven't done any for about twenty years. But Priscilla insisted on lending me her paints and brushes, and suddenly this morning I knew that that's what I wanted to do. The view from my balcony, to be precise.'

'You'll find it very difficult, you know, to paint something you're looking down on from such a height. Unless you particularly want to try a bird's eye view.'

'No, I don't. I hadn't really thought about it. I could probably get the same view from the end of the garden. You know, where it runs into a piece of wasteland?'

'Yes. I had a walk round before breakfast. There are good views from there across the river, and trees to sit under. Look, we could set up there together, if you like. Well, I mean a bit apart, but I think if you're quite alone you might get pestered.'

'Yes, thank you. That would be lovely. They do tend to pester rather, don't they? They don't mean any harm, but it's a bit of a bore.'

They set up chairs and makeshift easels under the line of trees at the end of the lawn where the parkland gave way to scrub which, in turn, petered out into sand. Corinne settled herself, choosing a view looking down the river. Somewhere behind her, under the trees, an old man sat puffing contentedly at his bubble-pipe. But he did not intrude, he in his world, she in hers. Feluccas gently crossed and recrossed the Nile; she wished that one would ride at anchor for a while, so that she could study the billowing of the sail and the reflection of the boat in the water. She did not notice how time slipped by. Only a sudden burning on the back of her neck told her that the sun had moved. It was nearly three o'clock. She was very stiff. She got up and stretched. Bernard waved.

She strolled across to him. He had drawn the view directly across the river, taking in the far bank and the mountains beyond, which rose steeply from the shore and were tunnelled with tombs. The ruins of a temple topped the hills to the left. In the foreground, men were at work in the fields, furrowing the light, sandy soil.

'You're allowed to be honest,' he said, smiling up at her.

'I think it's all wonderful, the temple and the hills and the landscape, but I'm not so sure about the men.'

'Dead right. I told you I can't do figures.'

'At least you've tried. I painted them out. I've just done the furrows and pretended the chaps had gone home for lunch.'

'Speaking of lunch – but let's look at your painting first.'

'I've put in one man,' she said as they walked back to her chair, 'a kind of representative figure in the boat, but otherwise nobody.'

74

But seeing the painting afresh, walking up to it, she observed, in a detached kind of way, as if it was somebody else's work, that it was quite good. At least the general effect was. It was alive, somehow, the water sparkled, it really did. Beginner's luck.

'You do have a gift, you know,' Bernard said. 'Water and sky are notoriously difficult.'

'But there's something a bit flat, isn't there? I mean the boat. Look,' she pointed, 'it doesn't seem quite *forward* enough, does it?'

'Frankly, the perspective isn't quite right. But that's not something to worry about too much. It really isn't difficult once you've got the idea.'

'What idea?'

He laughed. 'The way it was explained to me was this. Think of two lines on a blackboard, one starting at the top left-hand corner, and the other somewhere in the middle, and both careering off on the right to what they call the vanishing point where they join each other. Rather like an arrowhead disappearing off the board. Inside the arrowhead you draw your buildings or whatever, the biggest one in the front, getting smaller as you get nearer to the arrowpoint.'

As he talked he pointed out where the lines would go in her picture.

'Yes,' Corinne said slowly. 'I see that now. That part, nearer to the arrowhead, should have been smaller, and that would have brought the boat forward, wouldn't it?'

'Yes, that's really all there is to it. Well, obviously it gets more complicated if the shapes aren't rectangular buildings, but irregular things like human bodies. Why not try a few simple sketches in pencil, starting with your basic arrowhead lines and then filling in with detail? It's quite a good exercise, then later, it becomes instinctive.'

'I'll do that. Thanks. I'm really grateful. I'm so ignorant; I've always suffered from being untaught.'

'But that's not really important, Corinne. What matters is

75

the love of the thing and the eye to see what you want to paint. You have that – the rest can be learned. Now, aren't you hungry, or would you rather have a swim?'

'Both, swim first. Doesn't the Nile look tempting?'

'The Nile!' he exclaimed. 'You wouldn't think of going in, would you? Seriously? It's dangerous. You can get bilharzia.'

'Bill who?'

He burst out laughing. Then, 'It's an illness,' he said. 'You get it from little snails that live in the water. I'm sorry, there's no reason you should have heard of it. But you'll be safer in the pool.'

They had the grounds to themselves; the rest of the world seemed to be sleeping. He was ready by the side of the pool when she came out of the changing room.

He pretended to examine the water, then, 'No sign of Bill,' he called to her.

'You're not going to let me forget that, are you?' she said, and ran to push him in, but he was too quick for her and dived in before she reached him. He had a nice, quiet dive and swam with easy, clean strokes, she noticed as she thrashed about in her usual inexpert way. In fact he was a nice chap altogether, she thought, he'd really taken trouble to explain about painting to her, seemed to think that it mattered. Fancy any woman leaving a man like that. She got out first and ordered lime juice and sandwiches. Then they lay in the shade of the trees which flanked one side of the pool, eating and drinking and talking about perspective.

'It's a bit of a bother,' she said, 'when the sun moves. I mean it makes it jolly difficult to get the shadows right.'

'Yes, that's why people make sketches, then work on them slowly indoors. But you've got to do pretty exact sketches, especially if there're water and reflections.'

'Why especially?' she asked, biting into another sandwich. 'I'm still hungry. Are you? Let's ask for some more.'

He called the waiter over and, when he had given the order, went on, 'Well, say you were painting a church set back from the water's edge, you might only see its spire reflected in the water, because the view from the water would be much lower than the level of your eyes from where you're sitting viewing the landscape. Now, indoors, later on, you might forget that and paint the reflection of the whole church.'

'Yes, I can see what you mean. I hadn't thought of that. Reflections are very effective, though, aren't they, in pictures?'

'Oh yes. If the water is glassy you get a near-perfect reproduction upside down. But if the surface of the water is broken, the image becomes very distorted and – how can I describe it? – sort of discontinuous. Something I've promised myself is to go and see the Impressionists in Paris now they've been moved from the Jeu de Paume to the Musée d'Orsay. Would you like to come?' he asked suddenly.

She was taken aback. 'What me? Now?' she said.

He laughed, a nice laugh, a really amused kind of laugh. 'Well, not now, this moment,' he said. 'Just sometime.'

'Now, this moment, I just want to get back to my painting,' she said. 'It's a kind of obsession. Sorry. I do want to finish it today and start the perspective exercises tomorrow.'

'Don't apologise. I understand it very well.'

They painted until it was too dark to see, then he helped her to carry her things up to her room and again discussed the painting.

'It's there,' he said, pointing to the far end of the boat, 'that it goes wrong from the perspective point of view. If you just moved that edge up, so, the rim of the wood there, you see?'

'Go on. You draw it in.'

He hesitated. 'No,' he said, putting the pencil down. 'You can't have paintings drawn by committees. And it's your picture and the boat has a nice feel about it, a kind of – I don't know – buoyancy. I might spoil that.'

She looked at it, head on one side. Yes, it was a jolly little boat, her boat was. She nodded, happy after all to have it left alone.

'Do you know that Browning poem about Andrea del Sarto?' he asked.

'No. I don't really know any poems about anything,' she said.

'There should be a special word for people like you – the opposite of pretentious,' he said, and stood for a moment looking at her. Then he went on, 'Anyway, del Sarto used to be nicknamed the perfect painter, because he got everything technically right, and in this poem Browning imagines him standing in front of a Raphael Madonna and knowing that the arm is not exactly right, not anatomically correct, standing there wanting to alter it and realising that it's so essentially right, so lovingly an arm, that to try to give it perfection of line would spoil it.'

'You're putting us in rather grand company, aren't you?'

He laughed. 'You know what I mean,' he said. 'That maybe technique and the spirit of love in anything are incompatible. Even that good technique can destroy love.'

'*What* did you say?'

'Technique can destroy love. I meant that something too well done is too self-conscious.'

'Yes, of course, I'm sorry. Yes, I do see.'

She was flustered, for a moment she'd thought he'd been explaining about Grover. Because somewhere at the back of her mind all day that dream had lingered.

'I'm going to fly up to Abu Simbel one day this week,' he said. 'Do you want to come?'

'*Abu Simbel.* Goodness, I nearly forgot. Yes, of course I must go. I promised Priscilla I'd go and take lots of photos. I meant to book for it.'

The planes were booked for days ahead, the clerk at the reception told them, the only seats were on a special early flight the next morning.

'It would mean crossing over at about six-thirty,' Bernard told her. 'What do you think?'

'I'm game, if it's the only chance we've got of getting there. But I shan't come down to breakfast.'

'Right, I'll see you down by the landing stage then.'

* * *

She was there first. The ferry boat was lying at anchor, waiting. In fact there was a feeling of waiting about the whole scene, she thought, as she walked down the steps to the little quay, a wonderful stillness before the day's bustle began. Mist softened the banks, pink and wispy. A cluster of feluccas was tied up alongside the ferry, their masts rising like a copse of slender trees into the mist. One or two had already ventured out into the stream; their sails, partly unfurled, thrust like white blades into the pale blue sky of the early morning.

'Doesn't it make you want to paint it?' she said to Bernard when he joined her. 'Just stay here and paint now?'

'No, we're going to Abu Simbel,' he said, taking her hand as if to make sure she got on the ferry.

She laughed. 'It's all right, I'm coming. I couldn't face Priscilla ever again if I didn't.'

'Do you know what puzzles me about you?' he said later, as they flew over the desert.

'What's that?'

'How you managed *not* to paint all these years. I mean, here you are, I can see the whole time that you're just itching to get those scenes down on paper, aren't you? Yet you tell me that you haven't painted since you were at school. Or did I misunderstand you?'

'No. I mean I used to draw and paint a bit with Priscilla when she was little. You know, she'd want me to draw her houses and animals, the way children do. Then she began doing her own and was very good—'

'But you, what about *your* painting?' he insisted.

She shrugged. 'I don't know. There just didn't seem to be time.'

'Did you have a job?'

'No. But it's amazing how time disappears when you've got a home to run and a family. Men don't realise—'

'I'm not being critical,' he interrupted. 'Please don't think that.' He sounded really worried lest he had hurt her. His eyes were anxious. How could she have thought he was toffee-nosed? He was reserved with strangers, perhaps just shy, but so caring, once you got to know him.

'I just wondered,' he was saying, 'how you managed not to paint when the need is so much in you?'

There had been time, plenty of it, but she'd filled it with other things, broken it up so that it never seemed worth settling down for the odd hour. She always told herself that she'd get down to it when she had days at a stretch, but they never seemed to happen. She'd thought she'd paint in term-time when Priscilla started school, but there were always interruptions. People asked her to do things like help with the guides or collect money or drive the disabled to hospital. She liked to think of herself as one who would always lend a hand, good old Corinne, a willing horse. So she didn't ever have those hours at a stretch. She herself had ensured that she didn't.

Why, she wondered now, trying to be honest, had she prevented herself doing what she most wanted to do? Because she had been afraid of doing it badly, that was why. You have to be very confident to risk doing badly something you desperately want to do well. And she wasn't very confident.

'You're right,' she said slowly. 'Of course I could have made time. I think that underneath I was afraid to try in case I found out that I wasn't good enough.'

'And who would judge that except yourself?' he asked gently.

Grover, she thought, he would have judged. He would have weighed it up and found it wanting. Although he knew nothing about painting, still she had feared his judgement. All that time and mess, he'd have thought, and expense too, just for *this*? No, she'd been safer helping with the coffee morning in aid of the new scanner for the hospital, and baking cakes for the guides' tea. She was a good cook and so long as you followed the recipe nothing went wrong. Not like painting.

'But when you get back, you'll keep it up, won't you?' he said when she didn't reply. 'Because you *are* good; it's wrong to waste a talent, you know, Corinne.'

It wouldn't have mattered to Grover if the paintings had been good or bad, of course. If she'd sold them he would have been very impressed; popular painters, best-selling writers, he approved of. They had made it; you could count their success in dollars. What else was there to judge them by? The idea that a painting might be a success just in itself, because it was as good as she could make it, would have been quite alien to him; she hadn't dared risk it. She could see now that it had been wrong, indeed she had often thought so at the time, but it was by Grover's standards that they had lived.

'It might be a good idea to go to classes,' Bernard was saying. 'Apart from what you learn, it encourages you to go on trying.'

'But don't you have to be rather good to be accepted at a class?'

'But you *are* rather good,' he said, exasperated. 'I'm sure your local council will run evening – and probably afternoon – art classes.'

Grover hadn't approved of classes subsidised by ratepayers like himself, he had said. Yet his own education had been paid for by ratepayers, who had long ago provided him with the scholarships which had enabled him to prosper. She had said so once, but he had made it pretty clear that self-made men should always kick away the ladder that helped them up in case anybody else climbed up it. She had seen the sense of that; there wasn't, as he had said, all that much room at the top.

'A good teacher can help a great deal with perspective and technique. They're things you'd find out yourself eventually, but why waste time and maybe get discouraged when there are people around who can help you?'

He was right, she knew it. And it was absurd to let Grover's disapproval haunt her memory.

'Right, that's settled,' she said suddenly. 'Art classes when I get back. It's just that I'm not very good at organising myself.'

He looked at her thoughtfully. 'You strike me as being a very well-organised person,' he said. He hesitated before adding, 'But perhaps one who underestimates herself.'

'I'll try to rethink me,' she promised.

'I didn't mean that, you're perfectly all right as you are—'

'It's all right,' she interrupted, 'I'm not offended. Look, coffee and After Eights.'

'Actually, those little brown envelopes contain bits of flannel for wiping sticky fingers. I shouldn't try to eat them,' he said, and they laughed and talked about things other than painting until they landed at Abu Simbel.

It was not at all as she had imagined. There was no village, nothing beyond the airstrip except barren rock and sand and the river winding below. As they set off behind the others along the dusty track, she thought what a picture it would make, with this line of people, like a straggling band of pilgrims, wending their way slowly round the side of the hill, their heads bent as if the heat was crushing them down while the sun bounced in fierce, dazzling light off the rocks. How tiny the people seemed in the desert wilderness, under the harsh blue dome of the sky.

Tiny they seemed too as they stood, heads strained back, looking up at the colossal figures in front of the first great rock temple. The four seated statues of Rameses the Second gazed out impassively into the distance, oblivious of the little people moving like ants on the ground below them.

'They're over sixty feet tall,' Bernard told her. 'About three times as high as the average house. If Charlie Paste were here he'd tell you how many multi-storey car parks you could pack into that.'

She laughed. 'I do miss his comments, don't you?' she said.

'The small statue here is Rameses' wife,' the guide said. 'Her name is Nefertari.'

Very diminutive, Nefertari seemed, at a mere twenty feet. She nestled at the side of her seated lord, reaching his knees.

'She had a temple of her own, which we'll see soon,' Bernard said as they went under a great façade and into the temple which had been fashioned inside the rock itself. 'But even there he's got four statues of himself and only two of her.'

The light was dim inside the rock temple, the air cooler despite the crowd. The ceilings and walls were beautifully decorated, the colours fresh. Corinne marvelled at it all as the guide explained the scenes of battles, of the first recorded peace treaty between nations, of slaughter and of marriage, of offerings to the gods and to men. On the roof, above her head, painted birds hovered among constellations of stars. The same stars as ours.

Bernard seemed more intrigued by the fact that the temples had been moved from their former site down by the river to safety up here when the Nile was flooded by the building of the Aswan dam.

'I hadn't realised quite what a task it was,' he said, shaking his head. 'You do realise, don't you, that they moved everything, the statues, the temple, and even the rock it's built into?'

'How did he say they did it? I couldn't hear very well.'

'They carved it up into blocks, cutting the front inch with handsaws, would you believe? Then they lifted it, block by block, with cranes, and rebuilt it up here.'

'But you can't see any joins, can you?'

They went carefully around walls and statues, but couldn't see as much as a hair's breadth of a crack or line anywhere in the stone.

'I don't believe it,' she said simply.

Bernard burst out laughing. Heads turned.

'All the same, it's true,' he said. 'It's just that they cut it so exactly, so finely, that the two edges come together perfectly. About forty nations were involved and it cost as many million dollars, so really you can't deny it happened.'

He was still enthusing about it as they flew back. Corinne, tired after the walk and the heat, was half asleep and only half listening.

'I've a postcard,' he said, 'of how it used to be before they moved it. Absolutely identical. I'll show you when we get back. It just looks as if the whole mountainside had been shifted.

And I once saw a very old photograph of how it was even earlier, when they were uncovering the statues in the middle of the last century. It's in a book by Flaubert. He came with a friend who was a keen photographer, in the very early days of photography, and he took a shot of those statues when they were still down there by the river, with their feet practically in the water, and their heads just being uncovered from the sand. Up till then they'd been completely hidden. Just think, for all those centuries they'd been buried in sand. I must say it worries me to think of the damage we may be doing to them now. I suppose the dry air preserves all the temple paintings but, all the same, I wonder what the effect must be of all these tourists breathing on them.'

'Well, they've got to breathe, poor things,' Corinne said, and yawned.

He laughed. 'I wasn't suggesting that they shouldn't. There,' he added, moving his shoulder so that she could lean her head against it. 'Go to sleep.' Thus she sat dozing until the coffee was brought round.

'I liked that row of baboons outside the temple,' she said, 'at the top of the façade on the first temple.'

'Twenty thousand years ago,' he remarked, 'there were more baboons than men.'

'You know a lot, don't you?'

'Not all of it particularly useful. Sugar?'

'No, thanks. Rameses was a bit full of himself, wasn't he? Statues everywhere and his little wife firmly in her place.'

'Yes, everywhere the same, wherever we've been. The thing that really riled me was at Queen Hatsphetsut's temple – do you remember the tiered one in the Valley of the Kings? She was one of the best rulers they ever had. She didn't waste money on wars, gave them peace and prosperity, yet even she had to have herself carved with a beard to show she was as good as a man.'

'When she was so much better.'

'Yes. That sort of thing sickens me. Like George Eliot and

the Brontës having to be published under men's names. Thank goodness we live in more enlightened times.'

'Do we?'

'Of course. Nobody thinks like that any more.'

She didn't argue: maybe his neck of the woods had been more enlightened than hers.

'You're tired,' he said when the bus dropped them near the far end of the town. 'We'll take a garrya back.'

So they sat under the awning of the little cart and went clopping gently along the front between the river and the town. Then they turned inland and drove through the souk, down little streets, weaving their way between shoppers and vendors, between other garryas and donkeys and bicycles, past tiny shops stuffed with brassware and spices and perfumes, the air smelling hot and aromatic and sweet. Every time they had to stop, people pressed upon them, holding out clothes and jewellery, eager to sell. She was wide-awake now, intrigued by everything and everyone, overwhelmed by the colour and movement of it all.

'Do you want to get out and buy things?' he asked. 'Or come another day?'

'I've lots of presents to buy,' she said. 'Better come back another time, don't you think?'

'Yes. Back to the hotel for lunch now.'

It was only a narrow stretch of water between them and the island. They didn't go and sit under cover, but stood on the side of the boat, enjoying the breeze. In midstream it livened and suddenly a gust of wind snatched the coolie hat off her head, spun it up into the air like a flying saucer, let it hover for a moment as if undecided what to do with it, then gently deposited it on the water a few yards behind the boat.

She watched it and then turned to Bernard. But he wasn't there. There was a splash and she saw that he had jumped into the water.

'Oh, no! Come back.'

Idiot man, just for a hat.

The boatman shouted, waved his arms, making signs to keep away from the boat. 'Propeller,' he bawled. 'Danger.'

But Bernard kept well clear of the water churning around the boat and caught up with the hat which was bobbing slowly downstream.

The boatman shouted again and turned off the engine, obviously terrified he was going to swim back to the boat, but Bernard was heading for the shore. He got there first and was waiting for her at the landing stage, dripping with mud and dirty water. She was too angry to thank him.

'That was an absolutely mad thing to do,' she said. 'You could have been chopped to pieces by the propeller.'

'I kept well clear of it and—'

'You said yourself the water was dangerous, and now you'll get bilharzia and—'

'No, I won't. Not in that short time.'

'You can't be sure.'

They plodded on up the path, in silence, she hot and angry, he dripping ridiculously and still clutching the wretched coolie hat. All the friendly understanding there had been between them was lost.

'You're going to have a bath straight away,' she nagged on, bossy as if she'd been dealing with a daughter newly arrived back from foreign parts. 'At once, before the germs get a chance to sink in.'

'I'd rather wait outside until I've dried off a bit. I don't really want to go dripping across the reception hall.'

'I've got my key with me, you can use my bath. We'll go in the side door by the lift.'

Grimly she led the way. In silence they went into the lift, along the corridor and into her room.

She opened the bathroom door, turned on the taps. 'There's heaps of towels and soap and everything in there,' she said, and shut the door on him.

'I've nothing to wear afterwards,' he shouted after a few minutes.

'I'll go down when you're ready, get your key and collect some of your clothes. You can wear towels until then. And do wash off all the snails and things. Shove a wet flannel into your ears and up your nose.'

There were roars of laughter from the other side of the door at this.

'And it's not funny either,' she called back. 'I'll make some tea. I've got a gadget for boiling water.'

She filled a jug from the drinking bottle and switched on the portable immersion heater. She put cups and teabags ready alongside.

'I'll go and get your clothes now,' she shouted. 'What shall I bring, and where do I look for them? It's room 528, isn't it?'

He came out of the bathroom, wrapped in towels. 'I'm sorry,' he said. 'I do realise I've upset you.'

She shrugged. 'I know you're a good swimmer,' she said, 'but you could have been carried away on the tide, or the water could have dragged you under the propeller. You'd have been snarled up in it—'

She stopped, horrified at the thought of it, and suddenly remembering how Grover had looked, smashed to pieces on the rocks.

'Truly, I'm sorry,' he said again, coming across to her.

'I mean, if it had been for a child who had fallen in, it would have been different, but for a *hat*.'

'But it wasn't just any old hat,' he sad. 'It was *your* hat.'

He put his arms around her. Upset, surprised, relieved that he was safe, she was disarmed. And his face was all moist and fresh too, his hair ruffled up. Even so, it might not have happened if the towels hadn't slipped off.

She remembered wondering what Priscilla would think of her and hearing herself say rather childishly, 'You haven't got Aids, have you?' and he had smiled and said, 'She left me two years ago and there hasn't been anybody since.' It occurred to her that he hadn't asked the same question, which was either nice and perceptive of him, or, from the pamphlet's point of view, merely irresponsible. Then she forgot about it.

The sun was setting; they lay watching it through the open window. The lace curtains stirred in the breeze and the last rays of the sun, slanting through the balustrade, painted slatted lines of paler grey across the balcony. She turned towards him and they looked at each other as he gently stroked her hair back off her face. 'You're so beautiful,' he said. 'I've wanted to tell you for so long.'

'You've only known me for a week,' she said, tracing his mouth with her finger. 'It's not long to wait.'

'You get to know each other more quickly on a boat,' he told her. 'I've watched you and thought about you all the time. You've been hurt, haven't you? I suppose you wouldn't let me look after you?'

'No, thanks.'

'Why not?'

'I've learned about this looking-after business. Men don't.'

'Have you known so many that you can generalise?'

'One's enough. Let's not think about it. It's nice just like this.'

'I just thought that one day you might perhaps think of marrying me?'

'No, thank you. It's kind of you to ask. But we can be friends like we are now.'

He paused, then seemed to decide to go along with her. 'All right. We can meet in London, can't we? And go to see the Impressionists at Easter?'

'Priscilla will be home at Easter.'

'She can come too.'

She laughed and shook her head. 'Oh, no. Mothers have to be tolerant of daughters, but daughters are very strait-laced about their mothers.'

'Try her,' he said.

'But I wouldn't mind going on one of those painting holidays,' she said. 'Maybe we could go on one together in the summer?'

'And in the winter we could go somewhere warm, where there are things to see and paint but time to laze as well. Have you been to India, or maybe Sri Lanka would be more restful . . .'

'No, I've been there,' she said quickly.

'Have you? On holiday? When?'

'Three or four months ago. It wasn't exactly a holiday. My husband had work to do there and I went too.'

He drew away, surprised. 'You mean your husband only died a few months ago?'

'Yes.'

'Corinne, I'm so sorry. I didn't know it was so recent. I thought it was a long time ago. I mean, you must still be shocked and lonely and—'

'Don't be upset. It didn't make all that difference to me. I mean, he was away a lot when he was alive.'

It sounded heartless, she realised that, but it was the plain truth and she didn't want to mislead him.

So they lay, not talking. The sun slipped down behind the horizon, rimming with gold the sandstone mountains on the western bank. The sky lost its warmth, turned cool and pearly grey. The moon rose. And still he lay, a little apart, watching her.

'You're not to worry about it,' she said, and to reassure him she slipped her right arm under his head and her left across his chest and drew him to her. 'Truly, I'm all right.'

'Oh, yes,' he said. 'You're all right,' and he took hold of her tightly again. 'Oh, Corinne, I never thought I'd love anyone again.'

She recognised it, the pain in his voice. She knew that hurt, couldn't explain how, just that she recognised it as the pain she had felt years ago. It returned to her now, although she had thought it long dead. The special pain when someone you love turns their back on you, preferring another. Something similar had happened to him. She was sure of it. Suddenly the significance of his saying that she had been hurt came to her:

he recognised her pain as she had recognised his. She clung to him, consoling and consoled.

Later she said, 'It's past eight o'clock and we haven't had lunch yet.'

'We'll go down and have a splendid celebration supper,' he said. 'You'll be my guest and we'll have champagne.'

'Oh, lovely. And Bernard . . .'

'Yes?'

'I'm sorry I was so cross.'

'You were, weren't you? I felt like a ten-year-old, you were so bossy.'

She laughed. 'Once a mother, always a mother,' she said.

'And now I'll be bossy. You've got to get up, get dressed and go and fetch my clothes. I can't go down like this.'

She reached for the light. Nothing happened.

'There's no electricity,' she said. 'Oh, *no*. I thought there was a funny sort of burning smell.'

She jumped out of bed and ran across to the table. The jug of water had boiled dry, the little heater was a blackened lump of metal and molten plastic.

'I think I've fused the whole hotel,' she said.

She had. They drank their champagne by candlelight and accepted the head waiter's apologies graciously.

'It's awful,' she whispered to Bernard. 'I mean considering it was all my fault.'

'It might have been a coincidence.'

She shook her head. 'You jolly well know it wasn't,' she said. 'I should have warned you. I'm a bit accident-prone.'

'Don't change. Stay just as you are. Where shall we paint tomorrow?'

'The other side of the island?'

And so the days passed, painting in the garden or on the shore, walking, love-making, swimming in the pool and, on the last day, driving in a little carriage through the narrow streets of Aswan. How differently the holiday had turned out from what she had planned, she thought, how unexpected it all was. She had stopped mulling over the past; something was healed. She remembered how she had thought, that first day in Cairo, that it was a far better thing to be Grover's widow that his wife. Certainly it was, and she didn't regret it. It was just that she had ceased now even to feel like his widow. She was simply herself.

They were leaving early the next morning to fly back to Cairo. She set the alarm for five-thirty, although she knew she'd wake early. In fact she woke with a start in the middle of a very convincing dream, sure that she had missed the only plane of the day. Except that it was the plane to Sri Lanka, not to Cairo, and she knew that Priscilla and Becky Portman were waiting at the other end and there was no way of getting in touch with them. For some reason it was desperately urgent that she should. She had let them down; it was all her fault. She was begging someone to let her get on another plane, she was crying. She woke up sweating, her heart thumping. The phosphorescent figures on the little clock by the bed showed that it was half-past four.

She lay, not wanting to sleep again in case the dream returned. Why had she confused Cairo and Sri Lanka? And where did Becky Portman come into it? Well, maybe she associated her with aeroplanes and disaster, she thought, staring into the darkness, wide-awake now and remembering.

She hadn't really wanted to go with Grover to Sri Lanka, not really. It had been one of her stupidities; if he was going on a business trip to this exotic place, she'd told herself sourly, she'd jolly well go too. It would cramp his style a bit, having the wife in tow. Of course, when she'd got there she'd realised that even Grover couldn't get up to much in that benighted spot, in that awful sticky heat, which he'd failed to warn her about. The only exotic things they'd seen had been the paintings of the Sigiriya maidens, which he'd drooled over on that last climb.

These seductive creatures had been painted fifteen hundred

years ago, near the base of the rock, on stone so highly polished that it still gleamed like glass. Protected from the elements by the overhanging cliff, the maidens, their colours still brilliant, smiled knowingly from their polished wall. Nothing very maidenly about that lot, Corinne had thought. Bare-breasted, narrow-waisted, they offered gifts of pomegranates and fingered leaves of frangipani, as they had done for hundreds of years.

Grover had tried to finger the maidens, but the guide would not let him touch. 'Not allowed,' he had said, then added by way of consolation, 'also not nice – looks soft but feels hard.'

So Grover had just stood there, feeling the breasts with his eyes instead. It had made her so cross that she hadn't actually been able to enjoy the beauty of them and the way the colours had kept so fresh after all these centuries, though of course they were modern compared with what she had just seen in Egypt.

She'd been pretty bad-tempered on the whole trip, she thought now, smiling as she remembered her former self. How she'd resented the presence of the Portmans! God knows what they were doing here at the back of beyond, she'd thought, hardly the place for a holiday. And it was infuriating the way Becky managed to look so cool and elegant despite the heat. Even on that awful climb, scrabbling up the rock, she'd kept some sort of poise, a kind of dignity. Sickening really. And the way Matthew doted on her, always watching over her, that was an added irritation in the circumstances. Yet all the time, unbeknownst to her, unforeseen even as she climbed the rock, fate was preparing for her this great chance, this offer of freedom which she had seized: not to be Grover's wife any more but to be his widow.

It had changed Bill Anderson's life too, of course, Grover's death had. For she had heard the mighty row they'd had the night before they went to Sigiriya. The guest-house, which she and Grover had been given, next to Bill's, was pretty basic, with partition walls that didn't reach the ceiling, so that the air could circulate. Not only the air, as it turned out. Conversations circulated too.

Grover had invited Bill round for a nightcap. She'd gone to bed and left them to their talk, which drifted in snatches along the corridor to her bedroom. At first she hadn't paid much attention, was just aware of voices droning on as she half dozed beneath her mosquito net. She liked Bill, a decent sort of chap, she reckoned. He really loved his work; it was a challenging job building a whole sugar estate out there, roads, factories the lot. A straight-dealing man too. Not like Grover. Widowed recently. Apparently Becky had been a friend of his wife, Eleanor. That's why the Portmans had come to stay with him.

She hadn't thought much about why Grover had had to come out to Sri Lanka; something to do with Chemtec's taking over the firm that Bill was working for. It was quite funny really, lying listening to the pair of them, Bill talking about the engineering work, assuming Grover would be interested, and Grover bored to tears with all that, just interested in the assets and the money to be made. Rather like listening to a radio play when you're half asleep, piecing it together. Evidently Grover was trying to persuade Bill to cut out all the testing processes in the sugar factory; that way they would claim the million-pound bonus the clients were offering if they got sugar production going ahead of schedule. Bill was obviously appalled by the idea; he talked of the dangers, of exploding boilers, of fractured pipes and escapes of steam, of burns and scaldings to the workers, even of putting the men's lives at risk.

Their voices had grown louder; even though she couldn't see them, she sensed that Grover was plying Bill with liquor; he'd stocked up with vodka at the duty free. He was used to it; Bill wasn't. Chalk and cheese, they were. She wouldn't reckon Bill's chances very high if it came to a showdown. Nice guys didn't have much hope against Grover.

'How many staff could you sack if you dispensed with the testing?' she heard Grover ask.

'I've told you we can't dispense with the testing. It's dangerous.'

Bill was sounding belligerent. The unaccustomed vodka was taking effect.

'But *if*,' Grover said, quietly, reasonably. 'Only *if*.'

'There'd be no point. They'd have to be given time to look around for another job and—'

'Given time!' Grover exploded. 'Given time. Give them time to do a lot of damage before they go? No, call them in without warning and give them half an hour to get out, that's the way to do it.'

'But that's a terrible thing to do to a man,' Bill objected. 'I wouldn't want to work for a company that treated people like that.'

'I don't mind admitting that I shared your views once,' Grover went on, placatory now. 'I remember when I first joined Chemtec being told there was a saying in the company that when the boss comes up to you and puts an arm round your shoulder, it's because he's got a knife in his hand to stick in your back. I was quite shocked, I remember. But I've learned a lot since then.'

Corinne yawned; she'd heard all this before.

Bill hadn't. 'How can you sound so admiring?' he asked. 'I'd push off rather than work for bastards like that,' he added, his voice thickened with anger and vodka.

'You've a lot to learn, my friend,' Grover said, and his voice by contrast was smooth and controlled.

'Don't trust him,' Corinne wanted to shout over the partition. 'Especially when he calls you friend.'

'The point about the story of the knife is that it illustrates the advantage of surprise. Keep his confidence right up till the last minute, then you catch him off guard. In business, as in everything else, surprise is your strongest weapon. Never throw it away.'

Bill said nothing and Grover went on, 'It's the same in personal matters. Say you want to end an affair . . .'

She hadn't heard this one before. Corinne was wide-awake now, listening hard. She sat up in bed to improve her hearing.

'You don't go giving the woman warning signs, letting her think you're cooling off, do you?' Grover was expounding. 'That would give her time to get alarmed, start arguing, maybe put you in the wrong—'

'You might in fact be in the wrong?' Bill interrupted.

Behind the partition, Corinne gave a little crow of delight. They didn't hear.

'Nobody puts me in the wrong,' Grover told Bill brusquely. 'Man or woman. So you take her by surprise. She's expecting a loving telephone call or a tender heart-to-heart over lunch, because that's what you've led her to expect, so when you turn on the cold tap, give her the icy voice treatment, she's too shocked to argue.'

Corinne could hear the chair scrape as he leaned forward to fill up the glasses again. He was warming to his theme, 'Some people say,' he went on, 'that a woman's best weapons are her tears. Right. So you turn her weapons against her, as you always should. When a woman's shocked like that, expecting tenderness and getting the cold shoulder, the shock makes her cry, or rather feel like crying. A man would start getting mad, but a woman feels very weak, undermined and tearful. Now she won't want to show it. Women have this self-respect about not making scenes, so she'll have a great battle with herself not to cry. She's so busy fighting herself she won't attack you. I was told this years ago and it's the best advice I've ever been given. I've followed it many times. I'm speaking of a good class of woman, of course. You know, not some common tart who wouldn't mind howling and shrieking down the phone or at the restaurant.'

There was a long silence, which Bill broke by saying, as if after considerable reflection and very slowly, 'It's simple really. You're a shit.'

Corinne had almost cheered aloud as she sat up there in bed. She remembered having to bury her face in the pillow, taking care, of course, not to cover her ears.

'What did you say?' she heard Grover ask.

Bill now enunciated very carefully, navigating his words like boats on a sea of alcohol.

'Shit,' he replied. 'S-H-I-T spells shit. In vodka veritas,' he added, and she knew he was lifting his glass as if drinking a toast to Grover. She could picture it all.

'You're fired,' she heard Grover say.

'Don't be stupid. You can't fire me.'

'I can and I do. Once I've got back home and handed in my report, you'll be out. I didn't like your attitude from the moment I arrived and now I'm sure your face won't fit.'

There was silence. Was Bill just stunned? She wished she knew how he was reacting to all this. It was tempting to get up and join them, but eavesdropping gave her a sense of power she didn't want to lose.

'Then there's the little matter of getting the factory on stream early,' Grover was saying. 'I want someone in charge who isn't afraid to cut corners, a man with a sense of urgency.'

'You've got a nerve,' Bill burst out. 'You've engineered all this, haven't you? You know damned well it's not a matter of not having a sense of urgency. It's a matter of refusing to put men's lives at risk.'

'There's a risk in all construction work of this nature,' Grover began.

'God, you're devious,' Bill cut in. 'You know as well as I do that there's the world of difference between doing a dangerous job, taking every precaution you can and this, this murderous business. It's very easy for you, isn't it, to talk about taking risks when you'll be nowhere near the factory by then.'

'And neither will you,' Grover said. 'Now push off and get some sleep. You're drunk. And Chemtec doesn't look favourably on having drunkards in charge of its jobs abroad.'

She heard Bill leave; she waited for Grover to join her. But he didn't come, he stayed up drinking and she fell asleep before he came to bed.

Bill had looked awful the next day. He wasn't used to drinking and obviously had a fearful hangover. Grover, by contrast, seemed to be in rude health. His system must have become immune, she thought. Or maybe he was elated with last night's victory.

'Are you sure you're fit to drive the jeep all the way to Sigiriya?' Becky asked Bill after breakfast. 'You've had nothing but black coffee.'

Bill hesitated, glancing at Grover, obviously not sure if he would still want to go.

She too had looked at Grover: he can't want to go ahead with this trip, she had thought, not when he's just sacked Bill. It would be too awful.

'Well, I hope you're up to it, Bill,' Grover said affably. 'I'm certainly looking forward to it very much indeed. I'm sure the others are too.'

Then the innocent Becky joined in with, 'Yes, and maybe we could get up to Polonnarhua the next day. We'd like to see as much as we can while we're here,' she added, strolling over to the veranda to gaze out across the scrubland to the distant hills beyond, as if trying to absorb it all into her memory.

Matthew joined her, as Corinne knew he would. 'Hard to believe we'll be back in England in four days' time,' he said, putting his hand over his wife's on the rail. 'First day of term a week tomorrow.'

'Try not to think about it,' Becky advised, then added, illogically it seemed to Corinne, 'it's the Old Boys' Reunion the next weekend, isn't it?'

'Yes, and these are the very old boys. It's the turn of the pre-war generation this time. Some of them were at school in the twenties.'

'In that case,' Becky told him, 'I shall wear my blue lace dress. I always feel like my own great-aunt in it.'

It was weird, all this chat and normality. Corinne wanted to shout out that Grover had got Bill drunk last night, and provoked him into getting himself sacked and it was bloody unfair. She desperately wanted to talk to Bill, find some way of saving his job. Good God, the man lived for his work, and he'd nothing else now that his wife was dead. Grover mustn't get away with this. But there they all were, milling about, packing up and preparing, too busy to think about anything except loading up the jeep to get to Sigiriya.

And as for Grover, nobody could have been more friendly and charming than Grover as he'd set out on his last journey.

It was nearly half-past five. As she lay waiting for the alarm to go off, she found herself wondering what Becky was doing now. They hadn't met since that gruesome journey back, the four of them on the plane: Becky, Matthew, herself and Grover, with Grover travelling in the hold, of course, in a coffin made, so Bill had told her in a tone which suggested that he thought it a shocking misuse of such a precious timber, of jakwood.

She had said goodbye to the others at Heathrow, and she had been whisked away in a company car by a company driver back home to Priscilla. She had written to the Portmans to thank them, as she had done to Bill, for their help. They had all been very kind; maybe she'd invite Becky to see her new little house when she had settled in. Apart from anything else, she thought now as she lay in bed waiting for the alarm to go off, she would quite like to find out how much, if anything, Becky knew about what had actually happened to Grover in his last moments of life on top of Sigiriya.

Chapter Six

The pre-Second World War Old Boys were enjoying their pre-dinner sherry. Becky, resplendent in the blue lace, watched them for a moment before mingling: black evening dress, shining bald heads, mottled hands, hearing aids, grey-haired wives in dresses long and floral, expressions discreet but interested. Not that there was much discreet about Colonel Rigby (Crumms House 1919–1923), president of the pre-war Old Boys, and extremely deaf.

'You used to work in a bookshop, Mrs Er . . .' he surprised Becky by remarking.

'Well, almost, Colonel. It was a library actually. Not *selling* books, just *lending* them.'

'Come again,' he ordered, adjusting his hearing aid.

'I said *lending them*,' she shouted.

'Oh, pawnshop, was it? Sorry. Thought it was books.'

Becky heard Juliet, dutifully handing round nuts and crisps, say to her friend, Jo, 'Imagine Mummy in a porn shop? What does he mean?'

'No, Colonel. A *library*.'

'Oh, *library*. Thought so. Met your husband there, didn't you? I remember that. Never heard about that pawnshop. Used to call it "Uncle's" in my day. Gone out now, welfare state and all that. No call for 'em. People aren't properly poor any more. Suppose it's progress.'

He dipped the great mottled nose into the tiny glass and went on, 'I've got a book I'm very fond of. *Rob Roy*. Read it at school. In Ledbetter's time. Remember old Ledbetter? Head of English? Old chap with whiskers?'

'No,' Becky said, pretending to try to remember. 'He would

be before our time, Colonel. Matthew's only been here six years.'

'Yes, course. Dead long ago. Bit of an old fool really, Ledbetter was. No discipline. Still, introduced me to *Rob Roy*, grateful for that. Read it dozens of times since.'

'Really? Do you enjoy Scott's other books?'

'Who?'

'Scott.'

'Antarctic chap?'

'No, I meant Sir Walter Scott, who wrote *Rob Roy*.'

'Did he? Funny how you never think of anyone actually writing the book, do you?'

'I just thought you might enjoy his others. Do you have a good local library?'

The colonel shook his head. The drip on the end of his nose, which Becky had watched as it hovered, now saw its chance and plopped into the sherry.

'No, never read anything else. Only *Rob Roy*. I'm a one-book chap, myself, Mrs Er . . . Can't understand chaps poking round in libraries. I'm a one-woman chap too. Ask Mabel. She'll tell you. Can't understand these political chaps always messing about with other women. Must be something about politics makes 'em do it. Causes trouble, you know. Stick to one woman and one book, that's my advice.'

'The Bible?' Jackson Minor, once bishop of Hinnington, asked, coming up on Becky's right.

'Bugger the Bible. *Rob Roy*. Oh, it's you, Jackson. Forgotten you were a padre. Sorry. Soldier's language, don't you know?'

'That's all right.'

'Course you're in mufti, so a chap don't recognise you for what you are. Why don't you wear a dog-collar then? Ashamed of it, are you?'

'You haven't changed at all,' Jackson Minor said.

'D'you know Mrs Er . . . ?'

'But of course I do.'

The episcopal smile was extra warm, as if to make up for the colonel's supposing he might have forgotten. 'Of course I know our esteemed headmaster's good lady. Where would we be without her help in the library and in the production of our school plays?'

'Met her husband in a bookshop,' the colonel said.

Dinner was announced; Becky excused herself and left them reminiscing, assuring each other that they hadn't changed at all. In that case, she thought as she led the way into the dining room, they must have been very strange little boys indeed.

The colonel made a very good after-dinner speech. In the matter of after-dinner speeches, she reflected, deafness is no disadvantage. Confidence matters more, and he had that in abundance. His memory of times past was extraordinary too; he told anecdotes of the 1920s, remembering the names of boys and masters without a note, he who could never remember the present headmaster's name. He had remembered about the library too, or anyway associated her with the book trade and meeting Matthew among books; no doubt he'd been told that when he was introduced to them six years ago.

Matthew had always needed help finding books in the public library, where she had worked in Hampstead: the assistant English master at the local school, he had come in often, requiring things to be looked up, books sent for. Tall, donnish, bespectacled, he was a deceptively vague-looking man. Yet he had an air of authority; she had taken him to be much older than she was, though in fact there was only a couple of years' difference. Love had come to her as a kind of recognition. There had been no doubt about it, as there had been with Josh, the geologist she had known in her student days, who had loved her and had for three years tried to persuade her to marry him. Dear Josh, unchanging, dependable, ever-faithful Josh, how she had sometimes envied his certainty about her, as she wondered if the affection she felt for him might in fact be love, and had worried for both their sakes about what she should do. But there was no doubt at all when it came to Matthew. Now she herself was possessed of that enviable certainty. Yes,

Matthew, of course I'll marry you. Yes, Matthew. Yes, please.

The colonel chose to end his speech with a rousing attack on the young.

'They've got white of egg in their veins,' he was declaiming, 'and their spunk is that watery it's a marvel they can breed.'

Listening to him, Becky thought that the old are as unpredictable as the young in their utterances. The colonel was long past caring what he said or others thought. Actually the audience thought as he did: there was much clapping of frail hands and frequent barks of 'Hear, hear,' as he laid into modern youth.

Once she might have been embarrassed for Matthew's sake, but now she knew he would handle it easily. Soon he was up, replying, thanking, turning away the Old Boys' wrath with easy assurance. Nothing was ever as good as it had been, he reminded them, especially the young. Hadn't Bede written in the eighth century that the flowers didn't smell as good as when he was a lad, and the songs didn't have such good tunes? As for what flowed in the veins and other parts of young men, hadn't that been said by Orwell over sixty years ago, when the Old Boys themselves were youngsters?

'Thought you went a bit too far,' Jackson Minor said to the colonel afterwards. 'But there's something in what you said.'

'Of course there's something in what I said. Take books, for example. The names in *Rob Roy* are top-hole. Sir Hildebrand Osbaldistone, how's that for a name?'

'And you remember it so easily,' Becky remarked.

'What? No, they don't write 'em like that any more. Same with women. Don't breed 'em like my Mabel any more. Of course we had that Mrs Er for a woman prime minister. Good luck to 'em. Give the ladies a chance, that's what I say.'

He leaned over Becky and added confidentially, 'Had cause to write to her once. Heard her talking to this chappie on the television about the Ruskies and she said, "I can't understand anyone *ever* wanting to invade Afghanistan." Yes, that's what she said.'

He shook his head in remembered astonishment.

'So I wrote and told her Britain spent the last century invading Afghanistan. My father, grandfather and great-grandfather probably killed more Afghans between them than she'd had hot dinners. Whenever the emir wasn't pro-British enough, in we went and topped him. Put in someone else who was. She should've known that.'

He paused and then added reflectively, 'Now take Mabel. Mabel would've made a splendid woman prime minister. Where's she got to? Ah, there we are.'

Like a battleship, Mabel came towards them. 'Bedtime,' she boomed when she got within hailing distance, moving all in one piece like a heavy item of furniture on rollers. 'Come along now,' she said, taking her husband under one elbow and propelling him towards the door.

Becky watched them go. All around her, old men were talking, thin yellow hands were slicing the air, hearing aid arguing with hearing aid. She stood for a moment observing them, and suddenly it seemed unbearably sad; there were too many old people gathered together, segregated like old men and women in an old people's home. It's all very well to speak cheerfully of the winter of your life when it's still summer, or even autumn, but when it takes hold, that cold, leafless winter, which contains no hope of spring, it's a different matter altogether.

The air was sharp, the moon a pale, cold sickle in a starless sky as they locked the door on the empty hall and set off across the courtyard. It was only a short walk to the headmaster's house, but the very fact of going out of doors to another building was important to Becky, symbolising as it did the break between the world of school and the world of home. She was glad that the two buildings were so unalike; the headmaster's house was built of old stone, having been the lodge to a mansion which had burnt down a hundred years ago and been replaced by the present brickwork of the school.

She knew that Matthew didn't feel like this; as far as he was concerned the house went with the job and that was all there was to it. But she had learned the need to keep the two worlds separate, otherwise work and home would merge and she would exist only as the headmaster's wife.

Yet it was Becky who was still worrying about the Old Boys as they walked home.

'Matthew,' she said, as he unlocked their front door, 'do you think it's really a good idea to have these reunions in age groups? I mean, it's all right for the young ones, but it's sad somehow when they're all so old and frail.'

'But they love it, Becky,' Matthew told her, surprised. 'They love meeting all their contemporaries and condemning any one younger than they are.'

'Yes, I suppose so,' she sighed as she followed him upstairs. 'Yes, of course you're right. The sadness is in the eye of the beholder.'

The newspaper still lay where she had left it that morning on the bedside table, folded back at the report of Grover Blackford's death, but neither of them, for different reasons, referred to it.

'Have a look at this, Dad, before you go to school,' Ben said after breakfast, proffering a postcard.

'Pretty impressive,' Matthew remarked. 'Where is it?'

'Some place in Peru. James is there, James Carteris. He's backpacking before he goes to college.'

'Who's James Carteris?' his sister asked.

'You *know*, Juliet. The one who led the climbing expedition to the Lake District that I went on last summer. *And* he went up Sigiriya like Mum and Dad. Don't you ever remember anything?'

'I can't be expected to memorise all your sporting idols, baby brother.'

'He's not an idol. Just jolly good at climbing. Gosh, I wish I could go off to somewhere like Peru.'

'You will,' Matthew told him from the doorway. 'When you're eighteen and waiting to go to college.'

'Some hope,' Ben said gloomily after his father had gone.

'Oh, I don't know,' Juliet told him. 'You might find a university that'll give you a degree in cricket scores and rugby teams and how to navigate a skateboard.'

'There's plenty of time, Ben,' Becky encouraged automatically as she wiped the breakfast table.

Juliet lifted the toast-rack to make way for the journeying dish-cloth and then replaced it, scattering crumbs.

'You know that caseful of washing I brought home at the end of term, Mummy?' she asked.

'Yes.'

'Where is it? I mean, I know it's washed. But where is it?'

'Where did you put it, Juliet?'

'That's the funny thing. I can't remember. I mean I didn't need any of it at the time. It was duvet covers and stuff like that from college.'

'I'll have a hunt later.'

Ben looked up from the newspaper he was unwrapping from round his hiking boots. 'You ought to have something done about your amnesia, Juliet,' he said.

'When I want your advice, baby brother, I'll ask for it. What's that stuff you're reading?'

'What stuff?'

'You've got your nose in a chunk of gutter press.'

'Actually it's an article about statistics in the paper they wrapped my boots in at the menders.'

'What sort of statistics?'

'On adultery. It's very interesting. It says that fifty-seven per cent of married men commit adultery, and forty-three per cent of married women.'

'Cor, what an example our elders do give us, don't they?'

'It can't be right, of course.'

'Why not?'

'Well, obviously, they have to be the same percentages. I mean, it stands to reason. You can't have more men committing adultery than women.'

'Of course you can.'

'No. You can't. It's done in pairs.'

'Ben, you're so *stupid*. Mummy, don't you think you ought to have his brain tested or something?'

'Don't be silly, Juliet. I think, Ben, that what she is trying to explain is that they wouldn't necessarily have the same partners.'

She began carrying the dishes into the kitchen.

'You see,' Juliet said. 'I told you.'

'No, I don't see actually. And I do know something about it, because we have done statistics in Maths and—'

'Look, here's a bit of paper. Here's your Mr A committing adultery with Miss X, Y and Z,' Juliet explained, drawing crosses.

'All right. So then Mrs A has adultery with—'

'You don't *have* adultery, you *commit* it. Who teaches you English?'

'Dad. And Mr Walpole sometimes. Oh, I see what you mean. Yes, I get it. There might be lots of people.'

'Anyway, how do they know all these statistics?'

'They interview people. It was a poll. It goes on to say that, of the hundred women interviewed, forty-seven per cent said they'd slept with someone who wasn't their husband in the last month, and fifty per cent said they hadn't.'

'That's not right. It doesn't add up.'

'But you've just said it didn't have to add up.'

'This has to add up to a hundred, clot. What about the missing three per cent?'

'Oh, wait a minute.'

He spread the paper out. 'Oh yes, here it is on this crumpled piece. It says that three per cent of the women didn't know.'

'*Didn't know*? Let me see. Gosh, Mummy, did you hear that? This rag of Ben's—'

'It isn't my rag. It was wrapped round my climbing boots.'

'Says that three per cent of married women actually didn't know if they'd slept with someone who wasn't their husband in the past month? That really is quite surprising.'

'Women don't have such good memories as men,' Ben told her. 'I expect they just forgot. Because of their hormones and things,' he added vaguely.

'Rubbish. They probably couldn't be bothered to tell the people doing the poll. Anyway, most men aren't all that memorable.'

'They are. It's just that they look more alike than women because they dress more alike. Without their clothes on they're just as different as women.'

'You are just incapable of logical argument. We're discussing adultery and you yatter on about men's clothes. They wouldn't have their clothes on, idiot boy.'

'It doesn't say,' Ben said, perusing the paper, 'if the adulteries were clad or unclad. I mean if—'

'If you two haven't anything better to do than to argue about that rubbish,' Becky interrupted, 'maybe you could see to the washing-up.'

'Actually, Mum, I've got to get my Latin prose done by ten o'clock.'

'And I really ought to get my stuff together for next term. And you're a rotten little swine, Ben. You said yesterday that the prose didn't matter till next week.'

'And you've got all day to pack. You don't go back to college till Wednesday.'

'If neither of you wants to help,' Becky said, 'just go away, will you, and let me get on? I'd sooner do it myself than have you two fighting to get out of it.'

Juliet went up and sniffed her mother. 'Do I catch the odour of burning martyr?' she said, and hugged her.

'I'll wash,' Ben said, 'and you dry, Juliet.'

'It's a bit mean, actually, considering I don't eat breakfast,' Juliet said, picking up the tea-towel.

'But you drink gallons of coffee. It's a jolly unhealthy sort of diet. You'll get anorexia and start vomiting and your hair will fall out.'

'Oh Christ, don't you know the difference between anorexia and alopecia? Honestly, Mum, he's hopeless.'

Becky laughed. 'He's also six foot two, weighs eleven stone, and has a mop of hair like a sweep's brush, so really anorexia and alopecia aren't your problems, are they, Ben?'

'All the same, he should know his words. You might as well say that the only people who should be able to spell diarrhoea are people with the trots.

'Actually,' she went on after he had gone out, 'it's a bit hard on him being so big for his age. I suppose we do expect him to be more grown-up than he is.'

'He does pretty well, Juliet. Try not to needle him so much.'

'He asks for it. He will make these stupid sexist remarks, bloody childish. Especially from a great big hairy bloke like him.'

'He's not unduly hairy.'

'Well, you know what I mean. Grown-up looking. Dad's quite hairy, so I suppose he takes after him.'

'Is he? Yes, I remember, come to think of it, being quite surprised on our wedding night at how hairy he was.'

Juliet dropped the tea-towel and the cutlery it contained on to the table and collapsed on a chair in gales of laughter.

'Oh, you are so funny,' she gasped.

'Now what?'

'Just the way you said that, about not knowing what he looked like until your wedding night. It's so *sweet*.'

Give me patience, Becky prayed. I can take everything from the young except their condescension.

'Not just you, of course,' Juliet went on, 'but all your generation.'

'The lot of us? All sweet?'

'Well, the innocence of you. I mean, I suppose it made sense in the pre-Pill days, but all the same, it just seems so Victorian now. And somehow primitive.'

'Primitive?'

'Yes, I mean you wouldn't go out and commit yourself to

having a word-processor without testing it, but you committed yourself to a man for the rest of your life without even trying him out. Nobody would do that nowadays. It's crazy. I mean, it's a big decision. You ought to have all the relevant facts. Sex is a relevant fact.'

'So that's why marriages have become so remarkably stable in these permissive times?'

'Oh, my sarcastic old mother,' Juliet said, getting up and retrieving the tea-towel. 'I'm glad you're getting back a bit of fighting spirit.'

Becky glanced at her inquiringly.

'I just meant,' her daughter reassured her, 'that you've been a bit, well, you know, since your illness and everything. Not quite with us sometimes. But you're really back to normal now.'

'Good. Thank you.'

'And you were always a bit of a dreamer anyway. It's your natural state. Will you miss me when I've gone?' she asked suddenly.

'It'll be quiet without you.'

'I'll pop back sometimes. There'll be my driving test soon. What are you going to do on your day off on Thursday?'

'I'm going up to London to see Mrs Doughtyman about the book.'

'It's dragging on a bit, isn't it?' Then, seeing her mother's face fall, added, 'But it'll be lovely in the end. And just think, *three* books to your credit.'

'Only two so far. And the publisher of the second went bankrupt.'

'That wasn't your fault. Arblaster's just happened to be no good at sums.'

'No, that's not fair, Juliet. They were very good as small publishers go—'

'And as small publishers go,' her daughter concluded for her, 'they went,' and she kissed her mother again and ran out, laughing.

Chapter Seven

Juliet was right, Becky thought as she sat on the train: it *had* dragged on. It was more than two years since her first visit to the Doughtymans'. Sometimes it seemed like a lifetime away, sometimes the memory of it was so sharp and clear that it felt like yesterday. She hadn't, of course, been used to their ways then: no wonder that first visit had made such an impact. She had expected an ordinary office, even though Mr Doughtyman had remarked, on the phone, that the family lived above the shop, which might have forewarned her.

Mr Doughtyman was a vague, sweet-looking man, possessed of a vague and sweet-looking wife and innumerable children. When asked how many, he had answered uncertainly. She suspected he didn't know, was just vaguely aware that an extra one was added unto him each year.

It was Mrs Doughtyman who edited the poetry list. So it was for her that Becky had waited in the little ante-room by the main office, that first time, two years ago. As she waited, the youngest child came staggering in, clearly delighted with his new-found skill of walking upright. He stood staring at her for a moment, then collapsed in a heap. His mother, coming in behind him, narrowly missed trampling her youngest son underfoot and greeted Becky warmly.

'I loved your poems,' she exclaimed, her face lighting up with what seemed to be genuine delight as she shook hands. 'We both did. We'd be proud to have you on our list.'

Every chair and most of the floor was covered with manuscripts. Mrs Doughtyman cleared a space for herself on the couch next to Becky and put the poems on the floor beside her.

A girl put her head round the door. 'Shall I take Emmanuel away, Mrs Doughtyman?' she asked.

'Oh, no. He's not doing any harm, are you, Emmanuel?'

Emmanuel, who was wearing nothing but a vest which reached to just above his genitals, was staggering about the room, collapsing now and then on to his podgy bottom, smiling good-humouredly while his mother talked.

'He's not house-trained yet,' Mrs Doughtyman remarked. 'We put him in nappies but he just takes them off, don't you, Emmanuel?'

Her son smiled his great, loopy, good-natured smile, and crawled away into the corner. There he hoisted himself up by a chair leg and set off again around the room with a rolling, sprawling, splay-legged, drunken movement.

'I see you as a nature poet,' Mrs Doughtyman said suddenly. 'It seemed to me at first that we could collect together enough of the ones about the Dales to make one long section. But then I did just wonder, do you have any others you might work on which you could let me see? It did just cross my mind that we might do a complete book of the nature poems.'

Becky had been amazed. 'Well, I do have others in the making,' she managed to say, 'but there's still a lot of work to be done on them. You know how it is, you get an idea, then you don't have time to see it through . . .'

'If you had a deadline for a book you'd make the time,' Mrs Doughtyman told her briskly, and Becky realised that behind this vague and sweetly smiling exterior there dwelt a tough woman.

She looked up and saw that Emmanuel was now standing astride her manuscript. He was stretching his arms in the air so that his vest was slipping up to reveal his slightly protuberant belly-button. Suddenly he clutched at his chubby, crinkly genitals. Simultaneously his mother shrieked, lunged and grabbed. Just in time; the fine jet which rose from him missed the poems but delicately sprayed the carpet and couch.

'Oh, wicked Emmanuel,' his mother said, hugging him.

The coffee arrived.

She had been remembering this scene, reliving it as she walked back to the tube station that same morning, not concentrating, not seeing the barrel on the pavement, but still seeing the chubby child, the piles of manuscripts, the pale, expressive face of Mrs Doughtyman, which registered dismay and joy in such rapid succession. And how quickly after Emmanuel had been removed, she had reverted to discussing poetry; how perceptive she was, how well she understood. Becky saw her again as she leant forward in her chair, frail yet vibrant, instilling hope and confidence while her coffee, ecstatically welcomed, grew cold in the untouched cup alongside her.

If only she had been concentrating on where she was going instead of dreaming, Becky realised now, none of it would ever have happened. As it was, she heard the rumbling sound fractionally too late.

The barrel caught her on the back of her leg, slap against her calf. It pushed her in the direction of the trap door which was open to reveal the blackness of the cellar. She staggered, then felt herself grabbed from behind and, overcompensating, nearly fell backwards, reeled for a moment and at last found her balance.

The burly man in a blue sweater, jeans and a leather apron launched into what was presumably meant as an apology but sounded more like an accusation.

'I thought you was bound to have seen me. I mean you was walking along with your head down, looking at the pavement. You had your eye on it. Gave me quite a turn, missus. Could've been nasty.'

'You should have made sure the pavement was clear before you pushed that barrel,' the man behind her interrupted, still holding her arm. She felt like a buffer between the two of them, these two warring men.

'It's all right, really,' she said, 'I'm not hurt at all. It was my fault. I wasn't looking where I was going. I'm so sorry.'

'That's all right, missus,' her assailant forgave her and went back to his lorry.

'My God, it's Becky,' the man behind her said.

She turned sharply, not recognising the voice. For Josh's voice had quite lost its strong Yorkshire accent. She turned to stare up at him.

It wasn't just the voice which had changed. His hair was grey and his face was much fuller. Another look revealed that the rest of him was much fuller too. Quite plump, Josh had become. She smiled up at this new Josh, this Josh in disguise, pretending to be a middle-aged chap in London.

'Whenever we meet you seem to have to pull me out of holes,' she said, laughing and remembering the misty hillside where he had found her years ago in the swirling fog and how he had dragged her out of the unseen pot-hole and taken her safely back to the cottage in Enderby where her father was waiting.

'Well, at least you didn't actually fall down this one,' Josh said, nodding towards the cellar and taking her arm. 'Let's go in and have a drink. They've got supplies, that's for sure.'

'Oh, I don't think . . .'

'Come on, aren't you pleased to have been rescued? Mind you, you weren't particularly pleased the first time, as I recall,' he added, leading her into the pub and sitting down with her at an empty table.

'Well, you were so bossy, demanding to know how old I was and everything.'

He laughed, shaking his head. 'I remember that,' he said, 'but honestly, I really did think you were about fourteen.'

Yes, she must have looked that, with her white ankle socks and sandals, her childish cotton dress, her face all red from the sun which had blazed all day until suddenly the mist came down and the hottest day of that very hot summer ended in a tremendous thunderstorm.

'I was horrified actually,' he admitted. 'It's a dangerous mountain, Gorfell, riddled with small pot-holes. I'd been over it quite a bit with other geologists, but still treated it with

114

respect. And to see a school-kid like you wandering about – what'll you have to drink, Becky?'

'I wasn't a school-kid, I was eighteen, and I'd been brought up in the Dales and I knew Gorfell quite well,' she pointed out indignantly. 'And a dry cider would be nice.'

'What are you doing in London?' he asked later as they sat, he with a beer, she with a cider.

'I live near Oxford. My husband's the headmaster of a boarding school there. I came up by train to Paddington.'

A shadow passed over his face. He hadn't liked her reference to a husband.

'And you,' she said. 'Are you down from the north?'

'Good Lord, no. Whatever made you think that? I work in London.'

'I don't know. I just associated you with the north, I suppose.'

'It's the second half of the twentieth century, Becky. There are cars and trains and people move about and—'

'All right, I've moved too.'

They looked at each other, amused. The Becky she had been years ago looked at him. And the real Josh, under the flimsy disguise, looked back at her out of the middle-aged mask, as if neither of them was deceived by it, this curious pretence of change which the years superimpose.

'Have you had lunch, Becky?'

'No, but I'm not hungry.'

'Then you should be. It's gone one o'clock.'

He looked her over carefully, up and down and up again. 'You're thinner,' he pronounced. 'Thinner than last time I saw you.'

She had made a conscious effort not to remember the last time they were together. It was dangerous. She wasn't sure why, just knew it was.

'Come on,' Josh was saying. 'We'll get something at the counter.'

It would be churlish to refuse. Dear, kind Josh, she couldn't hurt him by being stand-offish now; she'd hurt him once, long ago, she knew that, she thought, as they stood at the counter, selecting cold meat from plastic trays and instructing the barman about which of the assorted salads to scoop up.

'Tell me what you've done in all these years,' she requested when they sat down. 'Fill in the gap for me.'

He launched into an account of his progress from geology into business. Evidently he had prospered. He was married, had a child.

'And your parents?' she asked.

'Both dead.'

'I'm sorry,' she said. 'They were always kind to me.'

'Yes, I'm always sorry they didn't live to see my success.'

She glanced at him; it was the sort of remark people make ironically. But Josh was serious.

'I'll get refills,' he remarked, getting up and taking the empty glasses with him back to the now crowded bar. Becky, watching him, remembered his parents and wondered, as she had done all those years ago, why he was so ill-at-ease with them. To her, brought up in college rooms by an adored but academic and unworldly father, it had seemed enviable that Josh should have that comfortable little home to come back to, complete with well-matched, contented parents. She could see them now, in the little sitting room with its brightly flowered wallpaper, sitting one on each side of the tiled fireplace above which pot ducks flew in triplicate: Josh's mother, plump, woollen-slippered, her hands busy with her knitting, his father, also beslippered, smoking his pipe, an unread newspaper open on his knee.

'Do you knit, Becky?' Josh's mother had asked politely on her first visit.

'Not much,' she had replied, never having even tried. 'Would you like me to do some for you?' And she had reached out to take the half-knitted sweater, thinking that perhaps it was one of those things you offer to help with, like the washing-up.

'No, dear, thank you,' Josh's mother had said, holding the garment protectively to her bosom.

'She'll not have much time for such things as knitting at university,' his father pointed out. 'She'll be that busy with her book-learning.'

He had pronounced the word heavily, as if it was alien, even suspect.

'Of course, there was none of this university education around in our day, was there, Mother?' he had persisted, and Becky had thought of the thirteenth-century spires of her place of education and hadn't known how to reply.

'And your degree will count the same as our Joshua's, will it?' Josh's father had continued, undeterred.

'It'll be in English and his was in geology, but yes, they'll count the same,' she had said, not sure what was worrying him.

'Even though you're a girl?'

'Of course it makes no difference that she's a girl,' Josh had cut in impatiently.

'And what will you do with this degree afterwards?' his father had persisted. 'I mean, what's it for?'

She had chosen the easiest explanation. 'I want to be a librarian,' she said.

'But if you get married,' Josh's father had objected, 'it'll all have been wasted. A lass don't need a degree to get wed.'

His wife shot him a warning glance.

'I wasn't suggesting anything,' he told her defensively. 'I just meant it's a bit of a waste if she gets married. I meant married to *anyone*. You managed very well without a degree, Mother,' he had added to clinch it.

'That's as may be, but if Becky wants to be a lady in a library she'll no doubt need her qualifications. It's different from our day, Father, you need a piece of paper before you can get a job like that nowadays.'

Poor dead parents, Becky thought now, whatever could they have made of her, this undomesticated creature their only son had brought home?

'A penny for them,' Josh said, bringing the replenished

glasses back to the table. 'You were miles away.'

'I was thinking about your parents,' she said, 'and how tolerant they were of me. They must have thought I was very odd.'

'Well, I think the time my mother gave you a cake recipe and you said you'd take it to a confectioner's and get it made up rather took them aback,' Josh conceded, and they both laughed.

'That's better,' Josh said. 'It's good to see you laugh.'

She looked at him, puzzled.

'It's just that there's something sad about you,' Josh said, 'and you're too thin. Come on, eat up.'

The salads, which had all looked different in their glass bowls, tasted identical, and the differently-coloured assorted cold meats had been processed into the same texture and taste too. She pushed greenery around her plate and couldn't think of anything to say.

'Becky,' he said suddenly, 'you're not happy, are you?'

It was the way he spoke so directly from the past that did it. As if he had the right to say such things to her because they had once been close. If you've once been as close as that perhaps you can never again be distant from each other. It gave him a kind of power; anyway something not to be denied.

'There *is* something, Becky, isn't there?' he insisted.

'I could tell you,' she heard herself say. 'He said I should talk about it, the doctor did, I mean, but I couldn't.'

'Of course you can tell me, Becky. I'm an old friend.'

The words wrapped around her. How good they sounded, how comforting. An old friend, from the past, from before – but an old friend she had once hurt. There was something to be said first.

'Josh.'

'Yes?'

'I know that years ago I hurt you, because I wouldn't marry you. I'm sorry I hurt you.'

'You couldn't help it, Becky. You were always honest about

it. I loved you, my God how I loved you. But you didn't love me. You never pretended. These things happen. It was nobody's fault.'

He held her with his eyes. It seemed as if he hadn't changed at all. The disguise the years had imposed was adjusting, fitting itself to other features. Besides, eyes don't change, nor had the expression in his. Really he wasn't different at all.

'You haven't changed, Becky,' he said. 'You've hardly altered. It's amazing how young you've stayed.'

'How long is it?'

'Twenty-three years.'

She remembered saying goodbye to him when she left college. She'd been three years in the library and she'd been married to Matthew for twenty years. 'Yes, that must be right,' she said. 'I'm forty-four. I don't feel middle-aged.'

'You don't look it.'

'Come off it, Josh. We must. It stands to reason.'

Besides, didn't she, when the black dog came and sat on her shoulder, feel about a hundred? No, no, she didn't. She felt ageless then, out of time, out of space, out of everything.

'We can't talk here,' he said, suddenly impatient. 'Let's go into the park.'

'Talk?' she repeated. 'Now?' She wanted to get out of it, escape. She shouldn't have said anything about it.

'Why not? I'm free. I was taking the afternoon off to choose some prints for my office. But it doesn't matter. Another day, another dollar. What about you? Are you in a hurry? Are you expected back?'

'Well, no. I left it open as I didn't know how long things would take.'

'Shopping?'

'No. Work.'

'Work?'

'Poetry. I write a bit.'

'Really? Should I have known?'

'Of course not.'

'I don't read poetry much.'

'It's all right. Don't feel you should.'

Curious, staccato conversation. The air had become tense between them, their words shot about in it like crackles and sparks in an atmosphere taut with electricity. Then they were silent, just looking at each other. He wasn't deliberately casting this spell, she knew that. He was as bewildered by it as she was. He touched her arm, signalling that they should go.

She followed him obediently, seeming to have no will of her own. There was a stillness around them, as if they carried with them their own little isolated world. There must have been people about, there must have been traffic, they must have waited on pavements to let cars pass, but she saw none of it, aware only of the stillness as they walked up narrow streets, and once a particular square, quite small but magical with trees and railinged houses and on one side tall buildings, between which long shafts of sunlight slanted and lay in golden lines across their path. He took her hand and they fell into step, walking easily as they had always done.

'It's as if twenty-three years have vanished, not existed at all,' he said quietly, reading her thoughts. His hand felt just the same. She would have known its touch anywhere. It seemed to belong in hers.

'And your hand,' he said, 'it feels just the same.'

It was quiet in the park; little children were playing, the elderly were walking their dogs. They strolled, she and Josh, across the grass under the trees, making their way towards an empty seat, but an athletic old couple spotted it first, accelerated and beat them to it.

'Over there,' Josh said, pointing towards another under a tree, and he put his arm around her waist to hurry her along.

They spread their belongings along the bench, making it their own. Then he turned her towards him.

'Now we can talk,' he said.

She was silent. They were alone, it was private, there was nothing to stop her. But she couldn't speak.

'Oh, Josh, I'm sorry,' she said.

'You do keep on saying you're sorry nowadays,' he said. 'I don't remember that you used to be so apologetic.'

The rebuke hurt; she looked up at him doubtfully.

'Oh Becky, you're so beautiful,' he said.

She didn't know what she'd expected him to say; certainly not that. She waved it away.

'But I saw,' he went on, 'the minute I set eyes on you, I saw that something was wrong. You looked as if you'd suffered.'

She smiled. 'I looked older, you mean.'

'No, Becky. The fact is that you didn't. You do still look remarkably young. I'm not just saying that, and you've still got a fantastic figure and you smile a lot and generally look cheerful, but I saw something underneath all that, I tell you I *saw* it. When you love someone you can see these things.'

She drew away, shocked.

'Oh, yes, Becky. I loved you then and I love you still. I think I have never stopped loving you.'

'Don't, Josh. You musn't. You must have been happy in between. You have been happy, haven't you?'

'Look, Becky. Why should I pretend? After you got married I just went on looking for another of you, really a kind of duplicate. Don't smile. I tried to find a Mark Two Becky. But it was never the same as it had been with you. In the end, well, I was getting on and I wanted to be married, so I gave up the search and settled for second-best.'

'But you were happy, a little bit happy?'

'Oh, the adrenaline flowed at first,' he said dismissively. It can't be true, she thought, I don't believe this.

'And now?'

'Now we just co-exist. It's mutually convenient, but love doesn't enter into it.'

'I'm sorry.'

'For God's sake, Becky, do stop apologising. It's not your fault. Anyway we were going to talk about you and we're doing nothing but talk about my woes.'

She hesitated, started to say something, stopped. He put an arm around her shoulder. 'You mentioned the doctor,' he said. 'Why were you seeing the doctor?'

'I've had a kind of, well, a depression thing. I didn't tell anyone about it.'

'Why not?'

'I was ashamed, I suppose. I mean, when you've always coped and suddenly you can't, you feel ashamed of yourself. I think that does happen, Josh, I mean I don't think it's just me.'

'I'm sure it's not. It's just that I've no experience of it, so you must explain. Was the doctor trying to find a cause?'

She nodded.

'Do you know the cause?'

She thought of the unmentionable thing. She hesitated. No, loyalty forbade it, just as it had forbidden her to tell her doctor, guilty though she had felt at wasting his time by withholding vital information when he was trying so hard to help her.

So she just shrugged and said, 'There aren't rational explanations, Josh. It isn't as if it was a mental thing.'

'Clearly not. But there is something, isn't there, Becky? You yourself know it. You're going to tell me.'

'Yes. I mean – no, I can't.'

She just wanted to get out of this, be somewhere else. Why had she got in the way of that wretched barrel, or, if she had to, why hadn't she fallen into the cellar and broken her neck before Josh set eyes on her?

'Start at the beginning, Becky. From where we parted. Come on, just tell me step by step.'

Like a child she began her narrative, describing the library and how she had met Matthew there.

'You married him very quickly, didn't you? I mean, you can't have known him more than a few months.'

There was pain in his voice. She knew he was comparing the years he had known her, tried to persuade her to marry him, with the speed with which she had rushed into marrying Matthew.

'I'm sorry, Josh. But I felt sure. I know that must hurt. It's true I didn't know him anything like as well as I'd known you, but I just felt sure. You know, in the same way you'd felt sure about me.'

'What did he look like?' Josh demanded suddenly.

'Tall, dark, handsome, glasses, a bit vague maybe, kindly, donnish—'

'Like your father?'

'Maybe that had something to do with it.'

'So. And you were happy? At first, anyway?'

She was tempted to imitate his remark about adrenaline flowing or some equally meaningless phrase, some easy lie. But she couldn't.

'I realised straight away,' she whispered, 'that there was something wrong.'

He looked at her sharply. 'Wrong with *him*?' he asked.

'I didn't understand. Just something wrong. I realised that we were strangers.'

'Had you been to bed with him before you were married?'

'Of course not. We didn't in those days.'

'Mm. Some did. But all right, nice girls didn't. But you know, it was everything but with us, wasn't it?'

'Well, I didn't "everything but" with him, if that's what you mean.'

'You should have done.'

'Well, I'm sorry, but I didn't,' she said, and then wondered at herself for being made to feel guilty about the chastity which had seemed so obvious a virtue at the time. Who would have thought, in those far-off days, that all the virtuous restraint would one day have to be apologised for?

'Anyway, to go back to what you said. Wrong in what way?'

'I didn't know. I tell you I didn't understand. I just seemed to repel him somehow.'

'Oh, my God.'

He took both her arms, held her from him, scowling as he stared at her. '*Repelled*,' he repeated. 'Oh, Becky, Becky. You're lovely still, but then you were, I don't know, so delicate and dainty and peachlike and everything a man could desire. And you talk of being repellent. What sort of devil would make you feel like that? I just don't, I mean I can't—'

'I'm sorry, Josh, it's no good. This is only upsetting you and getting us nowhere. I shouldn't have started.'

'Yes, you should. That was my fault. I'm sorry. Go on. You must have asked him about it?'

'I tried, but he just said he was quite happy. He was very reasonable about everything. I tried to find out what was wrong, but you know when something like that happens you just blame yourself. I loved him very much and I thought I'd failed him somehow or other.'

'Go on,' Josh prompted again.

She hesitated, forced herself to speak; the words came out jerkily, in short sentences.

'Time passed. We had children and then, when they were about five and seven, his father came to stay. He was a widower but he'd been separated from his wife ever since Matthew was a baby. Matthew had lived with his mother until she was killed in a car crash when he was twelve. Then he had gone to his father. They were good friends, but I never felt Matthew quite thought of him as a father. Understandable, I suppose, when he'd grown up without knowing him.'

She stopped, lost in thought for a moment, then went on, 'His father was taken ill, in fact he stayed with us until he died. We got on well. He was very brave, very lively to talk to, and really only needed much nursing in the last few days.'

She looked across the park, at the children playing, at their elders walking their dogs. The first of the autumn leaves were beginning to fall, aimlessly drifting and turning in the light breeze.

'And?' Josh prompted.

'One evening, in that last week, I took a milk drink in to him and he began to talk. The children were in bed, Matthew was away at a two-day conference, so I was free to sit with him. I thought he was just postponing the night, the way sick people do.'

'I know.'

'Then he began to talk about Matthew, and I got the funny feeling that there was some purpose behind what he was saying, that he was leading up to something, you know how you do when people are trying to steer a conversation?'

'Yes.'

'And he asked me if I knew why Matthew had left his first job. It was at a boarding school, St James's, near Battlestead. Of course I didn't know – he was teaching in London by the time we met, at a day school. Then his father told me the headmaster had discreetly asked Matthew to leave, because he'd caught him beating one of the boys. I was stunned. If you knew Matthew you'd understand why. He's a very gentle man. Not weak, I don't mean that, but he really hates violence and I just couldn't believe that, even if he lost his temper, was provoked beyond endurance, he'd react violently. And I said so to his father.'

'And what did his father say?'

'He said that he hadn't meant Matthew was beating the living daylights out of this lad, or anything like that. That he was more or less gently chastising him. Oh,' she smiled suddenly, 'I was so relieved, that he hadn't been cruel. I mean, I'd thought he had been trying to tell me he was some sort of suppressed sadist—'

'But he wasn't, so—'

'So I said it seemed a bit strange to sack a master for gently chastising a boy. After all, he was *in loco parentis* and the boy's father might have done likewise – or words to that effect. I forget exactly, but I remember the way Matthew's father listened to me and how he looked.'

'And what he said?'

She turned to him. 'Oh, Josh, this is the impossible bit.'

'Difficult, not impossible. Why is it so hard to speak of?'

'Because it's disloyal. We all have some things which matter to us, rules we can't break. Loyalty matters to me.'

'Poor Becky. You always had more trouble with your virtues than your vices, didn't you?'

She managed to smile.

'There, that's better. Now just hold my hand and tell me.'

'His father said,' she began almost in a whisper, so he had to bend his head to hear her, 'he said that the headmaster might have overlooked one of his staff's having a boy in his room to beat him, but if he finds him patting the lad's buttocks with one hand and fondling him with the other it's a rather more serious matter.'

He held her close. It was said. After a few seconds, she went on and her voice was stronger. 'I don't know why he told me. Perhaps he wanted to warn me, you know, put me on my guard in case of further trouble. It would be understandable. He was very fond of Matthew and he must have felt that after he died there ought to be someone else who knew the truth, could be there to protect him, if need be.'

'You mean that someone else should know that his precious schoolmaster son was homosexual and you could spend the rest of your life shielding him?'

'Don't, don't sound so bitter. Matthew couldn't help it.'

'He might bloody well have told you, Becky, before he married you. Not just leave you to find out in this very touching deathbed scene.'

A middle-aged woman in charge of two children walked by. The children stopped by the seat and stared at Becky and Josh as they sat there, wrapped round each other. The woman hurried them on.

It brought them back into the present; they smiled at each other, seeing themselves as others must see them.

'What a sight we must look, Josh.'

'She probably wondered what that dirty old man's doing to that young girl.'

'Flatterer.'

'Good, you smiled again. So what did you do, now that you knew the truth?'

She paused, then said, 'It was funny really, part of me couldn't believe it. In fact, I said to his father that I thought it very strange of the headmaster to give Matthew a reference if this story was true.'

'Implying that it wasn't?'

'Yes. But he explained that the head only gave him a reference on condition that he applied to a day school. And warned him that if there were any further questions he would tell what had happened. But there was nothing like that ever again. And the headmaster died soon afterwards. Only Matthew's father knew about it.'

'So then did you believe it?'

'Oh, part of me had believed it instantly. It explained everything.'

'So what did you do?' Josh asked again. 'What did you say to Matthew?'

'I couldn't talk to him straight away. His father was very ill. He died a few days later. But afterwards, after the funeral was over and all the clearing up seen to and we'd settled down, I did tell him exactly what his father had said.'

'Did he deny it?'

'No. He was absolutely wonderful. And, actually I did say what you did, that he should have told me. But you see, Josh, it isn't as simple as that. He'd hoped it would be all right. He was afraid of losing me if he told me. And for some people it *is* all right. It might have worked. He'd no way of knowing. He hadn't loved a woman before. He was afraid that, if he spoke of it, it would bring about the situation he most feared. I can understand why he didn't tell me.'

'My God, Becky, you're so bloody charitable.'

Indignation seemed to burst out of him, his eyes were bright with it, his mouth was set, his hands gripped hers until they hurt.

'He hadn't the right to inflict this on you. Nobody has that right. It was his problem, not yours.'

'Well, once we were married it was *our* problem, Josh.'

'Why didn't you leave him? Nobody would have blamed you. You had grounds for divorce.'

She sighed. Maybe her unwillingness to tell had been based not just on loyalty but on the instinctive knowledge that nobody would understand. She must try to explain. 'Josh,' she began, 'you don't walk out on someone just like that. Women don't—'

'Well, they should. If it was the other way round a man would give a woman a year or two maybe to get herself sorted out, then he'd be off.'

'All right, so women don't behave like men. Leave it at that. And bear in mind that anyway by this time I had a son and a daughter and a feeling of commitment to Matthew and his work and all our friends. You don't smash up—'

'What about the way *you'd* been smashed up? You knew all this and you did nothing?'

'But you see, this thing that happened at his first school never happened again. And he didn't pervert that boy: he was a sixth-former and was like that already. Matthew was harming nobody.'

'Except you.'

'But he told me he'd control it. He promised me that so long as I was there he'd be all right. I believe that. He understands this thing better than you or I ever could. I trust him, Josh, really I do.'

'So you just have to stay around being made to feel repellent so he can bloody well stay on the straight and narrow?'

'It's been all right, not as dire as it sounds, because life goes on and there are other worries and joys and—'

'Spare me that, Becky.'

'I know it sounds corny, but it's *true*.'

'So it's been a bed of roses and that's why you got hit by depression and look like you look. Becky, I tell you I saw that look, of being marked.'

'It'll be better now I've talked to you. Really, already I find

I'm feeling more detached about the whole thing.'

'Couldn't you have talked to anyone years ago?'

'No.'

He sat for a while in silence, then he sighed and said, 'I've been thinking, really, once your father had died, there was no one for you to turn to.'

'Even if he'd been alive, I don't think I could have talked to him about a thing like that. He wouldn't have wanted me to. He cared a lot about loyalty too.'

'No, but I reckon he'd have noticed. You were very close, the two of you. He'd have seen that look that I've seen. And he was so wise and humane, he'd have helped somehow. I'd a great regard for your father, you know, Becky.'

She nodded, smiling.

'Do you remember,' he went on, 'coming down in the storm, back to the cottage he'd rented in Enderby?'

'And the electricity had failed and there was nothing to cook on and you did wonders with the primus stove?'

'He must have wondered who the hell I was.'

'He was very grateful to you for bringing me back. I know that. We never mentioned to him about the pot-hole, did we? I wonder why not?'

'We just felt guilty, like kids do. You knew jolly well you shouldn't have been clambering around a mountain on your own in the mist.'

'And you didn't tell on me.'

'And we sat by the fire and it was blowing half a gale outside and your father talked so wonderfully. I shall never forget it. I mean straight away he was talking about religion and ethics and—'

'—and treachery? And he said that it was the only thing he'd kill a man for? Yes, I remember.'

'You see, my folks would never talk like that. They'd have thought it a complete waste of time. I used to feel more at home with you and your father than I did with my own parents. I suppose I envied you really.'

She sat quietly, thinking that there was nobody but Josh to whom she had ever talked about her father. They hadn't really had any family friends, not in the way she and Matthew and the children had. Her father had had plenty of friends in the academic world, of course, but they hadn't kept in touch with her after he died, the way family friends would have done. So to the usual pleasure of remembering a shared past with an old friend, was added the special joy of hearing Josh speak of her father with such affection, admiration even.

'It's been lovely, Josh,' she said gratefully, 'talking like this. Thank you.'

'We shall talk more, Becky,' he said, and suddenly he leant towards her and took her in his arms, not as he had done before, to comfort her, but as he used to do all those years ago.

'We can't, Josh. I know you said just now that it's as if twenty-three years had never been, but in fact they have been, haven't they? And all the consequences of them are here with us now. And we can't undo them.'

'I can have a damned good try,' he said, holding her even closer.

A very large, very bouncy dog suddenly hurled itself upon them, slapping a paw on each of Josh's knees and nuzzling him between the legs.

'Down, Rufus, down,' a woman's voice commanded.

Reluctantly, Rufus obeyed.

Becky began to gather up her things from the bench. 'I'll have to go, Josh,' she said. 'Look, it's nearly five o'clock.'

'I'll take you back to Paddington. Becky . . .' he hesitated.

'Yes?'

'You said you were free on Thursdays. Come up next Thursday and I'll meet you off the train.'

'No, Josh, we can't.'

'Yes, we can. We're going to talk some more. You can't just crash into my life like this and disappear again. You can't do that, Becky.' There was an edge of desperation in his voice as he repeated, 'You just can't, Becky.'

No, that wouldn't be fair. Just to use his listening ear and then go away again.

'Well, I—'

'Becky, when are you in alone?'

'At lunch-time. Matthew has lunch over at school and I stay at home. And in the early afternoon usually I'm still there.'

'Then I'll try to ring you at one o'clock and, failing that, at two.'

'But Josh—'

'No buts. Leave it to me. And you're not committing yourself to anything, you know, so don't look like that. Just let me meet you, take you out to lunch, and we'll have an hour's walk in the park afterwards.'

Again she had the feeling that it would be churlish to refuse after the pain she had caused him all those years ago, and after his kindness to her this afternoon. Besides, he was so utterly determined and strong. Stronger than she was now. What was it that was different about him? He was more assured. Yes, that was it: he had authority now. She could feel the pressure of it.

'You can spare a couple of hours for an old friend, Becky,' he said confidently, 'can't you?'

'All right, Josh.'

'Good, then that's settled,' he said, getting up. 'We'll check the train times at Paddington.'

And he had taken her arm, tucked it proprietorially under his own, and set off with her across the park.

Back at school, Matthew had been overjoyed for her.

'It's great news, Becky,' he had said. 'A whole volume of the nature poems, they really merit that.'

He stood looking down at her, blinking slightly as he always did when something truly delighted him. He even bestowed a kiss on the top of her head.

'Great news,' he repeated. 'And you really deserve it.'

'But I haven't got them anything like done, there's so much

131

work still to be done on them and—'

'We must see you have more time, Becky. We must get more help for you in the library and there really is no need for the school play always to be your responsibility. It's too late to change this year, but next year we might.'

He went on and on with ideas to help her. It was awful the way he was suddenly so concerned for her, she who had been in Josh's arms in the park this afternoon: she should have felt guilty, but all she felt was a great longing to be there again.

'Let's give it a week's trial,' Matthew suggested. 'We'll clear the decks for you so you can really work hard on the poems this week. You said you had two that were nearly ready, didn't you? Why not see if you can get them into the post by next Thursday. Or better still, take them up yourself?'

'I might do that,' Becky said. 'I mean take them myself. In case there's anything to discuss.'

Matthew was delighted. 'It's really given you a lift, this trip to London today, hasn't it? You must do it more often.'

Becky, sitting in the train two years later, going up once again to see Mrs Doughtyman, thought that Matthew had practically pushed her into Josh's arms. For Josh had been there, waiting on the station platform. And although for a moment, observing him before he caught sight of her, she had seen him as a stranger, a middle-aged man gloomily surveying the passengers as they surged past him off the train, she had thought, I don't know him, not really, I did once, but not now, the moment that his arms were round her she had felt like someone who, after much buffeting in storms at sea, has come safely home to harbour. So that later when he said, 'You belong here, with me. After all these years I feel whole again,' she had known exactly what he meant.

They walked across the park, as they had the week before, only this time the sun was a little lower in the sky, the breeze a little fresher, more leaves falling. He caught one as it landed in her hair.

'Becky,' he said suddenly, 'I've told you I love you. I think you feel differently about me now, don't you, from when we were young? Please tell me.'

She had tried not to let herself think of him all this week, but it had been there all the time, the longing for him. But where would it lead if she admitted it? Chaos for two families, chaos spreading and spreading. She couldn't even contemplate doing such damage. She looked down.

He put his hand under her chin, forcing her head up. 'Tell me, Becky,' he insisted.

She had looked back at him, directly into his eyes, but said nothing.

'Look, Becky, I know you well enough to know you wouldn't have reacted as you did if you hadn't felt differently about me now. You're not a light woman. But I've got to know, you must see that, you must tell me the truth. Could you, do you, love me?'

Still she couldn't say the words. Like a child admitting to something it is too frightened to say for fear of the consequences, she nodded her head slowly up and down, her eyes held by his.

'Oh, Becky, my love, my only ever love,' he whispered, holding her close. 'For more than twenty years I've longed for this moment.'

Then, with a startling change of mood he said, 'Now, then, Becky, you must trust me. I'm going to make it work. Don't look so scared.'

He set off purposefully with her across the park, his arm easily encircling her waist, hers reaching only to somewhere about the middle of his back.

'I am quite unambiguous about this, Becky,' he told her. 'I want you and I'm going to have you. You are the most precious thing in the world to me.'

She knew that he wanted her to say the same, but she could not. 'I'm sorry, Josh. I couldn't say that. Not as long as I had children.'

He sighed. 'Oh well,' he said. 'I suppose it's different for a woman.'

She wondered. She couldn't imagine Matthew saying such a thing either. To Matthew, as to herself, she knew that Juliet and Ben were precious above all others.

'You know,' he was saying, 'how they say that the pull in families is between father and daughter, mother and son? I've never found that. My daughter is much closer to her mother than she is to me.'

Her mother, the mother of his child. This was the worst part of all. To come between him and his wife, to hurt this woman who had never harmed her. She had always thought it was an unforgivable thing to do.

'To hurt them so,' she blurted out. 'It's, it's unthinkable.'

'Then you've just got to start thinking the unthinkable. Other people have faced similar problems and managed it. It's going to be a hard road. I'm willing to take it.'

'It's not the hardness, truly it's not. It's just that it *feels* wrong. Oh, Josh, I know this sounds smug, but honestly I can't think of any time ever before when I've deliberately done something which I know will hurt somebody else. Maybe by mistake many times, not knowing, but that's different.' She glanced up at him. 'I feel I'm playing the wrong role,' she said. 'It would be easier for me to be the wronged wife in this play; I'd be better at being brave and forgiving, awful though that sounds. I'm just not cut out to be the "other woman".'

He turned on her angrily. 'Don't call yourself that. Never say that again, do you hear? You are the *only* woman.'

'That's not how she'll think of me.'

'If I don't care what she thinks, I really don't see why you should, Becky. You've never even met her.'

'But still I do care. Women do care about not hurting each other.'

Maybe men don't. Maybe that was why it was easier for Josh.

'She won't be hurt, Becky, not in the way that you mean.'

134

'But she *will*. This is a cruel way to hurt a woman. It goes deep, it damages her past as well as her future – it destroys what she once had with you.'

'Don't talk so daft,' he said, momentarily Yorkshire again. 'She won't be hurt because she doesn't love me.'

'Oh.'

That hadn't occurred to her. 'Are you sure?' she asked.

'She told me so.'

'People say these things sometimes if they're upset.'

'Oh, God, Becky, how can I make you believe? I tell you we have rows, she's spelled out what she thinks of me, she's always throwing up the past at me. It's ludicrous to think of yourself as breaking up my marriage. It's broken up already. Like yours.'

But it's not. She would never have spoken to Matthew like that: they were never unkind to each other. A problem, yes, but still they got on well. She couldn't explain, so she just said again, 'Maybe she says these things in anger and doesn't mean them.'

'For God's sake, Becky, she's my wife and I know her better than you do.'

I wonder, does any man know a woman better than any other woman knows her? In different ways they know her, exclusive ways. Who but another woman knows instinctively what hurts, what pleases?

'The point is, Becky, that this is my responsibility, not yours. Everyone who has knowledge of these situations says that each partner has to see his or her own side in their own way. I shan't interfere on your side and you shouldn't try to judge mine. That's the only sensible way to behave in a divorce.'

It was the first time the word had been spoken. A week ago they hadn't met and now here he was talking about divorce. How had it happened?

'Her pride may be hurt,' Josh went on, 'but there won't be the sort of hurt that you mean. When I tell her, I reckon her reaction will be to go out and get the smartest divorce lawyer in town and tell him to screw as much money out of me as he possibly can.'

'You mean she won't miss you at all?'

'No, not me. She'll miss being Queen Bee at official functions and all the prestige of being my wife, of course, but that's all.'

She tried to imagine the young Josh using such expressions. Tried and failed. It sounded very different from her world too, hers and Matthew's. Or from any world she knew.

'And at work, Josh, I mean among your colleagues, won't it be difficult for you?'

She knew how it would be if Matthew had despatched her, Becky, and installed another Mrs Portman in her place. The poor unfortunate woman wouldn't get much of a welcome from the staff, parents, children or friends or anybody. Would she be like that, resented as Josh's new wife?

'Remember, Becky, that most of my colleagues are American. The only thing that surprises them about an English divorce is that it takes so long.'

They were silent for a moment and then he said suddenly, 'Look, Becky, I've got to get back to the office, but I've arranged to go home late tonight in the hope you might meet me after work for an hour. Can you? Just for an hour? Please, Becky.'

There was such longing in his voice, and it wouldn't be difficult. It would be stupid, mean, to pretend otherwise.

'I'm going to Doughtymans' this afternoon,' she said, 'but I could meet you afterwards. It's just a question of ringing school and saying I'll be back nearer eight o'clock than seven.'

'Bless you, Becky. We'll drive to the Serpentine this evening and we'll talk by the water and make plans. It'll still be light. You do trust me, Becky, don't you? You will come?'

Of course she would come, how could he think otherwise, when she had promised?

She smiled up at him. 'I'll be there,' she said. 'I shan't be long at Doughtymans'. It's just a matter of leaving the poems, really.'

But Mrs Doughtyman was in a talkative mood.

'I've had time to study your poems more deeply since we last met,' she told Becky, nursing the folder of poems on her knee, like a child. 'You believe very much in the unchanging nature of things, and of people, don't you?'

Becky considered this, then, 'Yes,' she said slowly. 'I don't think people really change, not fundamentally. Superficially, yes, of course, with changing circumstances, but I think that life only strengthens what was there already.' She thought about Josh. 'Deep down,' she repeated more emphatically, 'they don't change at all. What do you think?' she asked.

Mrs Doughtyman laughed. 'Oh, it doesn't matter what I think,' she said, dismissing with a wave of her hand the very idea that it might. 'What is of interest is that the theme of permanence, of the unchanging nature of things, runs through all these poems.'

Becky, taken aback at having her poems so analysed, could only say, 'Does it? Does it really?'

'You don't agree?'

'No, it isn't that. It's just that I've never thought of having a theme, nothing as grand as a theme. I just think of each poem separately and try to get it down as right as I can.'

She hesitated. Mrs Doughtyman was waiting eagerly. So she forced herself to go on. 'But yes, I do see what you mean about the same theme running through all of them, now that you point it out. I don't know why I hadn't thought of it before.'

'Writer's don't,' Mrs Doughtyman said. 'Novelists, you know, work away, letting their characters have their head, and often it may be half-way through before they see where it's going, and not till it's finished that they can see the theme. But it must have been there in them from the start, mustn't it? It's a bit of a mystery.'

'Even to you?'

'Especially to me. The more I see of it, the more it amazes me.'

'But you seem to understand the process so much better than

I do. Doesn't that make you want to write yourself?'

Mrs Doughtyman shook her head. 'Oh, no,' she said. 'It's a different thing altogether, writing and editing. My joy, my kind of creativity if you like, is to take a manuscript, say a group of poems like this, and turn it into a book as near perfect as I can make it. Speaking of which, I have a suggestion to make to you. We publish art books, you know. And recently we've done some very beautiful illustrated books. I can see your book like that.'

Becky looked at her, startled.

'I don't mean,' Mrs Doughtyman went on, 'most emphatically I don't mean just little decorative end drawings. I'd like illustrations which are of value in themselves. I have one or two artists in mind. There's a very promising young man who has done some beautiful jackets for us. It may delay things a bit, of course, but I think we could make a really lovely book of it.'

She was leaning forward, her face glowing. Her enthusiasm was infectious. Becky's face glowed similarly.

'It's a marvellous idea,' she said. 'I'd be *very* happy about it.'

'Good, then I'll start putting things in motion. I'll get some roughs done by the young man I mentioned. Ideally I'd like him to interpret your poems in his own way. We don't tell our authors what to write, so we shouldn't tell our illustrators what to do either. No artist worth his salt will be dictated to. You do understand that, don't you?'

'Of course.'

'But you must have the final decision. After all, they are your poems, and it would damage you if you felt the spirit of them had been in some way betrayed.'

'Thank you.'

'And if you don't like them, we'll try somebody else.'

'Won't it be very expensive to print?' Becky asked.

'I had a little difficulty about that with our accountant,' Mrs Doughtyman admitted, as if referring to a household pet of uncertain temper. 'A nice enough young man, but a bit inclined to go on about what he calls "financial viability". It sounds important, but it only means making money,' she added with a dismissive little laugh.

Becky nodded.

'But you see,' Mrs Doughtyman went on, 'we *do* make money on our popular side. The crime and science-fiction do very well from that point of view. Some of it isn't frankly what we'd choose to read ourselves, but it does enable us to publish rather special things, like this book of yours.'

'Yes, I do realise,' Becky said, 'that I'm very lucky. I can't imagine most publishers doing an illustrated book of poetry unless it was by someone very famous.'

'Quite. They'll think us very idiosyncratic,' Mrs Doughtyman said. 'But what *fun* it's going to be.'

'It's a wonderful idea,' Becky said again. 'I'd never imagined anything like it. I can't tell you how thrilled I am.'

Matthew would be thrilled, she knew. And Josh, too, of course. But when she met him that evening he only inquired briefly, 'All went well, did it, with your publishers?' and she just said, 'Fine, thanks,' because suddenly, in Josh's presence, the whole project seemed less important.

It was cold by the water. She shivered as they got out of the car. The sun had almost set; as they walked, the sky changed from pearly blue to slate grey. The images were cold and hard. Even the sound of the water was cold as it lapped against the concrete shore.

His voice was harder too. 'We've got to make plans, Becky,' he said firmly. 'We can't mess about wasting time at our age. We're no longer young, but if we set about it sensibly we can still have twenty-five years of happiness together.'

'But the *others*, Josh.'

How could she explain? She did love him, but what of them? Matthew, Juliet, Ben and the school and all their friends, all of them expecting everything from her except this, this unthinkable thing. She thought of Bill, sitting by Eleanor's hospital bed, day and night, deserving comfort and support. And what would he find? That she had broken up her family, not as Eleanor had done, snatched away by disease and death, but of her own choice. It could only add to his despair. Oh yes, she would be breaking faith with everybody. Everybody except Josh.

'Don't look so scared,' he said. 'I'm perfectly happy to go home tonight and tell her. I've courage enough for both of us.'

'Oh no, Josh, no. There's so much to think about first, so many problems.'

He stopped and turned her to face him. 'I tell you, Becky, that there is no problem on my side, not with spouse, child or colleagues. At least no problem I'm not prepared to face. It's *you* who are the problem.'

He stared out across the water. The lights reflected coldly in the ripples, the last rays of the sun had vanished and the sky was grey. He slammed one fist down hard into the palm of the other hand.

'I'll *make* you see it my way, I'll *make* you,' he said suddenly. 'My God, I'll think of some way to *make* you, Becky. Come on, you're getting cold.'

He strode off back towards the car, so quickly that she could hardly keep up with him. She struggled to understand. She wasn't used to the idea of anyone wanting to *make* her think something. She couldn't imagine Matthew saying such a thing. Theirs was an equal sort of marriage, nobody ever tried to impose their ideas, not on the children either; persuade, maybe, argue, reason. Perhaps twenty years of living like that, reasonably, unemotionally, had unfitted her for this onslaught. Because it was an onslaught, she could feel the power of it. But Josh hadn't been like that, had he, before? She tried to remember. Certainly he had never tried to dominate her. Or was it just that she had changed? Perhaps as he had grown stronger, more authoritative, she had grown weaker? Perhaps having children, caring for them and for others, does weaken women?

She was several steps behind him when he reached the car, panting to keep up.

'In you go,' he ordered, 'and we'll discuss this thing in comfort. We've got to draw up a schedule, decide when we tell our families.'

Soon she would be back at school; it was a different world there.

'To smash so many lives just so that you and I can be together—'

'You'll probably be quite surprised at how well everyone takes it,' he remarked blandly.

'Oh, no, Josh. We can't deceive ourselves about that. They'll be shattered. The children—'

'My daughter's no fool. She knows we have rows and sleep in separate bedrooms. She won't be all that surprised.'

'My children will be, though. I think they would be good about it and try to understand. But Matthew – I don't know how he'll manage. A school is—'

'Look, Becky, I can understand your worries about children. That's fair enough for a woman, but I simply cannot understand why you should worry about Matthew – come here – damn the bloody gear lever. God, it's ridiculous at our age to be stuck in here like a couple of adolescents with nowhere to go.'

'But it's the pain, Josh,' she said later, when he had rearranged himself, 'to cause such pain. We have to weigh that against our happiness, don't we? I mean do we have the right?'

'You don't have the killer instinct,' he said.

'What?'

'You haven't heard the expression?'

She shook her head, not liking the sound of it much.

'It's commonplace at work. I suppose it's American. It means doing whatever is necessary to achieve your goal, even if it damages others. You mustn't be deflected by that consideration. You must always keep your own purpose in view and go straight for it.'

'Oh, Josh, it's like all other clichés of that sort, it just avoids the issue. That sort of thing is no guide, no real guide, Josh.'

'Why not?'

'Because if you're in a dilemma about how to treat someone and you think, say, *Do unto others*, it makes sense, because then you can try to imagine how you'd like to be treated in the same situation, if you were in their shoes. But the words *killer instinct* tells you nothing. You wouldn't want to be on the receiving end of someone else's killer instinct, would you, Josh?'

He laughed. 'I'd make damned sure I wasn't,' he said, and started up the engine.

They were silent as they drove back to the station, both downcast at the prospect of parting, and the knowledge that they were out of step with each other. Suddenly he turned into a side road, parked the car and took her in his arms.

'We can't part like this,' he said, holding her close. 'Must you catch the seven-thirty? When's the next train?'

'In half an hour. Yes, I can catch that one instead.'

'Bless you. Becky, we mustn't let ourselves get down. We've come a long way really, considering that we only met again a week ago.'

Seven little days, Becky had thought. Yet surely even so, one should be able to see a way forward if a way existed.

'When does your post get delivered?' he asked suddenly. 'And does it all go to school?'

'No, all our personal letters come to the lodge direct.'

'When?'

'About nine, never earlier.'

'So you collect them yourself?'

'Yes.'

'Then I'll write every day. And I'll ring when I can. Next week I'm abroad, so I shan't see you on Thursday. But the following Thursdays are clear. I've checked in my diary.'

'In a month I'm coming on a Tuesday instead. I'm up for a literary do, staying the night.'

'Where?'

'A place called the Lordern.'

'I know it. It's not very grand,' he added, disapproving.

'It's not a very grand do,' she said.

'Anyway, I'll try to join you there. We can arrange all that later. Next week is going to be awful without you. I shall think of you all the time I'm away, my Rebecca.'

She smiled. 'Only my headmistress calls me that,' she said.

'Like you're the only one who calls me Josh.'

'Am I? Do they call you Joshua like your parents did?'

'No. When I joined my present international firm fifteen years ago, I filled in forms and signed a letter in full: Grover Joshua Blackford. And being American they used the Grover as it was the first of the two names, and somehow it stuck. We decided we liked it, so that's what I've been called ever since.'

'Grover.' She tried it, then shook her head. 'No, Josh, I'll leave you as you are. Just my Josh.'

'That's good enough for me,' he said, rubbing his cheek against hers.

'Grover was your mother's maiden name, wasn't it?'

'Yes, fancy you remembering that.'

'I remember lots of Grover aunts and uncles. Do you still keep in touch with them?'

'Not much. I think they felt I didn't look after my mother as well as I should have done.'

'Oh, no!'

He shrugged. 'Well, I do wish I could have done better sometimes, but I was very busy with work at the time. She was in a home and the other inmates used to ring me up telling me I was a no-good son. Mind you, they were an idle bunch, with nothing much else to do except telephone sons and insult them.'

'Do you blame yourself?'

'I never blame myself, on principle. But maybe if you'd been alongside me I might have done better.'

'I'm sorry,' she said, instinctively taking the blame for it. 'I'd have liked to help her. She used to make me so welcome, though she must have thought I'd make a dreadful daughter-in-law.'

'No, that's not true. She wanted me to marry you. She liked you anyway, and knew how much I wanted you. She'd be pleased we're together now.'

She smiled, glad that Josh thought his mother would have approved of them being together now. Nobody else would.

'I've got to go, Josh,' she said. 'Or I'll miss this train as well.'

At school, Matthew was waiting anxiously. She told him quickly about the poems so that she could see his worry replaced by joy.

'It's marvellous, Becky,' he said, his enthusiasm, she realised later, in marked contrast to Josh's near indifference. But then Josh had other things on his mind.

'But what really is amazing, Becky,' Matthew said later, 'is that Doughtymans can even contemplate doing this. It *must* be uneconomic to illustrate a book of poetry. I never would have imagined that any publisher would do it.'

'Ah, but Doughtymans aren't just *any* publisher,' she had told him.

And now, two years later, she believed more than ever that Doughtymans weren't like any other publisher. But she did sometimes wish they were. Here she was, the book still unpublished, going to see Mrs Doughtyman yet again about the illustrations. Mrs Doughtyman seemed to have an endless supply of hopeful and promising young artists who deserved to be encouraged, offered opportunities to show what they could do. It was just that none of them had produced anything remotely suitable for the book. Becky tried to convince herself that it didn't really matter, that it had given her time to add extra poems, but she was finding it increasingly hard to accept.

'These roughs are quite awful, I'm afraid,' she told Becky today. 'And I had such high hopes of this young man. He's done some lovely jackets for us in the past. But just look at these, I know you won't like them. Just too chocolate-boxy aren't they?'

Becky saw immediately what she meant. 'Whimsical,' she agreed. 'Sentimental.'

'Exasperating. So we shall just have to try again,' Mrs Doughtyman said. 'After all,' she added, 'it isn't as if time mattered.'

Becky didn't reply. She no longer agreed with Mrs Doughtyman's cavalier dismissal of the importance of time. She wanted very much to see her poems published as soon as possible.

Chapter Eight

The car swung triumphantly down the drive, swerved to miss the pillar at the corner of the turning space, braked so suddenly that gravel flew up and spattered the paintwork and finally skidded to a halt outside the front door.

'It looks as if Juliet's passed her test,' Matthew said.

He and Becky stood for a moment by the French windows, watching as their daughter hugged her instructor, jumped out of the car, and began tearing off the L-plates.

'The examiner said I was rough but ready,' she called to them when they came out.

'Well done, both of you,' Matthew said, shaking hands with the instructor. 'Can we give you a lift home, Mr Shale?'

'No, thanks. I've left my car round the back.'

'Well, no doubt we'll be in touch again when it's Ben's turn,' Becky said, her arm round her daughter's waist.

'Ben?' Juliet repeated. 'He's deadly enough on a skateboard.'

'Before you start criticising your brother,' Becky told her as they went indoors, 'I don't mind telling you now that sitting beside you on practice drives has sometimes been pretty nerve-racking. So you just be a bit tolerant when his turn comes.'

'You wouldn't *relax*, Mummy. I always knew I could stop in time. Daddy was calmer.'

'Not inside, I wasn't,' Matthew assured her. 'I agree with your mother. There are times when your driving gives new meaning to the expression *femme fatale*.'

'I might have known you'd take her side,' Juliet said, laughing as they went into the sitting room. 'Oh, tea, *and* a fire.'

She looked appreciatively round the room and sighed

147

contentedly as she settled herself into the big shabby old armchair by the hearth.

'I thought a fire would cheer you up if you failed,' Becky explained, pouring tea.

'It's nice the way you oldies have such confidence in me,' Juliet remarked, helping herself to toast and putting her feet on the fender.

'It was *you* who said you'd fail,' Matthew pointed out. 'You didn't want to come home, you said, in the middle of term, just to fail again.'

'Well, it was a bit soon after the last test,' Juliet said. She sat up suddenly, nearly spilling her tea. 'Gosh, I've just realised. I'll be able to go out in the car whenever I like without all the hassle of having to have someone with me.'

'We do only have the one car,' Matthew pointed out.

Juliet yawned and stretched. 'Well, I'm glad I passed, even if you're not,' she said.

'Of course we're glad, goose,' Matthew told her. 'Apart from anything else I'm delighted not to have to pay for any more driving lessons. What are you going to do to celebrate?'

'I thought I'd go round and see if either of the Banham twins wants to go to the pictures. Oh, can I take the car? Much safer for coming home late.'

'Yes, if you drive very carefully.'

'I knew you'd say that. I just *knew*.'

'What should I say? Take it on condition you wrap it round the first lamppost you see?'

He got up, glancing at his watch. 'Time for my meeting,' he said, 'but I'll see you safely off first, Juliet. What are your plans, Becky? Why don't you treat yourself to a lazy evening by the fire?'

'I might do that,' Becky said, looking up at them as they stood in the doorway.

'She'll sit by the fire and dream, won't you?' Juliet said, coming back and kissing her before going out with her father.

* * *

Other Women

Becky listened to their footsteps receding, their gentle bickering, the sound of a door closing, a car starting. Then she lay back and relaxed. Juliet was right, she would sit and dream, seeing pictures in the shifting shapes and patterns of the fire. She remembered sitting like this two years ago, listening to them companionably arguing and thinking that, in this world of home and school, she couldn't believe that Josh's world really existed. Each world had been so real when she was in it: this world of her family, of Matthew and Ben and Juliet, all taking her presence for granted while all the time she was going to London, talking of things which would smash their world up, so that nothing would ever be the same for them again.

She remembered how she had looked around this room with its shabby, comfortable furniture and its worn carpet and shelves of books and everything here had seemed so right, so permanent, yet being with Josh had felt right, too. Oh, Josh, she had thought, if only I could explain to you how hard it is to do this thing: to make Matthew lonely as my father was lonely, to make Juliet ache with pity for her father as I once did for mine.

So she had lived in those two worlds, each with its different assumptions, as autumn changed to winter and the bundle of cream-coloured envelopes, which Josh always used, grew thicker and his calls more frequent. He rang her from airports, he rang her from the office, he rang her from cars and from telephone boxes in lonely places, reversing the charges. If someone came in as they talked, she switched the conversation, pretending someone else was on the line, and if anyone but she answered the phone, he said it was a wrong number and rang off and she waited anxiously, knowing that he would soon try again. The tension increased, but she was glad for his sake that she was the one to take the strain; no letters or phone calls entered his home to disturb his domestic peace and put him at risk.

'I'm amazed how *easy* it all is,' Josh had remarked that day at the Lordern.

'Easy?' she had repeated astonished. 'Oh, no, Josh. The deceit

149

and everything, it's all desperately difficult.'

'Well, I can't get over how easy it's been,' he said, stroking her hair back off her face. 'If anyone had told me that it would be possible to have an affair with the wife of the headmaster of a boarding school, to write every day and ring most days, I wouldn't have believed it.'

'Is that what it is, an *affair*?' The word shocked her.

'Well, it is now, if it wasn't before. And even before it wasn't exactly platonic, was it?'

'No.'

'I suppose it's been easy because a school has a predictable timetable. I mean, lunch always happens at the same time and masters are in certain places at certain hours on certain days.'

'But, Josh,' she interrupted. 'That isn't the point. It's the deception.'

'All right. I'm just saying it would have been more difficult if you'd been married to a vicar.'

She laughed because it was ridiculous, the different way they looked at things.

'Don't you see, Josh, it's the deceit itself which is awful? I mean, if it was the other way round and I was your wife, I'd understand if you fell in love with someone else. I could forgive that. But I know I couldn't stomach the deceit. That's the part that would make me feel like killing you.'

'But it's necessary, Becky. You can't just meet and go home and say I want a divorce so I can remarry on the strength of one meeting, in order to make it all open and above board. There *has* to be a time of deceiving.'

'Yes, but I loathe it all the same. I'm sorry, Josh. I know it must be as bad for you as for me.'

He shrugged. 'It doesn't bother me all that much,' he said. 'All right, it would be simpler not to have to meet secretly, but if the alternative is not to see you at all, then I'm willing to pay the price.'

He thought for a moment, then went on, 'Actually, you know, Becky, I *was* quite prepared to go back and make a public statement that very first day, but I couldn't be sure of you then. I had to persuade you, didn't I?'

'Yes.'

He hesitated, then, 'I have persuaded you, haven't I?'

'Yes, Josh.'

He sighed deeply; she could feel the relief, realised how frightened he always was of losing her. She held him close to reassure him, suddenly desperately wanting him not to worry, not to have any of the feeling of rejection that he had had all those years ago when they were young.

He leaned out of bed and took something from the pocket of his jacket on the chair. 'I got this for you when I was abroad,' he said. In the little box was a ring, which he slipped on her finger. 'Wear it for me,' he said.

'But I can't, Josh, you know I can't.'

'Well, wear it when you're with me,' he said. 'And when you're alone or anxious just wear it to remind yourself that I want you for my wife and I've vowed to you that it's going to be all right in the end.'

'Josh,' she said suddenly. 'Why don't we feel more guilty? I mean I don't, not really, when I'm with you like this.'

'Because we love each other and this is just an engagement time.'

'But it isn't like that. We're not free.'

'Well, that's how it feels to me.'

'All the same, when you do something which all your life you've considered to be wrong, you'd expect to feel more guilty, wouldn't you?'

'Have you ever done it before?'

'Of course not. Of course I've never been unfaithful to Matthew. How can you ask? Honestly, Josh!'

'I just thought that, in the circumstances, Matthew being what he is, it would be understandable.'

She shook her head. 'The very idea would have horrified me. That's what's so strange about this. I suppose it's because you had a kind of prior claim.' She was still shocked by his question. 'You haven't, have you?' she asked suddenly, 'done this before, I mean?'

He paused. 'Yes,' he said.

'Oh.'

She should have guessed. All the same it came as a shock.

He drew his forearm across his eyes in a world-weary gesture. 'It's the way of things in the business world, Becky,' he said. 'It's expected, really. Continental hotels have arrangements. In America they have these singles' bars where divorcees and widows and unattached women have drinks and you just join them and pair off for the evening.'

It was horrible; she didn't want to hear it.

'It's stopped, everything like that, since I met you again.'

'Does she know?'

Odd how they never referred to each other's partners by name. Adultery seems to prefer to deal in pronouns.

'No. But you asked me and I've been honest with you.'

Somehow he had turned a fault into a virtue. She held him close. 'Let's not think about it, please, Josh.'

'It's unimportant, I tell you. They were nothing to me. It goes on everywhere. I expect if a single man booked a room in this hotel they'd put a list of women's telephone numbers in it, available women. It's commonplace.'

'Please don't, Josh. It makes me feel like one of them.'

'Who?'

'The foreign floosies.'

'Don't be ridiculous. Anyway, they weren't floosies. They were perfectly nice women. Not tarts or anything like that. The sort of girl you could take out to dinner.'

'I think I'll make a cup of tea,' she said, slipping away from him. She filled the kettle at the basin, plugged it in and stood beside it, naked.

'Come here, Becky.'

'No, I'm waiting for the kettle to boil.' It had a nice familiar sound in this unfamiliar world which Josh inhabited and she was a stranger in.

Suddenly he was beside her, had picked her up, and dumped her on the bed. She had forgotten he was so strong, twice her weight, barrel-chested, powerful-shouldered, and that there was no point in resisting.

'They meant nothing, you silly bitch.'

Outraged, she found the strength to pull away from him. 'What did you call me?' she demanded.

'It's a term of affection.'

'No, it isn't. It's horrible.'

'I only meant you turn me on, Becky.'

'Oh, I see,' she said, partly mollified. There was so much she didn't understand about these things, married to Matthew as she had been.

'And they belong to the past, anyway.'

'All right, Josh,' she said, relaxing in his arms, happy to be at one with him again, 'but I have to tell you that, if I'd married you in those bygone days and you'd been unfaithful, I'd have left you.'

'But I wouldn't have been unfaithful if I'd been married to you,' he said indignantly. 'I'd have been a different sort of person.'

It was all her fault for not marrying him. He would have been a better man if she had, a faithful husband. All her fault.

'I'm sorry,' she said.

'But you're going to make up for it now, aren't you?'

'Yes, Josh. But there's one thing that puzzles me.'

'What's that?'

'You remember you said to me that, given that I had a homosexual husband, it would have been understandable if I'd been unfaithful? Well, you had a normal marriage, so why couldn't you spend a few nights abroad without having to find other women to sleep with?'

He thought for a while, then, 'Curiosity,' he said.

Ah, if God had meant men to be faithful to their wives, He wouldn't have given them inquiring minds, Becky found herself reflecting, with unaccustomed cynicism.

'I'll let you make that tea now,' Josh said. 'Then we'll make plans.'

So they sat in bed sipping tea like an old married couple.

'But when I get back in early December, Becky,' he said, 'I think that's a good time for us to go public.'

'Oh, no, you're not going away again?'

'Only for five days. It's not long, don't look so tragic.'

'I hate it when you're away. I've always felt sorry for wives whose husbands are away a lot.'

'Mine likes it, actually. She says she can get on with things better when I'm not there.'

She hesitated: it was awful, the lovelessness of Josh's marriage, and yet, 'Josh,' she said, 'you don't think maybe it suits your way of life to have a wife who doesn't care much if you're away?'

'Nonsense, I love you for caring, don't you see?'

She nodded.

'Besides,' he went on cheerfully, 'I've got into the habit of spending an extra night away rather than hurrying back, but when I've got you waiting at home I shan't hang around abroad a minute longer than necessary, I can promise you that. And once we're married you can come with me.'

'Oh, Josh, that's a long way off.'

'All the more reason to get started as soon as possible. Once we're together, Becky, there'll be no more problems.'

She looked at him, puzzled. Did he really believe that?

'There'll be heaps of problems,' she said. 'We're so different and we haven't had time together to grow alike, the way people do over the years. You know, how you adjust in a marriage, almost without thinking, don't you? It'll be so different for us.'

'Will it? I should think our life-styles are similar.'

'What?'

'Well, Matthew's a successful teacher, I'm a successful businessman, so our life-styles will have been similar.'

'But I've never had a life-style,' she objected.

154

'Of course you have.'

'I haven't, I tell you. I've never even thought about having one. I've just had a life.'

He shook his head at her and laughed. 'You're a funny old thing,' he said. 'Anyway, the sooner we get set up together the better. And that's what I was trying to say when we got side-tracked. I think that early December would be the best time to tell our two families and go public.'

'Before Christmas! We can't. We just can't do that.'

'First we can't because it's Christmas, then it'll be Easter—'

'No, that's not fair, Josh, I agree to after Christmas.'

'I go to the States in January. I don't want to tell her and then just go away. I want to be on the spot to see what she gets up to.'

'And to help her to understand, talk about it—'

'Oh, yes, well, that too, I suppose.'

He sat, scowling into his teacup. His heavy features looked sullen. She took away his cup, lifted the corners of his mouth with her fingers.

'It'll be three months, Becky.'

'Three months is bearable.'

'But it isn't just three months, is it? It means we don't even make a start for three months.'

'I know, Josh, I do know. Honestly, I feel it just as much as you do. Maybe I hate the secrecy more than you do. As you say, you've deceived before.'

'Only abroad,' he said dismissively.

Strange that adultery to Josh didn't really count as long as it was committed abroad and wasn't found out.

'We'll have our own celebration at the pub on the Thursday before Christmas,' she said to cheer him up.

'No, we'll go somewhere special, candles and champagne and all that sort of thing.'

'No.' She had been firm, not wanting money spent on her which belonged to another, so they had gone to the pub as usual and exchanged presents and Josh brought a little

Christmas candle shaped like a house and put it on the table where it glowed throughout the meal. And somehow their world seemed smaller and simpler and safer than it had been before.

'It's hardly burnt down at all,' Josh remarked, picking it up. 'I shall keep it and light it for you, Becky, every Christmas as long as I live.' And he wrapped it up carefully and took it with him when they went to walk in the park.

It was as clear and sunny and crisp an afternoon as any they had spent there. Almost all the benches were empty; they chose one by the lake, huddling together because it was cold.

'I'd like to buy you a lovely fur coat,' Josh said, 'and wrap it round you so you can sit here on this bench all winter.'

She laughed, but she was alarmed all the same. 'You wouldn't do anything so stupid, would you, really Josh?'

'What's stupid about giving the woman you love a fur coat?'

'Everything,' she told him. She didn't want some animal hunted and killed so that she could wear its fur anyway, but that wasn't the point at the moment. 'You must never get anything that costs much. You know I don't care about expensive things anyway.'

'You look really cross,' he said, watching her. 'I rather like it.'

She shrugged. 'I've never been much good at anger,' she said. 'But I really do mean it about presents. I don't want you to give me things.'

'You mean you're cooling off?'

She looked at him, bewildered. 'Whatever do you mean?' she asked.

He sighed. 'Oh, just sometimes I think you're cooling off. When I rang you from the States – when was it? About ten days ago – you sounded a bit off-hand and I thought, Aha, now we're entering the cooling-off period.'

'How could you think such a thing? It was just that when you rang I was in the kitchen with the rest of the family, two of Ben's friends and the games master.'

They'd all been there, fresh off the rugby pitch, jubilant because they'd won, starving hungry, pulling off boots, shedding mud, while she hunted for towels and prepared the tea and listened to their talk of tries and conversions and in the midst of all this the telephone had rung: Josh making one of his unscheduled calls.

'I thought I managed to get through to you what was going on. I mean they were all there, listening. I tried to get you to understand.'

'Well, yes, you did convey that, but all the same I felt a lack of loving warmth in your voice. I'd desperately wanted to hear you, Becky. I was aching for you, so I took the risk of ringing at an unscheduled time and then felt let down because you sounded so casual.'

'But Josh, you can't imagine, can you, that if I *was* for some reason loving you less that I'd just speak unkindly on the telephone? For God's sake, what sort of person would do that? It would be a horrible way to behave. Unforgivable.'

'All right, forget it. I'm just telling you how I felt.'

But she sat amazed at the way, when they seemed so close, such enormous differences could suddenly appear. Why was he so suspicious of everybody, including her? He seemed to trust nobody.

'Actually, Josh,' she said slowly, 'if it's any kind of reassurance, I promise you I'd be the last person to say anything on the telephone that might upset you. Do you remember what happened when my father died? How they rang me?'

'Yes. Yes, I remember.'

'I had terrible dreams for months afterwards. Always the telephone ringing and somehow it became my fault because I picked it up and that seemed to kill him. I think it was the shock. I don't know why, but it's especially dreadful to get news like that on the phone. It's the disembodied voice coming to you, like some evil thing you can't see. I can't explain it, but it left me terrified that something like that would happen again.'

'Oh, Becky, love, I didn't know. What a lot you've had to

suffer, haven't you? You've had more than your share. I vow to you that I'll never hurt you. And most especially I'll never, never say anything on the phone that might distress you.'

'It's all right, Josh. I know you never would.'

He thought for a moment and then took a little note-pad from his pocket.

'I think it would be sensible to agree some basic ground rules, Becky. Maybe we should write them down? Don't look so surprised. It's quite normal business practice that certain things should be established and agreed.'

'But we're not a business. We're just *us.*'

'We're a partnership, aren't we? Or should be. You see, Becky, our lines of communication aren't easy at the moment, so we have to safeguard against misunderstanding. Agreed? I could rough out a few headings for us.' He began to jot words down on the pad.

'Firstly, that we'll always discuss any anxiety quite openly with the other. Secondly, we'll never reach a unilateral decision. Thirdly, we won't raise any issue that might be hurtful to the other except when we're together, preferably holding hands. Never on the telephone.'

'But Josh, I don't need this,' she protested. 'Truly I wouldn't do any of those things anyway.'

'You must bear with my business background, Becky. I do like things cut and dried. It's safer that way. And one of the things you must learn about me is that I'm a very dependable, reliable sort of guy. What Josh says he will do, Josh does—'

'Oh, don't say that—'

'Why ever not?'

'Because surely you've noticed that people who say they're reliable or honest, or whatever, never are. People who really are don't need to go on about it.'

'Maybe I'm the exception that proves the rule?'

He put the pad away. 'I'll clarify them over Christmas,' he said. 'And they can be our New Year Resolutions.'

'All right,' she conceded, 'if it makes you feel happier.'

'It does.'

He put his arms around her again and drew her head down on his shoulder.

'It's going to be a long time apart over Christmas,' he said. 'If ever you feel scared or anxious, just imagine your head is here on my shoulder. It's always yours, Becky, for the rest of my life, reserved for you.'

This was more reassuring than all that stuff about agreements on notepads. She leant against him, as comforted by the solid, rocklike bulk of him as she had been years ago on that bleak hillside when he had found her and brought her safely home.

'We must make the most of our last hour together this year,' he said, gently rubbing his cheek against her hair. 'And what a year it's been. The most wonderful year of my life. I wonder where we'll be, you and I, this time next year?'

She shivered, frightened of the unknown. 'We'll be together, that's all that matters,' he added. 'So there's nothing to be afraid of.'

When you're young, yes. She remembered marrying Matthew without a fear or doubt, not knowing where they'd live, moving away from friends and colleagues, without a backward glance. But middle-aged love had more to fear, more hostages to lose, more past, less future.

'I never thought I would be happy again,' Josh said suddenly.

'You've really been unhappy?'

'No, just a nothingness, you know. I was half dead, I realise now. You brought me back to life, Becky. Yes, you gave me life. You'll never take it from me, will you? I couldn't bear it.'

Perhaps that was why he was so afraid, so untrusting and suspicious. Because he was afraid of losing her again.

'Of course I won't. I'm yours: you know that.'

'If we could be anywhere in the world now, where it's warm and sunny, where would you like to be?' he asked suddenly.

'Jamaica?' she suggested at random.

'No.'

'Why not?'

He hesitated. 'We went there for a holiday once, fitted it into a business trip. It was soon after she found out about some woman abroad and we had a great row and then tried to make a go of it again. It didn't work.'

'But Josh, you said she didn't know. About the women abroad, I mean?'

'Did I? I must have forgotten. Not all of them certainly, but she must have found out about that one because we had this awful row about it.'

How could he forget such a thing? It must have been traumatic for both of them. He was so casual sometimes, about things which seemed to her important.

'I never found out how she discovered. Somebody at the office told her, maybe, or some colleague's wife. I don't know.'

Poor woman. The humiliation of it, the hurt. At least she herself had been spared anything like that, anything public, with Matthew.

'It's going to be awful over Christmas,' Josh said suddenly. 'No chance of meeting, is there, Becky?'

'None. Truly. I can't get away. And our friend Bill's coming to stay. He's recently widowed and is going abroad to work in January. So obviously we must do all we can to help him. I've got to be at home every day, Josh.'

'I can ring you up, can't I? Well, I shall risk it anyway,' he added as they got up and set off across the park, for the hour was up.

The park was deserted except for one old man who was walking towards them along the path by the water. He was a compact little man, pink-cheeked, very clean-looking and neat. He paused in front of them, smiled, and said, 'You look very contented.'

She smiled back, delighted with the unexpected remark.

'Well,' Josh said when the old man had passed, 'I think that's the first time anybody had ever accused me of looking contented.'

'It's a good omen,' Becky said, smiling up at him.

'Yes, roll on February when we shall be on our way.'

She thought of something. 'Oh, Josh,' she said, 'not February. It's the school play.'

He stared at her dumbfounded, his face flushed, eyes bright; when he was indignant there was a look about him of a bewildered bull.

'The bloody school bloody play. Look, Becky, I accept that Christmas matters, it's a special family time and I can see how you feel about not upsetting it, but a *play*—'

'But I'm in charge of it, I'm producing it. It runs for a week and the strain and, oh, Josh, I'm sorry, can't we wait until the end of term?'

The wind had got up: she could hear it soughing in the trees and rattling the loose catch on the gate into the side garden. They had been going to fix it for months but always forgot between storms.

The fire creaked and settled. Becky put on more logs, glancing at the clock to see if it was worth building up a bigger fire. No, it was gone ten; Matthew would be home soon, tired, ready for bed, and Juliet had long passed the age when she wanted to come and sit by the fire drinking hot chocolate and gossiping with her mother when she came in at night.

The logs were old and dry, the last of the wood from the ash tree which had blown down in a storm three years ago. The flames flared up around and above them, long and yellow. Why are some memories so clear, Becky wondered as she gazed into the fire, so real that you feel you can reach out and touch the people in them, hear their very words, catch their expressions, their tone of voice? Yet other memories, more outwardly important, fade into nothingness, leaving just a few facts behind like debris.

On such a night as this, with the wind blowing a gale outside, they had sat, she and Josh, by the fire in the cottage at Enderby, listening to her father as he talked about treachery, the three of them encircled in the warm glow of the oil lamp which stood on the damask cloth on the old oak table, while the wind made even the heavy portière curtain move gently in the draught that found its way under the cottage door. Such memories stay golden, unchanged, like scenes set in amber, while all the rest merge into the common greyness of the past.

She had been back to that old cottage, had seen it gutted, had seen it renewed, done up beyond all recognition. She had seen it supplied with a new kitchen, a modern bathroom, she had seen it adorned with formica and plastic, furnished with pine. But once away from it, even a day later, she couldn't picture it as it now was, she could only see it as it once had been. That was her reality and there was no changing it.

It sometimes seemed to Becky that she could look back on her life and see it as a series of scenes, like vignettes, each memory indestructible, established for all time, like a poem which takes experience and preserves it exactly as it was, safe from nostalgia and distortion.

Safe from what comes after, too, she thought, seeing again in her mind's eye Josh, the rescuer, looming out of the mist, and the pair of them struggling down the mountainside in the storm, seeing again his parents sitting companionably by the fire, baffled by education, and all those walks in the park merging into a single walk except for the one very cold memory of walking by the Serpentine, Josh striding grimly ahead, leading her she knew not where, while the icy water slapped against the concrete bank.

And there were all the memories of school, too: of being beside Matthew at countless functions, on platforms, at dinner tables, at garden parties, attentive as he spoke, proud of him, confident in him. And always in the background there were bells and voices and the sound of feet in corridors, the excitement of matches, the urgency of small, everyday things, the tension of the school plays, from which last year's stood apart not only because the cast included the best actors they had ever had in the school, but also because with every rehearsal and then with each performance, the moment for

telling Matthew had grown nearer, throwing its dark shadow
ahead until, at the final curtain, as she stood holding her
bouquet of flowers and acknowledging the applause, she had
felt nothing but a black awareness that there was now nothing
between her and the inflicting of that awful pain. Yet
somewhere in all the gloom there had flickered a little flame of
relief that it was all over, the play was done.

Chapter Nine

She had walked with Matthew down the empty corridors, past deserted classrooms, chairs up on desks, awaiting the cleaners. For the moment the school was theirs, hers and Matthew's. The office staff had long since departed and even the caretaker had gone to earth.

'My favourite moment,' Matthew had said, as they crossed the courtyard back to the lodge. 'Time to breathe and assess and appreciate. It's been a good term.'

It had seemed terrible to do it to him now; cruel to choose the moment when he was at his happiest, most relaxed and unsuspecting. He deserved a little time to enjoy looking back on the achievements of the term. But she had promised Josh.

He was taking a bunch of keys out of his pocket, separating the one for their front door. He was looking down at her, smiling. 'Thank you for everything, Becky,' he was saying. 'And especially for the play. Your last production was the best ever.'

She took a deep breath. 'Matthew,' she made herself say. 'There's something I—'

'Yes?' he inquired absently, pushing open the door and then stooping to pick up an airmail letter off the mat.

'Looks like Bill's writing,' he remarked, neatly slicing the envelope open with a letter knife from the hall table.

It was only a short note; Bill was no letter-writer.

'He's still very keen that we should go and stay with him in Sri Lanka. I think he's lonely, for all he's so busy. You know, I've been thinking about it. It might be possible to go out there next winter if—'

'Matthew,' she said urgently. '*Please.* There's something I must talk to you about. It's important. Can we go into the drawing room for a while? Now.'

He had listened quietly as she told him, not interrupting. He didn't move, the clear-cut features didn't change expression. A stranger might have thought him impassive, but she who was so familiar with that thoughtful, disciplined face, saw it very clearly: the shock, the pain deep behind the eyes.

Yet at the same time she felt a weight being lifted as she talked. She had always hated the deception, but it was not until now that she realised how physically burdensome it had been. She felt lighter, easier now that things were honest between them again.

'I've been very blind,' Matthew said, when she stopped.

'I'm sorry, Matthew. I know what a shock it is. I utterly understand if you feel hurt and angry—'

'No, no, no. No, I don't feel that. You mustn't blame yourself. I'm grateful for these twenty years you've given me. It's your turn now.'

'Thank you.'

He got up and went and stood by the French windows, overlooking the lodge garden and the playing fields beyond. She could feel the pain in his very bones.

'Can we walk in the garden?' he said at last.

The doors weren't locked. She pushed them open.

They went slowly, as they had so often done, along the narrow brick paths, by the rose bed, round to the rockery. It was smoothed over now, as it had so recently been with the snows of a late winter, under drifts of aubretia, purple and mauve and blue, and arabis and yellow candytuft.

'Last week,' he said suddenly, 'I looked at that and I thought I should have cut them all back last year. *And it seemed to matter.*'

'I'm sorry, Matthew. Oh, God, I'm sorry.'

'No,' he said firmly. 'You're not to say that. Never again. I am entirely responsible, we both know it.'

He turned to face her. 'I want to redeem my life,' he said. 'I want to redeem what I've done to you, by helping you now. Do you understand?'

She nodded.

She should have known, should not have underestimated the nobility of this man.

'So what do you want me to do, Becky? How can I help?'

'You've already helped me. Just by saying that. Oh, Matthew, I do feel so much better now that I've told you. It's been awful, the deceit of it.'

'Forgive me for putting you in a position where you had to deceive. For such an honest, straightforward person as you it must have been dreadful.'

He took her hand and they stood for a moment, saying nothing. She felt drained, numb.

'But in practical ways, Becky, that's what I meant really. How to help in practical matters and – oh, the children.'

So shocked had he been, she realised, that it had taken him all this time to remember they had children.

'It makes me realise,' he said slowly, 'how sure you are about this. I mean, for you to be prepared to do this to the children, you must be very sure.'

'They're both away for three weeks, Matthew. It gives us time to adjust and work out what's the best way to handle everything.'

They had reached the little sunken patio with its uneven paving, unprofessionally laid by the four of them during their first summer holiday there. In the centre wobbled a garden seat which Ben had made in woodwork classes. Automatically Matthew ran his hand along it to check that the wood was dry enough to sit on.

'Don't think I'm going back on what I said, Becky, but are you quite sure you're doing what's best for *you*? Will he make you happy? You've only met him for such a short time, and obviously in fraught and unnatural circumstances. Do you really *know* him?'

She thought for a while and then, 'No,' she said.

'Do you love him?'

'Yes,' she said without hesitating.

'I see.' He paused, then went on. 'I couldn't bear you to be hurt twice. Don't take this amiss, but have you asked yourself why his first marriage failed? Has he explained?'

No, that was something she didn't understand. Josh's answers, if not exactly evasive, certainly didn't bear the kind of intellectual scrutiny that Matthew would subject them to, or that she herself would once have done.

'Has he deceived his wife before?'

'Yes.'

'Oh, Becky, are you sure you know what you're doing?'

'No. I'm not. I only know I have to do it.'

It was not yet six o'clock: only an hour since she had told him. It had taken hardly any time at all to destroy what had taken years to build.

Days and nights merged after that. At night they were wide-awake, and during the day so tired that they moved about like zombies, heavy-eyed and leaden-footed as they did the everyday things. She could see he was getting more distraught, though he tried not to show it. She herself kept going by constantly reminding herself that soon she would see Josh again. All her strength seemed to come from him now.

On the fourth night they both took sleeping tablets, but still lay awake.

'You're not asleep, are you?' she said in the early hours of the morning.

'No.' He hesitated, then, 'Becky?' he asked.

'Yes?'

'I can just hold you, can't I, Becky? Please?'

'Yes, it's all right.'

He clung to her like a child. He was cold and she could feel that he was thinner. As she would have comforted the children when they were little, she tried to comfort him now, but could think of nothing to say except, 'It'll be all right. In the end, it'll be all right.'

'I'm sorry, Becky, I don't mean to be like this. I'm trying, I mean I want to help you, not to be a drag . . .'

'Sh – it's all right. It's the shock, too, you know. I mean I've had months to get used to the idea of parting, but for you, it's different, so sudden.'

'The will to live. It goes, doesn't it? I don't know how I shall manage without you. You know, don't you, that you've always been everything to me? I've never thought of anyone else, man or woman? So long as I've had you?'

No, that wasn't a fair weapon to use. Maybe he hadn't intended it.

'I've left it a bit late to tell you, haven't I, Becky?'

'Yes.'

'Oh, God, what a fool I've been.'

'If I'd died, Matthew, you'd have gone on at school and—'

'Different, quite different.'

Her eyes felt hot and prickly, as if they were full of dust and grit and burning, unshed tears. His too, certainly.

'You've got everything ready for your day in London tomorrow?'

'Yes.' She hesitated, then, 'I'm sorry; I realise it makes it worse that I'm going to meet him there.'

'Oddly enough, I'm not jealous. I don't seem to have room for that. I just can't envisage a life without you. That's all there is to it. That rules out everything except anxiety for you. To think that you might be hurt again and I wouldn't be able to help you. When someone doesn't love you any more, you can't help them any more, can you?'

'Or hurt them any more either.'

'That's true. Oh, God, that's true.'

They lay in silence; tired eyelids on tired eyes, she kept thinking to herself. It hurt to close them; the lids seemed rough, rasping against her eyes. It was easier to stare wide-eyed into the blackness.

'I suppose,' Matthew said hesitantly, 'you wouldn't consider staying here permanently and just visiting him? I wouldn't mind what arrangements you made, I'd help you in every way I could. I'd cover for you, find reasons, everything. Please, Becky,' he went on with increasing desperation, 'I wouldn't interfere in any way, just if you wouldn't leave me entirely. Rather than lose you, Becky, I'd agree to anything. I wouldn't mind at all.'

But Josh would.

'It wouldn't work, Matthew. I'm sorry.'

There was silence, then a whispered, despairing, 'No, but I had to ask.'

'I was surprised at the way she took it,' Josh had said when they met the next day.

'But you hadn't expected anything different?'

'No, but I didn't think she'd say, "There's the door" quite so abruptly. I mean, to want me out so *fast*.'

It was what she had expected. If she'd been in Corinne's place she'd have felt just the same. What's the point in prolonging the agony, she'd have thought. She had told Josh so, but he hadn't believed it.

'And, dammit,' he said now, 'it's *my* door as much as hers.'

He crossed over, putting her on the inside of the pavement. Then, 'That's one complication you're spared,' he went on as they walked towards the wine bar. 'Since it's only a school house that you live in, you won't have the business of selling up and dividing the proceeds. I mean, you don't have a matrimonial home.'

He sounded so dismissive; she wanted to cry out that she did have a home, that it was full of all the belongings they had gathered around them over the years, all the accumulation of family life. She thought of it all, oh, everything: the presents the children had made her, those clumsy, treasured objects; and she thought of the garden, the paths and terraces they had laid, the little rockery, the wooden seat which Ben had made for them in his carpentry lessons.

'No, there'll be no property complications,' she made herself say, knowing that he would not understand. 'Nothing like that.'

'You'll just claim half the capital. We'll get you a good lawyer.'

'Don't worry, Josh, Matthew will be absolutely fair. Maybe it sounds old-fashioned, but he is in every way an honourable man.'

'You could have fooled me.'

'That was different, that was something he couldn't help . . .'

'All right, forget it.'

After they had collected their plastic meat and salad, he said, 'Right, so what did he say?'

'He was very good about it. He's quite agreeable that I should come and see you when you get the cottage next week and all that, but he's just afraid that I don't know you, don't know enough about you—'

'That's pretty cool from a chap who kept a basic flaw from you before he married you.'

'Oh, Josh, he isn't trying to get at you. You're so aggressive about everything.'

'He isn't, I suppose?'

'No, not at all. Actually, you are about as different as two men could possibly be. I'm always amazed at it.'

'And I'm always amazed at how alike you and Corinne are.'

She had picked up her glass of cider, but now put it down again. 'In what way?'

'In every way. Time and again you make some remark and I think, That's just what Corinne would say. It's quite creepy. Sometimes I think it'll be a case of out of the frying-pan into the fire, marrying you.'

'What?'

'Don't look like that.'

'But are you sure you want—'

'I'm sure I'm sure,' he interrupted. 'Didn't I tell you that years ago? You wait until I get you all to myself in that cottage next week and I'll show you how much I want you.'

'Do be serious, Josh.'

'Right, you were saying I was the subject of certain inquiries by your husband?'

'He just wondered why your marriage had gone wrong. That's a fair enough thing to wonder about in the circumstances. He is genuinely afraid for me.'

Josh shrugged. 'Well, how many middle-aged people are happily married?' he asked rhetorically.

'Lots.'

'Oh, they pretend, but they mostly stick together for lack of an alternative.'

She didn't reply. It sometimes seemed to her that Josh just didn't have the knack of looking at anything honestly where emotions were concerned. He seemed to veer off. Or he took hold of any argument that seemed to suit his purpose for the moment, as if scoring points mattered more than getting at the truth of things. It was frightening to think of starting again, at their age, the two of them so different. Or was it exciting?

He surprised her now by saying, in one of his sudden eruptions of honesty, 'My other vices, apart from a lifetime's womanising, are food and alcohol.'

She laughed out loud. 'Oh, Josh, what sudden baring of the soul. You're plump all right, but I can't say I ever noticed you rolling about drunk.'

'I keep sober when you're around.'

'And you don't smell like an alcoholic. Don't alcoholics smell?'

'Not if they drink vodka, they don't.'

'Idiot.'

He looked at her hard. She saw that he was in earnest, as if he wanted to make sure that she really understood.

'It's not a joke, actually,' he said, and there was a critical edge to his voice when he went on. 'Sometimes you're surprisingly ignorant of quite commonplace facts, my love. But anyway, if the saintly Matthew inquires, I hereby promise never to have vodka in any house I share with you.'

'And no puddings either?'

'You put me on to a diet, Becky, and I'll stick to it, I promise.'

'Have you ever tried before?'

He shrugged. 'Every doctor I go to showers me with little pamphlets about calories, but till now what's been the point? I like my job and all the perks that go with it, which include a lot of good food and drink, so I thought I might just as well enjoy life and drop down dead at sixty-five.'

She turned on him, outraged. 'You've no right to talk like that. You're never to say such a thing again.'

'Hi,' he took hold of her wrists. 'That's the second time I've seen you angry. You're coming on, aren't you, kitten?'

'Don't, Josh. Tell me about the cottage. I must be off to Doughtymans soon.'

'It was amazing really,' he said, releasing her hands. 'This chap just mentioned to me that he had a cottage which he didn't want to leave empty for three months while he was abroad. It's got some quite good antiques in it. He asked me if I knew anyone who'd be interested. I couldn't believe my luck. So we've set the thing in motion and I'm in next Monday. Just as well in view of the line Corinne has taken.'

'And it's near the motorway?'

'Yes, the village is about two miles from it. I'll have a much easier journey into London than I did from home. Less than an hour. Anyway, you'll see it soon. You are coming for the weekend, aren't you?'

'Yes, Matthew says he will drop me off on his way to the conference. He has this three-day conference at—'

'He'll bring you to me?' Josh repeated, disbelieving.

'Not to the door, but, as you say, it's only a few minutes to the village from the motorway, which he'll be on anyway, so it makes sense.'

'All the same, it's not what I'd have done for my wife if things had been the other way round. I'd have told her to bloody well find her own way to her new chap.'

'Not if you loved her, you wouldn't.'

'Even more if I loved her. Anyway, what are we arguing about?'

'I wasn't arguing.'

She sipped her cider. 'Josh,' she said. 'Do you argue with everyone at work?'

'Yes.'

'But you get on with people?'

'No, I wouldn't say so. Most people think I'm an arrogant bastard.'

'I don't believe that.'

'Believe it or not, as you like. It's true.'

How strange after having a husband that everyone liked and respected, to have one who was regarded as an arrogant bastard. No. She didn't believe it. Josh just said these things.

'It's odd how we've never seen each other with other people, isn't it?' she remarked.

'Not really, Becky. People in our situation never do. They have to meet secretly.'

People in our situation; so there were recognised rules and procedures which Josh knew and understood, as if it was commonplace, their situation. But to her it had always seemed unique.

'I must go, Josh. Mrs Doughtyman will be waiting,' she said, picking up her folder. For a moment she held it close, this folder of her poems, and oh, it had a reassuring feel, belonging as it did to a different, safer world.

Something odd had been going on outside the Doughtymans' offices. On the pavement, Mr Doughtyman was pacing alongside what looked like a line of about fifteen bundles which, as she drew nearer, she could distinguish as being a briefcase, a small hold-all with a broken zip, a gaping canvas sailing bag, a succession of plastic carriers bulging with books and finally an assortment of brown paper parcels tied with hairy yellow string.

As she approached, a taxi pulled up alongside and simultaneously Mrs Doughtyman flew out of the house and began to pace behind her husband, wringing her hands.

'Oh, if only you'd put it all into proper cases,' she wailed. 'It would probably even go into one big case. Oh hello, Mrs Portman, how simply lovely to see you. We're a bit distracted. We're getting Cedric off, you see. Getting Cedric off is always a little traumatic. I'm sure you understand. Oh dear.' She broke off to answer a query from the cab driver. 'Yes, *all* of it, yes, every one of them. Yes, and him too. Do get in, dear. Yes, Victoria, it's Victoria station he's to be taken to. Do go indoors, Mrs Portman, I shall join you in no time at all.'

Becky let herself into the house and then hesitated about whether to close the door behind her. Looking back she saw that an altercation had broken out between Mr Doughtyman and the cab driver. She didn't want to add to the difficulties of Mrs Doughtyman's life by locking her out of her own home. The narrow hall, she observed, was further narrowed by having stacks of newspapers piled up against one wall. She took a few and used them to jam the door open just a little.

Crossing the passage, she noticed a lavatory on the half-landing, the door ajar. It seemed sensible to use it while she waited for Mrs Doughtyman. She climbed the few stairs quietly, feeling guilty, like an uninvited guest, and closed the door softly behind her. It wouldn't shut properly; she pushed her bag against it. Afterwards, still feeling like an intruder, she pulled the chain as gently as she could.

There was a tremendous crash which seemed to come from the rusty cistern high up on the wall above the lavatory, followed by a great juddering of pipes and whooshing of water somewhere above it, then a roaring, clattering sound which shook the whole house. She heard running footsteps. She stood, horrified, her eyes tightly closed, waiting for the ceiling to fall in on her, followed perhaps by a water tank or two and even the rest of the system. Nothing happened. She opened her eyes and crept out on to the landing, expecting to see the entire office staff running for safety into the street.

Only Mrs Doughtyman stood at the foot of the stairs.

'I'm so sorry,' she said. 'I should have warned you, if I'd known. We always warn people. These old houses, you know. Last year the whole front fell off.'

'The front of the lavatory?'

'No, the front of the house.'

She opened the door into her office. 'Yes, indeed the whole façade,' she added, shaking her head. 'Such a bother.'

Her office overlooked the road. Outside the window a car door slammed and a taxi drove away.

'Ah, that's all right,' Mrs Doughtyman said, suddenly smiling her sweet smile. 'There was a little trouble over charging extra for each of the bundles, even the smallest ones. It's no bother getting Cedric off, no bother at all. It's his bundles which always cause the difficulties. He likes to keep everything separate, you see.'

Then, with startling abruptness, she turned her mind to Becky and the poems, becoming instantly a different person. Becky could never get used to it, this transformation from the chaotic Mrs Doughtyman, whom she wanted to organise, sort out, take in hand, to the marvellously perceptive and knowledgeable Mrs Doughtyman who, with her inner calm, could enter Becky's mind, explain to her what was confused, clarify her vague ideas. If there was a line in a poem that Becky knew was somehow wrong and had tried repeatedly to make better and eventually given up and left as it was, Mrs Doughtyman would spot it straight away. 'You're not quite happy about that, are you?' she would ask gently. She seemed to be on the same wavelength and yet detached, so that it would seem to Becky that it was her own conscience that had spoken and told her to try once more. And she always did manage to get it better: Mrs Doughtyman never asked the impossible. It was as if she knew what Becky was capable of better than she did herself.

Certainly, she reflected, she would have written no poetry

in these last few terrible weeks if it hadn't been for the imperative of Mrs Doughtyman expecting it of her.

'So you've brought, how many did you say, two more?' she was asking now, taking the folder.

'There should have been a third,' Becky said. 'But it wouldn't work.' Mrs Doughtyman looked at her, bright-eyed, inquiring.

'It's an image which keeps coming back to me,' Becky said. 'I mean, when I'm trying to turn to something else, it comes back, but it won't work out. There was a tree which grew out of a rock. I mean, literally, its roots were embedded in the rock. I remember it when I was little. And it's still there, the tree I mean. I suppose the seed must have fallen into the crevice in the limestone years ago and germinated, and the roots must have pushed down and found a little bit of soil, or even just fed on the rock. It's about roots really,' she ended lamely, her voice trailing off.

'I'll look forward to seeing it one day,' Mrs Doughtyman said.

They sat in silence for a while, Becky regretting having talked about the poem. Trying to explain the inexplicable was so pointless and only made you feel stupid. And had probably driven away the poem for good.

'The themes are linked, aren't they?' Mrs Doughtyman remarked.

'What? What themes?'

'The idea of the roots in the rock and of the unchanging nature of things?'

'Oh, yes, I see. Because we all put down roots, don't we, when we're small, and that forms us, doesn't it, the soil we grew up in. What we draw from that gives us strength.'

She thought of the strength it gave her, going back to Enderby, the nourishment, the feeling of permanence.

'Yes,' she said. 'I suppose I *am* trying to say something like that in the poem, about the connection between permanence and strength and roots. I'm sorry I can't explain.'

'If you could explain it,' Mrs Doughtyman said, 'you wouldn't need to write the poem.'

* * *

Matthew had been pale, very composed when he dropped her off in the village on his way to the conference. She ached for him.

'You're quite sure you don't want me to pick you up on my way back on Tuesday?' he asked.

'Quite. I shall make my own way home and be there before you.'

'Thank you.'

'I've things to do,' she said, but they both knew she was sparing him going back to an empty house, the foretaste of things to come.

He kissed her, handed her the small case from the back seat, and drove off. She stood for a moment and then turned, walked down a narrow lane and knocked on the door of Number One, Petts Row.

'Oh, thank God you've come, Becky,' Josh greeted her. 'It's awful. There aren't enough wardrobes and there isn't one of those things that dries clothes, you know that goes round and round, full of hot air—'

'Tumble-dryer?' she supplied. 'It doesn't matter. Can I come in?'

There were windows looking out on to the back.

'Look, there's a garden,' she said. 'We'll put up a clothes-line.'

'And the washing-machine doesn't work. It's my shirts I'm worried about. If only we were in America they have that special stuff there, you can wash your shirts in a basin—'

'It's called soap, Josh.'

'No, in England they go in machines, but over there it's all right to put them in a basin to wash. I could ring up some hotel in New York when I'm back in the office and ask them what the stuff's called. I mean, they all have it.'

He was pounding round the room, head thrust forward, glowering.

Amused and astonished, she couldn't help laughing.

178

'Oh, Josh, what a fuss about nothing. I'll see to it in a minute.'

'But what about when you're not here? Can't you move in permanently now?'

'No, Josh, I can only stay three days. I've things to sort out first at home. You know that. You said you understood.'

'Home? I've no home but with you. You've no home but with me. Oh, I'm sorry, I haven't exactly welcomed you warmly, have I?'

'Actually, you haven't welcomed me at all.'

'Come here.' He held her close, kissing her but, opening her eyes, she saw that he was looking distractedly over the top of her head.

'What's the matter?'

'What's that going round for?'

'It's the electric meter.'

'But why's it going round? There aren't any lights on.'

'There must be something else on. An immersion heater, maybe.'

'The water isn't hot. That's another thing.'

'You're not very relaxed, are you?'

'No, I'm so worried about my shirts. And that meter's puzzling.'

'It could be the refrigerator.'

'Yes, you're right. I've put provisions in it.'

'Let's see what you've got.'

The fridge contained six bottles of wine and a very small piece of cheese.

'Oh, what a deal of sack,' she said.

'What?'

'Never mind. Is there a shop near, Josh?'

'I don't know.'

'Come on, let's go out and look for one before they close. I expect there'll be a general store in the village.'

'Since we're in the country, I thought I'd wear this,' he said, taking a cap out of his pocket as they set off. He put it on and grinned at her. 'Like it?' he asked. She smiled and nodded. He fancies himself in that cap, she thought fondly. I will not tell him he looks like Mr Toad.

They found a general store in the high street. 'It's easier than I realised,' Josh said as they gathered tins and packages off shelves and dipped into freezers. 'Nothing to it, really.

'All the same,' he said as they walked back, 'I didn't see any of that stuff for shirts.'

'I've got some detergent. I'll wash your shirts tomorrow and put them out to dry.'

It was amazing to think how often he had said he wanted nothing except to look after her, but now the only problem seemed to be how to bridge the gap between having himself looked after by Corinne and having himself looked after by Becky.

'God, I could do with a drink,' he said as they got back into the cottage.

'I'll put the kettle on.'

He gave her a pained look.

'Didn't you say you wanted a cup of tea?'

'No, a drink, woman, a drink.'

'Oh.' In different households, the same words have different meanings.

'You mean you want some of this wine?' she asked, busy packing eggs and butter into the fridge door, vegetables into the basket, meat on the shelves.

'No, actually what I really want is vodka, but since I've banned it from any house I share with you, I suppose wine it must be. I'd rather have alcohol, though. Now what's funny?'

'Oh Josh, *you* are.'

'Come here and I'll show you something funny.'

He took her by the shoulders and propelled her towards the door at the bottom of the stairs. It was a semi-spiral staircase, with just one room at the top, a bathroom opening out of it.

'I haven't even unpacked. My nightie's in the case in the kitch—'

'You don't need a nightie. Look, I've got something for you. It's under your pillow.'

It was the key of the cottage, a huge thing made of iron.

'There's only one door,' he said, 'and two keys.' He put it into her hand. 'Nobody can come in here except you and me, Becky,' he said solemnly. 'It is the key of the cottage and my heart and everything. Don't part with it. Ever.'

He pressed it into her hand so hard as he kissed her that it made a mark like a key in her palm.

For a moment the next morning she couldn't think where she was. Light was shafting in through the thin curtains; she blinked and looked at her watch. Six o'clock and quite cold. She crept up closer to Josh, put her arm around him.

He turned, instantly awake. He smiled at her. 'I've dreamed so often of you, Becky, I wasn't sure.'

'Were you asleep?'

'Yes. It was wonderful. I just felt this little arm come creeping round me. Bless you for being here.'

This is where I belong, she thought, here with Josh. He had always said so, but she had never quite believed it. She believed it now as she lay peacefully in his arms and watched as the sun slanted in through the window, lighting up the brass bedstead.

'It's a nice old bed,' she remarked.

'Mm. We'll get one like it. Brass knobs and all.'

'It's such a cosy cottage, Josh. When you said the chap had antiques in it, I thought you meant something a bit museumish and forbidding, but it's nice old homely stuff, isn't it?'

'Nothing of any value. I think it was just that he didn't want to leave the place empty for three months. He only comes here at weekends when he is in the UK, so we could probably go on renting it if we haven't got fixed up by then.'

'We will have.'

'Yes. It's a funny thing, but you know, when we were first married, Corinne and I had a furnished place lent to us, much better stuff in it than this, really elegant. And I used to think of you and how you'd have graced it all and how I'd have loved to share it with you.'

'Don't, Josh.'

'Oh, it's just that sometimes I think of the lost opportunities, the wasted years, and it gets me by the throat.'

'Sh. It came right in the end for you.'

'Yes. Oh yes.'

Later she said, 'Shall I make some tea?'

'No. I hate it, especially if it takes you out of my bed. I made plans in the night. I thought we'd stay in bed all morning and then go for a walk.'

'Where?'

'Somewhere where we could get a pub lunch.'

'We could take a picnic. I brought a thermos flask.'

'No, Becky. Pub lunch with beer.'

'All right.'

'Two whole days to ourselves, I can scarcely believe it,' he said, and sighed. 'I can't tell you how wonderful it will be to come back to you here on Monday evening. By the way, I've to go to Africa next week. I'll be away about ten days.'

'Oh, no!'

'It's all right, I'll be back. I didn't tell you last night because I thought you might be upset.'

In separate countries again; she hated it when he was away. It frightened her.

'It'll be horrible for Corinne too,' she said, 'in all this upset. There'll be things she needs to discuss with you.'

'She's not well either, which doesn't help. And worried about Priscilla, who's off on some boat somewhere or other. And there were storms in that area the night before last.'

Poor Corinne, she thought. She must feel as if her whole world is falling apart.

'There is a phone here, isn't there, Josh? I mean, she can ring you if she's worried about Priscilla?'

'Yes. It's in the kitchen. I gave her the number in a sealed envelope.'

'In a *what*?'

'It's the right way to do these things.'

'But why didn't you just give her the number?'

'This way it can only be used in a crisis. If it's a matter of life and death she'd be justified in using it.'

For a moment she was filled with outrage on behalf of this other woman. Steam it open, Corinne, she thought. No, be a devil, tear it open clumsily for all to see. Preferably with your thumb. Defy him with its jagged edges, him and his silly rules. We live by different laws, you and I.

'I do things correctly, Becky, that's one of the things you'll have to learn about me.'

She struggled to understand. If you start with a suspicious nature, trusting nobody, then maybe it is correct to put telephone numbers in sealed envelopes. But how much simpler to trust in human sanity.

'And she isn't well, you said. Is she on her own? I mean with Priscilla away and you gone—'

'She's in bed. I saw to her before I left. I did everything a husband should. I took her a cup of tea and some Perrier water.'

Oh, lucky Corinne! Tea *and* Perrier water. Oh God.

'And I stayed till her friend arrived. That seemed the right thing to do.'

'You could ring her, in case she doesn't like to break the seal,' she said. 'I suppose the telephone's by her bed?'

'No. I'm against that. If someone rang from the States in the early morning she'd have to go and get me and they'd know we sleep apart.'

'What's it got to do with them?'

'Everything. That's why one doesn't tell too much to the company doctor.'

'But that's awful . . .'

'They pay him, so they have a right to know what he says or prescribes, I suppose.'

She shook her head. 'I remember my father telling me that, when the National Health Service was being set up after the war, there was a campaign against it, telling people there'd be a government spy in every surgery. It wasn't true, of course, but isn't it odd that these great companies are now more like that than the government?'

'I can tell you these companies *are* like governments in the way they control our lives.'

'But surely it matters more for her to have a telephone by the bed than to worry about the effects on your career and—'

'It's an academic point now,' Josh said.

It wasn't: it was what lay behind it.

'Anyway, she isn't alone. I stayed until her friend Paula arrived. That seemed the correct thing to do.'

If I were her friend, I would hate you, Josh, for leaving her now. But, of course, I would hate me even more.

He came back distraught on Monday evening.

'I've got to go sooner than I thought,' he said. 'It's a real crisis situation. The job's in dire trouble money-wise. I'll have to leave on Wednesday, go home and pick up my tropical kit tomorrow. Oh God, what a muddle it all is. Did you make the washing-machine work?'

'Yes, I've done the washing.'

'Clever girl.'

'Not really. One washing-machine is very like another. And there are instructions for the uninitiated.'

He laughed. 'You're good for me,' he said. 'You can always raise a smile. Come here.'

'I didn't realise,' she said, leaning against him, 'that you'd become so unpractical.'

'What, *me*? I'm very practical, people have often commented on it.'

'Are you sure?'

'Yes. I give them advice and they say, that was very practical advice you gave me. Really, Becky, it's happened several times. What are you laughing at?'

He sat drinking wine and watching while she cooked in the

little kitchen. There were blue and white gingham curtains at the window.

'Something's different,' he said.

'Yes, it's the curtains. They were a bit limp and grubby so I washed and starched them.'

'Do you think you should have done that? I mean, they're not ours, are they? I'm not sure that legally—'

'Oh, Josh, of course it's all right. Just leave it to me.'

'Are *you* practical then, Becky? I mean, poets aren't supposed to be, are they?'

'I don't think I'm practical by instinct, but any women who's had a family and run a home just ends up being practical, because she has to be. But you've got much less so,' she added, looking at him thoughtfully. 'I mean, you used to be good with primus stoves and all sorts of things like that.'

He shrugged. 'Oh, I leave all the practical chores for others now,' he said. 'Isn't that what wives and secretaries are for? I mean, why keep a dog and do your own barking? Don't look so shocked.' He got up and kissed her.

After a while he said, 'You know, Becky, I'm not looking forward to going home tomorrow to collect my stuff. I don't relish it, I can tell you.'

'It'll be all right, Josh.'

'It's easy enough for you to say that. I'm the one who's in the dog-house.'

Becky shook her head. 'No,' she said. 'You're not. I'll get the blame.'

'*You*? What rubbish. What have you done?'

'I suppose I've done what you wanted me to do, haven't I?'

'You have, my darling.'

'But that's got nothing to do with it. It's women who get the blame.'

'Why?'

'Because they're willing to accept it, and men aren't.'

'Why should they accept it?'

She hesitated. 'I suppose,' she said slowly, 'because they feel

185

responsible for other people, worry about them. So when things go wrong they blame themselves.'

'More fool them,' Josh had said.

The fire had almost burnt out. Only a few glowing embers remained among the powdery grey ash at the bottom of the grate. Becky stirred them gently, watching them fall through the bars. No more fires this year, she thought, once these storms are over; soon we shall be living outdoors. For there always seemed to come a moment in the Easter holidays, a certain day when the garden called, when the soil looked dry enough to work on and the grass ready for its first cut.

Last year, despite everything, they had still recognised that day, that day when the earth was turning a paler brown and beginning to send up weeds. They had worked together on the rockery, she and Matthew, that afternoon in the Easter holidays, trying to do the normal every-year things.

He was tracing a long branching strand of couch grass; it led him under a large stone. He looked up from shifting it and said, 'Becky, what are those little things, weeds or plants?'

She peered at them. 'I think they're seedlings from the campanula. They must have sown themselves from that clump over there and survived the winter.'

'Shall I chuck them out?'

'No, I'll dig them up and replant them ready for next year.'

He didn't answer. Silently he lived this pain. She knew he was unable to conceive of a next year without her, of new plants flowering which she had planted but was not there to see. Yet she couldn't help him. How much easier to be Josh, to be shown the door. Anything rather than this grief: anger, jealousy, recrimination, blame, anything would be easier to bear.

Sometimes she could feel the strength draining out of her, feared she could not last out. But tomorrow Josh would be back, give her some of his strength, his emotional toughness. He would offer that shoulder, dependable, rocklike. He had been right when he had told her that, whenever he was not there, she must just think of her head on his shoulder. She had smiled at the time, but it worked, it did work. She had used it a lot this week. But now she needed the reality of him.

'I've got to go in now,' Matthew said. 'I'm going to see the bursar at four. Don't stay out too long. It's getting cool.'

'All right. I'll finish off that patch you've been working on.'

It was soothing, the deadening repetitiveness of weeding. The soil was just right for pulling up the annual weeds, their roots slipped out as if they were oiled and the soil didn't cling to them. She worked on until she could feel the cool dampness of the evening in the air, and then gathered up the trowels and forks into the trug and clambered down from the rockery. The grass below was messy with bits of weeds and deadheads, but the rockery looked better. She looked at it with satisfaction; the rocks were visible now, especially the quartz ones near the front and the curiously shaped ones that the locals called cats' brains.

She took the bucketful of weeds down to the compost heap and stood catching the last of the sunlight, separating out the pernicious weeds for burning, especially the sinister white roots of couch grass, thinking what evil-looking things they were.

Years ago they'd had an old retired gardener as a neighbour, who used to come and inspect what they had done. George, he was called. Nearly all her gardening lore had been learned from him. It was he who had taught her to sort out the good weeds from the bad. Only bad gardeners burn good weeds, he said. They make good compost. They're only plants in the wrong place.

And hoeing before the weeds appear, that was another of his rules, hoeing in the morning early so the sun shrivels them up. He hated chemical death. Doing things in the garden before they needed doing, he'd say, is the way to save work, not chucking chemicals about. And how to make a fine tilth, he'd taught her that too. And how to plant seeds. She could remember him now, instructing her to sow peas in staggered rows, not straight lines, rebuking her for not doing so although in fact they hadn't come up. 'How did you know I planted them in a straight line?' she had asked. 'Because the mouse that ate them before they could germinate walked down the soil in a straight line. See?' And, looking where he pointed, she saw the little paw marks on the bare soil.

A garden tells you a lot about a person, he had said. She had the feeling that he viewed a person's life as a garden, all things in their season. Dear George, long dead, what would you think of me now? I wonder, would you understand? Somehow his approval mattered. Matthew would understand that. Josh would think it ridiculous. A good old man, but not powerful, not important or rich; in Josh's scale of values he would come pretty low. She would know better than to try to explain. Her father, too, although he scarcely knew a rose from a hydrangea, would have valued George.

In one of the gardens where George occasionally worked, there was a Judas tree. He took her to see it one spring when it was in flower, because it was rare and beautiful. 'But I wouldn't want one of them trees in my garden,' he had said. 'Symbol of treachery, they are.' And she had thought of her father saying that a man deserved to die for betraying a friend who trusted him. George, although a pacifist like Matthew, would have agreed with that.

She shivered as she went to collect the tools and the trug from the rockery; she'd been silly to hang around musing in the cold. The secateurs, as usual, had gone missing. She found them at last on the stone where she had left them.

She was still thinking about George and the Judas tree as she lay in the bath, thawing out. Afterwards she indulged in rereading Josh's last letter, written from the airport just before he went abroad. It was on top of the pile in the drawer of her dressing table, the key of the cottage alongside. She was holding them both, the key and the letter, when the telephone rang.

'Becky?'

'Oh, Josh! You're home! Oh, welcome back!'

'Yes, I got back to UK earlier than I expected. Yesterday, actually.'

'Yesterday?'

'I went home to sort out my stuff. I had a lot of dirty washing as you can imagine. Anyway, the long and short of it is that I had a long talk with Corinne and I've decided it's all off. It seems that she could claim a much bigger proportion of my salary than I'd realised and I'd have to find a colossal sum to compensate her for loss of pension rights. Apparently these ridiculous old judges are prejudiced in favour of deserted wives nearing fifty.'

'It doesn't matter, Josh,' she whispered. 'It's only money. I'm not used to being rich.'

'Well, I am. One gets used to certain standards, Becky. No, it's hopeless. We've got to be practical.'

Silence. Then this strange, hard voice, which surely couldn't belong to Josh, went on, 'Of course, as my lawyer said, with people of our age, death sometimes solves the problem and the right couple gets together in the end. A very wise comment, that.'

He is wishing them dead, Corinne and Matthew. It's evil. Stupid, too, because he is the oldest of the four of us. How can he call it wise?

'I've got to be brief, Becky. I'm in a call-box and I haven't much change.'

Then it wasn't Josh. Josh always reversed the charges or got her to ring back. He never put money in. It was someone else. It was all a mistake.

She wanted to ask for the real Josh. Please let him speak. The one who promised that he'd always be there. Where is he now? The one who said, 'It is quite unthinkable that I should ever hurt you.' Please go and get him. But she could not form the words.

'The main purpose of this call, Becky, is to tell you to bring a case when you come on Saturday to collect your stuff. Just for the day, you'll come to the cottage on Saturday?'

'Case?'

What was this man on about? Please get Josh. Tell him that I need him.

'For your things. You left a few things at the cottage. You don't think I'm the sort of chap who'd let a woman go off with all her bits and pieces in a couple of carrier bags, do you?'

Disbelief, blackness. She stared down at her own body, hoping that she would see somebody else. She saw the ring on her finger. Suddenly it seemed important, this material thing.

'What shall I do about the engagement ring?' she asked, though really she was asking, 'What shall I do about me?'

'I never called it an engagement ring,' the hard voice said.

She tried to remember. Perhaps the words were true, but the spirit false, false, false.

'Perhaps you could give it to charity,' he said.

Near the hand which wore the ring, was lying the letter she had just read. His last written words to her were, 'My love is invincible.' Liar. Your love was very vincible; it was a poor little thing that crumpled at the first hurdle. For a moment anger flared up in her. She recognised the saving grace of it. Please God, vouchsafe me just a little anger to give me strength. But her prayer went unanswered; her anger flared up, flickered and died.

'And the key, Becky. You'll bring it back, won't you? I've only got two and I remember giving you one. You haven't lost it, have you?'

No, I had it pressed into my hand and on the palm are the marks of it still.

'Are you there? I said, have you still got the key?'

'Mm.'

The key has turned into a knife and it is twisting and turning in my heart. It is only the pain that is creating the tears which flow, like blood, of their own accord. I'm not really crying.

'Bring it with you then, would you? Look, I must go, the small change is running out.'

I trusted you, Josh. Entirely. Because you told me to. And

once you were a decent, honourable man. You don't exist any more. Only the memory of that man you once were. Or perhaps it was a case of mistaken identity. Or perhaps you killed him, you of the hard voice and no small change. Oh Josh, I trusted you so.

'Goodbye, Becky.'

'Goodbye.'

She could not say his name. There was no more Josh. Only Judas. Judas Blackford. Judas Blackford. Judas. Judas. Judas.

Chapter Ten

It was ridiculous, Corinne thought as she flew back to Cairo, to be haunted still by that dream about Becky. Bernard, alongside her, had very sensibly gone to sleep. Why did she have to be so wide-awake and plagued with memories? Why couldn't she just forget that awful flight home from Sri Lanka which had seemed endless at the time and unreal? She remembered wondering what would happen at Heathrow and asking Becky if she thought that when they went to collect their luggage Grover would appear on the carousel. Becky had said she thought they probably had a special arrangement for coffins.

The first time, years ago, that she'd heard Becky's name, she had not realised its significance. They had been discussing, she and Grover, what to call their baby. A boy was to have her father's name, which happened to be the same as Grover's grandfather. So that was easy. Girls were more difficult.

'How about Rebecca?' Grover had suggested.

'Rebecca? Oh, I don't think so,' she had said, burping gently and stretching her legs out on the stool in front of her as the baby squirmed and kicked inside her. It seemed to be climbing higher and higher every day. Not long ago it had been way down there in her stomach. Now it seemed to be scrambling up into her chest. She watched, fascinated, as the magazine lying open on her front lifted itself up and down, taking on a life of its own. Then, 'There aren't any Rebeccas in your family, are there?' she asked. 'I'm sure there aren't any on my side. Have you known any Rebeccas?'

'No, not really. I just thought it was an attractive name. I rather like it.'

'Well, I don't,' she said. 'I'd rather have a name that means something, at least to one of us.'

He sighed and said, 'Well, perhaps it wasn't such a good idea. Besides, come to think of it, if we called our daughter Rebecca, people might think we were Jews.'

So when he told her, years later, about meeting Becky Portman, some ludicrous tale concerning a beer barrel – typical, come to think of it, liquor would just have to be involved, wouldn't it? – she had been taken unawares. She wasn't hurt like the first time; his affairs had ceased to worry her much. But this wasn't an affair. This wasn't a matter of some woman from a singles' bar going to bed with Grover in return for a good meal. Oh no, this was for real. The woman must be demented, she had thought.

In a way, part of her had been relieved. Right, she'd thought, or rather part of herself had thought, let somebody else cope with him and good luck to her. He needs someone as tough and hard as himself, as devious and unscrupulous. I hope she gives him hell.

But then she had watched, fascinated, as Grover thrashed about trying to get himself organised. He was totally unpractical, she realised now; he had always relied on her to sort out his day-to-day living arrangements. What a time it had been, how unable he had been to distinguish what mattered from what was trivial, how clumsily he had set about shattering her world, Becky's world and his own. How relatively calm she herself had been, detached, until a kind of pity, not unmixed with self-interest, made her hold out a hand to rescue him, save him from his own maudlin sentimentality. She realised for the first time that he simply could not cope with genuine emotion. He had always had appetites, not feelings: appetite for power, for money, for sex, and had used people – employees, colleagues, women – to satisfy them. But assailed by this feeling for Becky he couldn't cope; his usual methods were of no use to him. He floundered. Ah, well, she would not dwell upon it, she thought, for had it not all turned out for the best?

Besides, when, by the most extraordinary chance, she had met the Portman woman, she had really rather liked her. She had done her best not to, but simply couldn't help it. Becky wasn't at all as she had imagined. She was really rather sweet; she was gentle and dreamy, vulnerable really.

How the poor silly thing had got herself entangled with Grover she couldn't think; it was impossible to imagine a less compatible pair. At least when she herself had got hitched to him, she had had the excuse of immaturity. By the time you're pushing forty-five you've no right to be so bloody stupid.

It had clarified things in her mind, the Becky affair had. It had made her realise that she had her strengths too, that in fact she was stronger than Grover, for all his aggressive ways, and that she could manage perfectly well without him. Events had played into her hands, of course, but when they did she had been ready to seize her opportunity. Without that insight into herself which Becky had provided she might never have realised that she had the strength to take control of her life, might never even have come away here, never met Bernard, never found the courage to paint.

She owed a lot to Becky, in a funny sort of way. Yes, definitely, she would write and ask her to come to see her in her new home. So that's settled, she said to herself, and leaning her head comfortably against Bernard's shoulder, she slept soundly for the rest of the flight.

Matthew watched Becky as she sat alongside him on the garden seat reading Corinne's letter. He sipped his coffee, he gazed out across the rockery, he fingered his own letters. But all the time he was watching her out of the corner of his eye.

'Anything special?' he asked casually at last.

'It's from Corinne.'

'Oh, yes?'

He sounded mildly interested, no more.

'She suggests meeting.'

He paused, alert, and nervous for her. Then, 'She wants to

come here, does she?' he asked, picking up his coffee-cup.

'No, she's wondering if I might go and see her in her new house. She's moving to Hackney.'

'*Hackney*?'

The surprise was genuine. It wasn't an area you'd expect a widow of Grover's to move into.

'She says it's a convenient little house, near to a good art class and handy for buses.'

'All the same—'

'And she says she's never liked living in the country anyway.'

'Tell me,' he requested carefully, keeping his voice as unemotional as possible, 'do you really want to see her again?'

She hesitated. 'I'm not sure,' she said.

That made it easier; it allowed him to say, 'Don't force yourself to go if you think it might be – ' he searched for the right word, not wanting to sound patronising – 'well –*stressful*.'

She looked at him directly now. 'I think I'd like to go,' she said. 'And please, Matthew, don't worry about me. I'll be all right.'

'Of course you'll be all right. I just don't want Corinne upsetting you.'

She shook her head. 'The world would say that it's I who did the upsetting,' she said.

'The world usually gets these things wrong,' he told her.

When she didn't reply he went on, 'I just don't want you to find yourself in a difficult situation. Corinne can be very brusque, you know, and you're such a gentle person.'

'Don't worry,' she said again. 'I won't let her browbeat me.'

She picked up her other letter to show that the matter was dismissed. It was from Mrs Doughtyman, just a brief note to say that the new roughs were no better than the earlier ones had been.

Poor Mrs Doughtyman. Another promising young artist had let her down. She had warned him against producing anything soft and sentimental and he had evidently overreacted.

'They're so sketchy and harsh. There is something quite

abrasive about them,' Mrs Doughtyman wrote. 'Quite wrong, horrid in fact.'

She went on to say that Becky could come and see them if she liked, but she was quite sure she wouldn't approve of them either. Never mind, she would go on trying, it was important to get it absolutely right. That was all that mattered, however long it took.

'Do you agree with that?' Matthew asked Becky now. 'Does it worry you, the way it's dragging on?'

'I think if it was just up to me,' she said, 'I'd probably go ahead and publish the poems unillustrated, as we were going to do originally. But it isn't just up to me. And I think Mrs Doughtyman is one of those people who, when they get an idea in their heads that they are quite sure is right, simply won't be satisfied until they've seen it carried out. And she's far too much of a perfectionist to take second-best. It's reassuring to know that,' she added. 'She wouldn't let me down by using illustrations that didn't fit the poems; she would understand how much that would hurt.'

'You're very trusting still,' Matthew remarked. She thought it was a strange thing to say, and looked at him inquiringly, but he had turned back to the pile of letters he had brought out with him.

'I'll let you get on with those in peace,' she said. 'I'm going to prowl round the garden.'

She walked slowly across to the rockery. The aubretia and alyssum had died back now, the little campanula seedlings which she had planted out last year had spread and were filling the hollows with swathes of blue. Matthew watched her. It had become a habit with him since last summer, this watching, this listening, alert to catch the slightest sound of stress. He seemed always to be tensed, on his guard for her, ready to ward off danger. He feared for her all the time now, he who had for so many years taken her strength for granted.

It was that strength which had first drawn him to her, that gentle strength of hers, gentle but somehow implacable.

Instinctively he had known that Becky was one who wouldn't give in, would never let you down. Not so much would not, as could not. It was not in her nature. Yet at the same time, he realised now, he had feared it, this womanly strength of hers, was in awe of it and could not admit his need of it. So he had just used it, pretending it was his own.

He owed everything to her, of course; he could accept that now. Marriage to her had made him safe, safe in his dealing with other men, safe in his dealings with the boys, safe eventually to rejoin the boarding-school world where he excelled, for it suited him to live in this school community, almost a village it was, where he was at the centre of everything, turned to by everybody, the source of all authority; no wonder that it seemed to everyone that he was the sun around whom Becky's life revolved.

But it was not so, Matthew Portman acknowledged to himself as he sat on the bench, pretending to read his mail while watching his wife stroll around the garden. And in his heart he had always known that it was not so. The reality was that she was the source of his strength and he, like some cold moon, had circled her sphere, dependent on her warmth.

The moment of truth had come when she was first ill with depression. He had seen the signs of its coming, but instantly discounted what he had seen, refused to recognise the symptoms, refused even to listen when she made feeble attempts to talk about it, turning to him in vain for some emotional support. He had behaved like a child hoping that, if you pretend something isn't there, it will go away. Yes, that was the most sickening thing, he thought now, with sudden self-disgust, that in his panic he hadn't behaved like a grown man, he who was so mature about everything else, so wise in judgement, so readily available to everyone who needed help, had closed himself off from Becky in her great need.

And yet she was the most precious person in the world to him. And he had known it. And still he had turned his back on her. Oh God, how could he have been so blind? He remembered how he had walked away from her on the one occasion when she had broken down, literally walked away, and he remembered too the sudden knife-sharp guilt which had assailed him and which he had instantly suppressed, as he had always suppressed everything else.

So he had shrugged off all responsibility for her, and Grover had taken over the role that should have been his. He had deserved to lose her. He didn't try to make excuses for himself, there were none. What he had done was unforgivable; he saw it all clearly now. But he hadn't lost her. It was Bill, the ever-caring husband, who had lost his Eleanor, and there is no justice.

There was a letter from Bill among his pile on the bench; perhaps that was what had put the thought of him into his mind. He had always admired Bill; deep down, in a hopeless sort of way, he'd wished he had been made like him. No, it was more than that, he envied him and he felt uneasy with him and Eleanor. With them he was simply Becky's husband, and he was aware of not being a husband as Bill was a husband. He had felt it the very first time they had gone out together, the four of them, about six months after they had married. Bill was confident *as a man*, that was it. It was something you recognised, but couldn't explain. He knew that he would never have that kind of confidence. Meanly, he had tried to tell himself that Bill was aggressively masculine, but that wasn't fair, he knew it even at the time. It was just that Bill had a quality, a male assertiveness, that he himself lacked; you only had to look at Eleanor, relaxed and happy, to see that she was profoundly satisfied with her lot, the woman in her cheerfully dependent on him, sexually beholden. Typically he had told himself that he was glad Becky wasn't like that, that she was stronger and more independent. Never had he for one moment admitted to himself that she had to be independent of him because that was all he would ever let her be.

He didn't feel for Becky that sexual revulsion that he had felt for other women, that disgust at the over-abundant fleshiness of them. He didn't feel repelled by her body, thank

God, he just didn't feel anything about it. It was all perfectly manageable. It was just when he was with Eleanor and Bill that he most felt his lonely guilt. Fortunately they didn't meet very often. But when they did, he sometimes found himself watching Becky, trying to see if she envied Eleanor, to see if she showed signs of being hurt as she observed the other pair and perceived the contrast, as he did. But he dismissed such suspicions instantly, before the idea could even take shape. He would not let himself speculate about things he couldn't change. He had always been so obsessed by his own needs, he realised now, that he had blinded himself to Becky's.

No longer. It was the shock of thinking that he had lost her to Grover that had done it, and then her illness. He no longer took for granted either her presence or her strength. For the first time he understood about cherishing her. When he had taken that vow it had meant nothing to him; now the word had taken flesh. He couldn't *not* cherish her; it was as involuntary to him now as its lack had been before, as if his whole make-up had changed. He couldn't stop himself watching her, worrying over her, feeling responsible for her. Even when he was at school or in a meeting his concern for her was always there, at the back of his mind. She chided him for it sometimes, but he couldn't help it, he thought as he watched her now coming back along the brick path towards him.

Oh yes, the events of last year had shattered his world, and when it reassembled it was a different place and he was a different person in it. And, of course, with Grover shattered at the foot of Sigiriya and incapable of reassembly, Matthew reflected with satisfaction, it was a safer place too for all of them.

Becky paused by the pale green bush of southernwood, letting its leaves slide gently through her hand and then sniffing its fragrance on her fingers. She looked vulnerable, fragile and dreamy, as she stood there in her light blue dress, still holding Corinne's letter in her other hand. He tried to imagine this delicate, fine-boned wife of his next to the sturdy Corinne, a water-colour next to Corinne's tempera. It was no good; they belonged in different pictures. He wanted to keep them apart.

'Who's the airmail letter from?' she asked, coming back to sit next to him on the bench.

'Bill. He's inviting himself to stay for a couple of nights next month. But I'll find an excuse to put him off if it's too much for you.'

'Of course it's not. Bill's no trouble. But what's he doing back in England? He can't be coming home for good, can he?'

'Oh, no. He'll stay out there until the job's finished. He's just coming back for a week of consultations with his new bosses.'

She laughed. 'Knowing Bill,' she said, 'they'll be lucky if they get consulted at all.'

He smiled back at her, delighted that she sounded just like her old self again.

She saw the relief on his face. She took his hand. 'Please, do try not to worry about me,' she said. 'I'm fine now. And the more I think about it, the more I feel I'd like to meet Corinne again.'

'So long as she doesn't upset you,' he repeated.

'She won't. Remember she's had a fearful shock, poor thing. I mean, she's bound to be a bit subdued.'

'I wouldn't count on it,' he said.

'Considering that he never read anything except the financial columns, pornographic magazines and the lessons in church on Sunday,' Grover's widow said, 'he really did have a remarkable weakness for literary ladies.'

'I don't think I'd qualify as a literary lady,' Becky protested. 'A mere librarian with two slim volumes of poetry to her name, one of which bankrupted its publisher. And a manuscript mouldering away with Doughtymans.'

'But your successor was a novelist.'

'Oh,' she was shocked. 'I didn't know I had a successor,' she added feebly.

'Well, you wouldn't, would you? Mistresses don't know these

things. It's wives who keep the tally.'

She got up, picked up a log from the pile on the hearth, and threw it on the fire so vigorously that smoke and fine ash billowed out into the room. The hearth was tiled in pink and the walls covered with heavily patterned paper of a floral design, which gave way to stripes above the picture-rail. It was a 1930s room and reminded Becky of one she had visited years ago, but she couldn't remember where.

'She was called Nathalie Scorse, the novelist bint,' Corinne said, replenishing the coffee-cups from the percolator which stood, next to the logs, on the hearth. 'Do you know her?'

'Not personally, no,' Becky replied, wondering if she'd ever been referred to as 'the poetess bint', 'but I know *of* her. She wrote a very good first book, a kind of send-up of romantic fiction, a bit in the style of *Cold Comfort Farm*, but less witty. I don't remember the title, but the heroine's name was something like Selena Vomit. After that she's written straight fiction, I think, but she's not a popular novelist, not in paperbacks. She's the sort people read in libraries.'

'They get something now, don't they, writers I mean, when their books are borrowed? PLO, isn't it?'

'No, Corinne, that's the Arabs. What writers get is a public lending right which means they get paid every time a book is borrowed. A penny a read, actually.'

'A *penny*? How sweet!' Corinne exclaimed, and burst out laughing.

'You may think it's funny, but actually it's a huge percentage increase on nothing at all.'

She spoke sharply. Matthew had been right, Corinne wasn't in the least subdued. If anything she was spikier than she'd been before. Maybe bereavement had made her waspish. All the same, she liked her; she was a kind person underneath, Becky had decided, commonsensical and direct.

'Corinne,' she said abruptly, remembering that she had promised Matthew not to be browbeaten, 'I presume you had some purpose in asking me here? I mean, other than to discuss the remuneration of authors?'

'I wanted to talk,' Corinne said. 'After all, we did have something in common.'

'What?'

'My husband,' Corinne said.

There was silence. No, Becky decided, she would not be put down.

'Why not talk to Nathalie Scorse then?' she asked coldly. 'She'd be more up-to-date.'

'Oh, *her*,' Corinne dismissed her with a shrug. 'She was hopeless. I mean, I'd thought you were bad enough, but she was a total disaster.' She took a mouthful of coffee and then added, 'Actually, she really wrecked things.'

'How?'

'Well, after I got rid of you,' Corinne said, 'it dawned on me that I'd made a mistake. Life would have been much pleasanter without Grover. You know, America is just full of rich widows? The men work themselves into an early grave and the widows clean up the lolly. And I thought maybe I could learn something from that.'

'What, kill him?'

Corinne gave her a startled glance. 'Whatever made you say that?' she asked. 'No, of course not, there are plenty of rich divorcees too. That's what I had in mind. I'd done too much of this forgiving business and the let's-try-again thing, so I decided that next time it would be different. Next time I'd say "out", and I'd stick to it and not be talked round or anything.'

She got up and stood resting one arm on the mantelpiece. 'You know, Becky,' she said, 'I've thought a lot about it since Grover died. I don't know if you ever realised it, but he was sixteen stone of solid selfishness, Grover was. It was no good trying to reason with him. You might as well have argued with a tank.'

She looked thoughtful; she had quite dropped the bantering tone. 'I realised that it's selfishness that makes men like Grover so strong. They're blinkered, they see what they want and go for it. We just dither about, worrying about who'll get hurt, and in the end we choose whichever course will do the least damage, the least hurt, to everybody else. That's not the way to win. So I decided that, if you can't beat 'em, join 'em, and that next time I'd do what was best for *me*. And the rest of the world could fit in as best it could.'

She was flushed, excited, as she remembered. 'It was a great feeling, Becky. I'd really decided to take the initiative for once. And it was a marvellous prospect, the thought of having all the advantages of being his wife and none of the snags, just like those American widows and divorcees. Thanks to the business with you, I'd found out how much money I could get out of him. I'd be fairly rich and totally independent. And I'd never again have to go to another of those boring office functions,' she added.

Becky remembered Josh's words, *'She'll miss the prestige of being my wife, of being Queen Bee.'* Poor deluded Josh, poor unhappy little Queen Bee.

'So I'm grateful to you, Becky,' Corinne was saying. 'You clarified things for me. By the time the Scorse woman cropped up, I was ready with my plans.'

'How did she crop up?' Becky couldn't help asking, though she didn't really want to know.

'They were at college together, she was the only woman geologist that year and needed some information about courses for her son, so she rang Grover and came to see him at work. It was all above-board. Only being Grover, it naturally didn't stay that way. Then one day he was supposed to be flying back from the States, but in fact he'd come back the evening before and stayed the night with her at some pub or other. It was just his bad luck that the office rang him up at home. So I realised, of course. I went to the solicitor next morning.'

'Just like that?'

'Just like that. I'd made up my mind I'd go for a quick divorce on the grounds of adultery. I knew the civilised sort where you separate for two years would only give Grover time to get up to all sorts of tricks.'

'So what went wrong? I mean, you were still married when you came to Sri Lanka. Why didn't you get your divorce?'

'Because they were so bloody incompetent, that's why. They wrecked everything for me.'

'What happened?'

'Well, things were moving ahead nicely, when she rang up one day, would you believe it, the Scorse woman did, to speak to Grover? He was away, I forget where, anyway abroad for a while. So I sweetly asked if there was anything I could do to help. And, all upset and breathless, she said she didn't understand about the affidavit. So I said, "Well yes, that's to admit to adultery." "What adultery?" she asked. "Well," I said, "my husband has admitted that you stayed the weekend together at the Three Feathers, or whatever it was called".'

'Yes?'

'And she said . . . she said, honestly, Becky, you won't believe this . . .'

For a moment Becky thought she was going to burst into tears, but actually it was laughter that got in the way of Corinne's speech.

'She said, "Well, Mrs Blackford, impotent men can do many things, but committing adultery isn't one of them." '

Again she wiped her eyes. 'Oh, well I can laugh now, but I was pretty mad at the time. Don't you think it was grotesque that they couldn't get their act together when I'd made all my plans? I mean, you know how it is when you've taken a long time to decide something, get it all settled in your mind? Then to have it upset in this totally unexpected way. I told her she'd better wait till he came back and bloody well try a bit harder next time.'

'Corinne, you didn't.'

'I jolly well did. So stupid. I mean I'd just assumed it was *me* he didn't fancy. I suppose in fact it was middle age, obesity and vodka that had got him. It never entered my head that he was no longer capable of being unfaithful to me when for the first time in my life that's what I wanted him to be. What a thing to do to me, or not to do to her, rather.'

'So you just stayed together until you came out to Sri Lanka?'

'Oh, there was more hassle. He insisted that they'd committed adultery at the Feathers and she denied it. She said it was the sort of thing she'd have noticed. One has to agree with that. Well, you know Grover. He was a bit of a barrack-room lawyer. He turned all legalistic and said, according to the law, adultery involved penetration of one inch.'

'Corinne, are you making this up?'

'I swear to you Becky, it's the simple truth. He trundled off to see her, clutching his law book that had it all written down.'

'But why didn't she just agree? I mean, if they wanted to be married?'

'She wouldn't. She'd got this thing about honesty and she wouldn't pretend they'd committed adultery when they hadn't. The only alternative was the two years' separation and I wouldn't have that. I wanted it settled quickly. Poor old Grover, between her not being prepared to lie about the adultery, and me not being cooperative over the two years, he was a bit isolated. And really, Becky, such a little lie, but she wouldn't tell it.'

'I can understand that.'

'I can't. She was in love with him, but she wouldn't tell this one necessary little fib. I can't remember ever feeling so frustrated in all my life, because there was nothing I could do about it. I insisted he took her for another weekend at the Feathers. Mind you, I expect it was pretty frustrating for her, too, with a law book under her pillow and Grover being ineffectual and no doubt peering at her over his half-moon specs and taking measurements—'

'Sh, Corinne, he's dead—'

'What difference does that make? Well, yes, I do see your point, but you have to admit it was maddening. I knew he'd drop her rather than have the court debating how many inches he'd managed. Think of the fun the local papers would have had with that.'

She sat quietly for a moment and then said reflectively, 'It's odd, isn't it, that men can be unfaithful – deliberately and of their own free will break their most solemn promises, do what they've publicly vowed not to do – and feel no shame? Yet something like impotence, which they can't help, makes them feel ashamed. Why?'

'It's a different sort of shame, I suppose. It's a kind of instinctive sense of failure, like women feel who badly want children but don't conceive. They feel they've failed simply as women. It's no good telling them that it's not their fault; they still feel they've failed. It goes deep.'

'Well, poor old Grover didn't. His colourful sex life ended not with a bang but with a whimper.'

'Don't mock. You're not really a mocking person, Corinne.'

'Aren't I just? And why not a bit of mockery of men for a change? Look, Becky, I've heard men, not just Grover, speak slightingly of women who're plain, mock their poor looks. I've heard them laugh about rape, and abortion, and all the things that hurt women. All the things we couldn't ever make light of because we feel and share the humility and indignity and pain. But there's no equivalent for men, is there?'

She got up and began to walk around the little room, ending up by the fire. She threw on another log and then went on, 'I mean, when some pompous old judge tells a girl she's asked for it because she's been raped on a lonely road, don't you just wish some equally horrible and humiliating thing could happen to him, so he could experience the terror and shame, even if he can't imagine it? But there isn't an equivalent, is there? There isn't anything which gets at men in the depths of their being, not like these other things do to women. So all I'm saying is, OK, if there is something like impotence which humiliates *them*, why shouldn't we mock?'

'Because it doesn't help. It just adds to the sum total of cruelty. Honestly, Corinne, imitating their callousness won't help to make the world a better place.'

'It wasn't improving the world I had in mind, actually,' Corinne said, kicking a log, 'just making me feel a bit better.'

She laughed. 'Come on, we'd better have lunch or it'll be tea-time. It's all ready in the kitchen. We'll bring it in here by the fire. Talk about spring! It's cold enough to snow.'

'It's lovely and warm indoors, though,' Becky remarked, following her. 'Did you put in the central heating?'

'Yes, that's all I did. The old couple who lived here before hadn't altered anything since they moved in before the war. You can see the little holes where their flying ducks used to be.'

That was what it reminded her of: Grover's parents' house.

She told Corinne who laughed and said, 'Grover wouldn't have liked that at all – the idea that I'd brought Priscilla back to the kind of home he was brought up in. He did everything he could to break away from his roots. His idea of success was to live in some remote spot in the wilds, preferably at the end of an unmade-up road. He seemed to think that there was something upper class about being muddy.'

She measured oil and vinegar into a bowl and began to whisk, adding salt and pepper, then tossing the salad.

'But it's just right for me,' she went on. 'There's almost no housework and just a tiny bit of garden. The grass is growing quite well, isn't it?'

Becky looked out of the kitchen window. Pale blades of sickly green were struggling through the uneven, pebbly ground in what looked like patches of mould. Something Corinne had said was important. She tried to remember what it was, but couldn't grasp the elusive wisp of it.

Corinne came and stood behind her. 'Yes, I'm really pleased with it,' she said. 'It was full of bedsteads and rubble and old tins when we moved in, but they heaved it all into the next garden, Priscilla and her friends did. Luckily it's still empty next door. I expect someone will come and dig it up soon and chuck all the rubbish into the next garden.'

She laughed. 'It's been such fun. I sometimes feel that I'm having my student days at last, rather late on. Could you carry that tray with the cold meats and things? Oh, the wine, I nearly forgot.'

She took a bottle of white wine out of the refrigerator and began working on it with a bottle-opening gadget, screwing it into the cork and turning the knob.

'I think it should be the other way round,' Becky said. 'The cork isn't moving.'

Corinne started again. The cork still didn't move but began to look frayed.

'Grover just used an ordinary corkscrew,' she said, taking one out of a drawer. 'Maybe that would be better. Would you like to try? I'm not much good at this.'

Becky twisted the screw into the cork and then sat, the bottle between her knees, trying to heave it out.

'Don't risk rupturing yourself,' Corinne said. 'I'll have a go.'

She tucked the bottle under her left arm and pulled hard on the corkscrew with her right hand.

'Ah, it's moving,' she said suddenly. 'I felt it give.'

'Yes, but in the wrong direction,' Becky pointed out.

The cork had now sunk almost half an inch down the neck of the bottle and had begun to disintegrate.

'I should push it right in,' Becky suggested, and watched as Corinne took a wooden spoon and pressed the handle down on the cork, at the same time hitting the other end with her shoe. Slowly the cork slipped into the bottle, fragmenting into little pieces that bobbed about in the wine, which she then poured through a tea strainer into a milk jug.

'Grover would have had a fit,' she remarked with satisfaction as she led the way back to the sitting room.

'Anyway,' she went on, as if their conversation had been left by the fire, like a piece of knitting, ready for taking up where they had left off, 'that was the tale of the batty novelist.'

'On the strength of whom,' Becky said, helping her to arrange the lunch on a table between them, 'you accuse Grover of having a weakness for literary ladies. Unless there were others?'

Corinne laughed. 'I doubt if any of the foreign floosies were particularly bookish,' she said. 'Help yourself to everything.'

'Floosies? Oh, you mustn't call them that—'

'They were Very Nice Girls, the sort you could take out to dinner,' Corinne quoted, and they both laughed.

'God, men are ridiculous,' Corinne said. 'I wonder if he'd have thought *I* was being a Very Nice Girl if *I'd* gone off to a singles' bar when he was away and picked up anybody who would buy me a drink and taken him off to bed with me?'

'Different rules,' Becky said, helping herself to salad.

'Take more than that,' Corinne told her. 'This is all there is. It looks like hors d'oeuvres but it isn't. It's *it*, if you see what I mean.'

She filled their glasses from the milk jug and went on, 'No, it was only at home that he went up-market. Funny you being a librarian, really. You know he wouldn't touch library books?'

'Why ever not?'

'He said he didn't know where they'd been and he might pick up something nasty from them.'

'From *books*?'

'Oh, I know it's dotty. It's much more likely he'd have picked up something nasty from the foreign floosies. I mean, I don't expect he knew where they'd been either.'

'Weren't you frightened, of what he might pass on to you?'

'It wasn't a problem latterly. But I expect the Aids scare has altered the ways of international businessmen quite considerably. The women are probably stamped all over with government health warnings. Let's have some more wine. It makes me thirsty talking about the past.'

They ate and drank in silence for a while, then Corinne sighed contentedly and said, 'Anyway, it all worked out in the end. I just love it here. The shops are just around the corner and it's so handy for everything. A chap I met on holiday lives not far away and we often meet.'

'Oh. Might you marry again?'

'Oh, no. Once bitten. But he's a nice guy and we get on very well. I'm much richer than I expected to be, too.'

She went on talking about the joys of her widowhood, and Becky listened with increasing unease. Grover's death had been very convenient for Corinne. She must try to get her to talk about what happened at Sigiriya. But the more she tried to steer the conversation round to it, the more Corinne talked about earlier times. Once having started on her husband's infidelities, she seemed unable to stop. Not that she sounded in the least bitter; she seemed more amused than anything else. Perhaps it was the wine.

Becky listened, she made the right responses, but all the time she was wondering how much Corinne knew of those last moments. She tried, as they carried the dishes into the kitchen and made coffee, to bring the conversation round to the general topic of murder, but the conversation refused to be steered; like a supermarket trolley it kept veering off in the wrong direction.

'I heard an interesting thing on the radio the other day,' she said, trying again as Corinne put coffee-cups on a tray. 'It was a remark by P. D. James saying that, if you wanted to murder someone, you wouldn't do something difficult with poisons or guns, you'd just go for a walk with them and push them off a cliff and—'

'Who's Peedy James? Bring that bottle of liqueur, would you please? I've got glasses.'

'She's a crime writer who—'

'Funny name for a woman, Peedy. Funny name for a man too if it comes to that,' Corinne commented, leading the way out of the kitchen.

'I can see what she meant,' Becky persisted. 'I mean, if you were walking along the cliffs at Eastbourne, for example, the chances are that nobody would see if you gave your companion a little shove.'

'You often go there, do you?' Corinne asked, putting down the tray and pouring out the coffee.

'Where?'

'Eastbourne.'

'No. It was just that she was citing that as an example.'

'This Peedy woman?'

'Yes.'

'She lives there, does she?'

'No. I mean, I don't know where she lives.'

There was silence as Corinne waited, looking puzzled, and Becky realised how very difficult it is to broach a subject like murder in the pretty, chintzy sitting room of a pleasant woman who is even now offering you a mint chocolate.

'I mean it could be a cliff anywhere. She was just making the point that it would be easy.'

She took a deep breath. 'It could be Sigiriya, come to think of it.'

It was said.

'Funny you should say that,' Corinne said, helping herself to a mint. 'It's something I wanted to ask you about. I mean, Grover wasn't the adventurous type, not the sort who'd risk some balancing act on the edge of a cliff. Bill maybe, but not Grover. Have you any ideas about what might really have happened?'

Becky flushed deep red, guilty, despite herself. 'Well, I suppose he might have tripped,' she said.

'Or had a dizzy spell?' Corinne offered.

'Yes, or a dizzy spell.'

'On the other hand he might have been pushed.'

'Pushed?'

'That guide didn't look very friendly to me. But then would any guide work hard for a couple of hours then kill his charge before getting his tip? That's not my experience of guides, Becky. I reckon it was more likely a black-out.'

'Wouldn't that have shown in the post-mortem? I mean doctors can tell if you're dead already before you fall. You don't bleed as much, do you? And I expect there are other signs.'

'I doubt it. Grover had spread himself quite a bit. You know, he was scattered about, I mean. Anyway, it could have been just a momentary turn which made him lose his balance. He did have high blood pressure, you know.'

'Then why did you encourage him to go on up?'

'Did I?'

'When we rested for a while half way up, don't you remember? I remember it very clearly. I suggested he should stay down there and rest if he didn't want to go on. He didn't want to go up. But you said it was a pity not to go up to the top when he'd come so far. Yet you knew he wasn't fit.'

Corinne looked at her curiously.

'You're getting very het up about it,' she remarked coolly. 'Do you think I pushed him, or something?'

It was suddenly very quiet.

'You might have done,' Becky said, her voice coming out in a whisper.

The silence hung heavily. They could hear the tick of the clock. In the distance a car was having trouble starting.

'Becky,' Corinne said at last, 'are you really accusing me of murder?'

'You did say you wanted rid of him, Corinne,' Becky said, trying to sound reasonable. 'And since you'd now no hope of getting a divorce, well, it would be a possible alternative, wouldn't it?'

'I just can't get over you,' Corinne said, shaking her head. 'You sit there, all pretty and ladylike in your Laura Ashley dress, sipping my coffee and calling me a murderess.'

'Oh, no, I'm not saying that.'

'God, you're exasperating. If murdering your husband doesn't make you a murderess, what does? I mean, I'd like to know, if I'm to qualify.'

'I think to call someone a murderer or a murderess means that they're that sort of a person,' Becky said, trying to be precise. 'I don't think that just impulsively giving their husband a push is quite the same somehow.'

'Just a little push. But it happens to be six hundred feet up above a lot of spiky rocks.'

'It doesn't make them into a Bill Sikes,' Becky said. 'Any more than if someone tells a lie on the spur of the moment it means that they're a liar by nature.'

'Well, I hope a jury will make these fine distinctions on my behalf,' Corinne said drily. 'Would you like a liqueur? I'll drink mine first if that would put your mind at rest.'

'Oh, Corinne, *please don't* misunderstand me.'

Corinne poured the liqueur but deliberately took a sip of her own first, before giving Becky her glass.

'You're not handling this very well, are you?' she said kindly. 'Let's look at it another way. You didn't have much to thank him for either, did you? I think it would be very understandable if you gave him that little push you were at pains to minimise just now. All right, maybe I did have a financial motive, I concede that, but you had a motive too, Becky. And I don't mean revenge, you're not that sort of person, however much he'd hurt you. I think you're the sort who might kill on principle, though, as a matter of justice.'

She laughed suddenly. 'It's all right,' she said. 'I don't really believe it. I'm just theorising, the way you do, to show you how ridiculous it is. I'll tell you something more to the point. Grover and your friend Bill had a hell of a row the night before we went to Sigiriya.'

'Did they? Are you sure?'

'I heard some of it. But Grover often had ding-dongs like that, so at first I didn't give it much thought. But then I heard Grover say he was going to get Bill sacked when he got back home. So Bill had a very good motive for making sure he didn't get back to England.'

'Unthinkable,' Becky said.

'You're a loyal friend, I'll say that for you,' Corinne remarked, 'though you didn't pay *me* the compliment of being so sure of my innocence, did you?'

'I only meant Bill wouldn't kill to avoid being sacked. It was different for you. You'd been hurt and you didn't want him around any more. It might, in the last resort, have seemed the only way.'

Corinne smiled and shook her head. 'Becky,' she said, 'if I'd been going to kill Grover I assure you I'd have done it long ago.'

'Because of me, you mean? If I caused you any pain, I'm truly sorry.'

Corinne laughed, 'Oh, Becky you're so innocent,' she said. 'Of course not. I was well past caring by the time you arrived on the scene. It's the earlier ones that hurt, especially the first. There should be some sort of organisation,' she went on, standing up and leaning against the mantelpiece, her eyes bright, cheeks flushed and her voice getting harder until it had that edge of harshness, Becky thought, which creeps into a woman's voice when she is keeping tears at bay, 'Some sort of organisation for wronged wives, like Alcoholics Anonymous, shouldn't there? Then old stagers like me could go along and cheer them up a bit. "Courage, sisters," we'd say, "it gets easier each time and, when you reach the stage of not loving them at all, it simply becomes ridiculous." God, it's marvellous when you don't love them any more and don't give a tinker's cuss what they get up to. The freedom of not loving—'

She broke off suddenly and in a different voice added, 'You, of course, don't agree with any of this, do you, Becky? Idealist that you are.'

But I do, Becky thought, unable to reply. It *is* love which makes us vulnerable. And middle-aged love is the worst sort; it strikes mercilessly like an illness, regardless of whether the patient can withstand the pain or not. I used to think that Love Endureth All Things was a wonderful ideal. Now I know that it's a simple statement of a terrible truth. Love is devastating. It is much more powerful than hatred. Oh Josh, I walked one day last summer in the park where you and I once walked and I saw our old man coming towards me. Do you remember our old man, Josh, the one who smiled and stopped in front of us and said we looked contented? This time too he seemed to hesitate and I hoped, I just hoped, that he might remember and ask about you and so bring you back just for a moment. But he didn't stop. And I thought I might run after him and ask if he remembered that day. But I didn't. I wasn't even sure if it was the same old man.

'So you see,' Corinne was saying more calmly now, 'by the time your turn came I didn't care enough about him to be hurt. Worried, yes, about practical things, but not truly hurt in the way that you and I understand.'

She sat down on the couch near the hearth and, leaning forward, poked the logs about until they blazed up. Then, looking thoughtfully into the flames, she went on, 'I suppose that, in all those middle years, before you came on the scene and broke the mould, I'd jogged along with him quite comfortably because I'd ceased to love or trust him at all. My expectations were so low that even he could live up to them.'

Can this be Josh she is talking of? Could he once have been my Josh, this man he became? Matthew was right: I shouldn't have come here.

'It suited us both, if I'm honest. He needed a wife to come back to, the place where his clean clothes were, where his supper would be ready on a tray so that he could eat it while he watched the telly. He was really terribly boring, you know, Becky. He'd have sent you round the bend in no time at all. I reckon you had a narrow escape twice over. You ought to be grateful to me really.'

Twice? No, they were different people, Josh and Grover. It was a case of mistaken identity. This man of Corinne's wasn't Josh at all.

'And it was convenient for me too to stick with him,' Corinne was saying. 'It saved me having to do some boring job to earn my own living. I suppose that I thought that any marriage was better than none. That's what I'd been brought up to believe.'

Becky made herself listen, forced herself to forget herself, feel what Corinne was feeling, enter her world.

'Well?' Corinne asked abruptly, obviously requiring comment.

'I think,' Becky began tentatively, 'it can't have been quite like that. I mean, people can't live together, can they, without any real affection or regard or respect . . .'

She broke off, thinking how different this barren picture of marriage, which Corinne had presented, was from her own. Problems they had had, she and Matthew, but their lives had always been intertwined, bound together by shared values, trust and work.

'I mean,' she floundered on, as she saw that Corinne was waiting for her, 'it seems so empty, a denial of the oh, I don't know, human spirit.'

She stopped. Corinne was staring at her, wide-eyed. There was a whole world of sadness, emptiness in those eyes. The moment passed. The blankness was filled with anger.

'Of course I'd have preferred all that,' Corinne broke out. 'Of course I'd have liked to cherish a man I loved, a man I trusted, and who loved and cherished me, just *me*. What woman wouldn't? But we have to make do with men as they are, not men as they ought to be.'

Suddenly her anger seemed to leave her and quietly, very quietly, she began to cry. Becky crossed over and sat on the couch beside her, put her arms around her. Corinne leant against her, sobbing. 'I'm sorry,' she said after a while, snuffling and looking towards a box of paper handkerchiefs on a table nearby.

'Don't be sorry, there's nothing to be sorry about,' Becky told her, reaching for the box and handing it to her.

'I just meant,' Corinne said, blowing her nose, 'that it wasn't typical, that outburst.' She smiled and then pulled a face. 'I suppose it was just all this remembering brought it on. And the waste. Honestly, Becky, I really did nothing with all those years. And it's not true, what I said about not minding. I did mind. I never got used to it. It ate at me and stopped me doing anything useful or creative. And now I look back at all that waste of time. I mean, at our age, one sees how dreadful it was to waste a single day.'

'Yes, but you're not now, are you?' Becky said gently. 'You were telling me about the painting this morning. You're catching up. You can't do anything about the past, but you can make sure you don't waste a day of the future. I'm sorry,' she said humbly, 'I know it's the sort of advice we all hand out so glibly and can't follow ourselves, but I do think it's true.'

'Of course it's true,' Corinne said. 'It's the way I've seen things since Grover died. It's funny how I can talk to you,' she said unexpectedly. 'I suppose it's because you're so honest. Oh Becky, I wish you'd got in touch with me the minute you met Grover. We'd have sorted things out much better, you and I, wouldn't we?'

'With hindsight, maybe. But I doubt if you'd have felt that at the time.'

'Well, I'm sure of it now. We should have worked out what was best for the both of us. Instead we both tried to do what he wanted. And, being Grover, of course he didn't know what he wanted.'

'That's true.'

'Before anyone starts an affair, they should get together, the women should. They're the ones who'll get hurt, them and their children.'

There was nothing more to be said. They sat together in companionable silence by the fire, which was burning low now and hung with ash.

'He told me once,' Corinne remarked at last, 'that we were very alike, you and I.'

'He said that to me too. He said that marrying me could be a case of out of the frying-pan into the fire.'

Corinne grinned. 'Poor old Fire, did that hurt?'

'A bit, Pan, a bit. But I'm not allowing self-pity. It was worse for you.'

'Why?'

'Because you were married to him.'

'No, it was worse for you, Fire. Because you loved him.'

Becky didn't reply.

'Didn't you?' Corinne insisted. 'Even at Sigiriya, you still did, didn't you, despite what he'd done?'

' "Love is not love which alters when it alteration finds," ' Becky quoted softly.

'What?'

'Oh, nothing, nothing.'

'It's all right. I got the gist. What it boils down to is that women do have a disturbing tendency to go on loving bastards.'

She blew her nose, threw the paper handkerchief on the fire, put on another log. Then she seemed to gather herself together, squaring her shoulders and said, with a return to her former, more aggressive tone of voice, 'That's just typical, isn't it?'

'What is?'

'Well, people like the Nathalie woman and poets like you and academics and all bookish people and whoever wrote that thing you've just quoted about love—'

'Shakespeare.'

'Yes, him too. You take on board something like bereavement or an unhappy love affair or whatever and you pore over it and write about it and think you've somehow dealt with it. But it's still there. You haven't achieved anything at all.'

'Understanding?'

'No. You've understood your own little effort, but not the thing itself. Look how you misjudged Grover, so did the novelist bint. I bet you thought he was dependable because he had that solid look?'

For a moment a conspiratorial flicker of recognition passed between them as Becky remembered the rocklike shoulder he had offered her and how she had laid her head there, trusting him entirely. She would have done better to have thrust it into a nest of vipers.

'And you thought he was reliable,' Corinne went on relentlessly, 'because he said he was. But I could have told you the truth if you'd troubled to ask me. He was reliable about little things, he made up trivial rules and obeyed them, because he couldn't keep any of the rules that really matter. In fact I sometimes wondered if he even knew they existed, he was so immune to them.'

I am beginning, Becky thought with sinking heart, to recognise him. The Josh whom she had met again had also fretted about minutiae but had seemed immune to laws she had thought absolute.

'I mean, his rules allowed him to humiliate me with his unfaithfulness,' Corinne said, 'but he'd never, never let me walk on the outside of the pavement. He'd practically dance the hornpipe to save me that indignity.'

She laughed. 'So ridiculous,' she said cheerfully. 'It was always the showy things that mattered, like being on parade at church on Sundays.'

'But doing unto others?'

Corinne laughed again and shook her head. 'Oh, Becky,' she said, 'you're hopeless. Grover was all too well aware of what he was capable of doing to others to risk having it reciprocated. That wasn't at all the sort of thing he wanted to believe. No, I think that religion to Grover meant the sound of his own voice reading the lesson.'

And it wasn't even his own voice; even that was fabricated, Becky thought, but said nothing. It was overwhelming, the sense that she had now of recognising Josh in this man of Corinne's. They were beginning to seem like the same person. But how had he changed so? People don't change, not fundamentally, she had always been sure of it. Wasn't it the theme of her poems, as Mrs Doughtyman had pointed out? So he couldn't have changed; it didn't fit in with her beliefs.

'Appearances always mattered to him, Becky, much more than they did to me,' Corinne was saying. 'I mean, he really did judge people by their possessions. When the divorce thing was raised and it turned out that everyone would be worse off, that really scared him, Becky. It wasn't that he didn't love you. It was just that he couldn't make the sacrifice it entailed because he really did believe that if he had less money, he was worth less as a man.'

She paused and then added, 'But of course he couldn't admit that.'

'Why not? It would have helped me to know the truth.'

Corinne laughed. 'I'm afraid that once he had decided to ditch you, saving you pain wouldn't come very high on his list of priorities. Saving his own face would matter much more to him.'

She saw Becky flinch and thought how little Becky had known him if she did not know this.

'Of course a stronger man would have admitted he'd got into a situation he couldn't cope with, Becky,' she said kindly, 'and asked your forgiveness. But he wasn't such a man. He behaved ignobly because he was cornered, frightened, very frightened.'

'Poor Josh.'

'Must you be so bloody charitable?' Corinne exclaimed, echoing the words that Josh had once used to her. 'You really are exasperating, Becky. I think there was triumph as well as love in his feelings for you, you know, that after so many years he'd actually won you. He was a very acquisitive man.'

She laughed. 'It's just struck me that really having acquired you he didn't know what to do with you. Like money. He was always very keen on making it but never knew how to spend it once he'd got it. Look, I'm going to make some tea. And don't you go wasting your compassion on him. He showed precious little for you.'

'I ought to be going soon . . .'

'Oh, there's plenty of time.'

'Corinne, I do believe—'

'Yes?'

'I do believe what you say about him, and yes I do recognise, I mean, I accept it. But how did it happen? I've been trying to remember, something you said a while ago . . .'

'Did I? Well, I've said a lot of things today, haven't I?'

'It was something about wanting to get rid of his roots,' Becky said.

'Well, he would, wouldn't he, want to get rid of his roots, I mean? He'd be ashamed of them because he wanted to better himself.'

'*Better*?'

'That's what they say,' Corinne told her. 'You know, Becky, getting on, making money, it was the gospel of the eighties. It preached that there was nothing wrong with greed. You must have heard of it, even in your cloistered little academic world? It was about getting rich enough to afford too much to eat and drink so you could clog your arteries and wreck your liver; it was about getting rich enough to afford mistresses so you could break up your marriage. It was called *bettering* yourself, and I know about it because I've watched my husband actually doing it. And anyone who wouldn't listen to the Good News was a no-good waster without ambition.' She laughed suddenly, dropped the sarcastic tone, and said, 'Come on, Becky, let's have some tea.'

'No, Corinne, please, let me think it out. You see, you said he cut himself off from his roots, from everything that would have nourished him, if he'd let it.'

She got up and began pacing the room restlessly. 'Instead he had an image of what he wanted to be and he set about fabricating it. He was in every sense a *self-made* man. But we can't make ourselves like that—'

'Does it matter?' Corinne interrupted. 'It's all over now. He's dead. Must you tear yourself apart trying to work out the *why* of everything?'

'It matters,' Becky told her, 'because it left a great void. That's why he so easily absorbed this pernicious creed you've just been talking about. Oh, Corinne, at last I'm beginning to understand.'

Corinne shook her head. 'There you go again,' she said. 'It's what I was telling you just now. All you bookish types, you hunt around for reasons after the event and you don't see what's in front of your eyes at the time. You didn't see Grover as he was. If he'd been a book you wouldn't have been taken in by him for one moment. But he was only a human being so you got him all wrong.'

'It has been said,' Becky conceded, coming back and sitting down again on the couch beside her, 'that writers don't understand anything about human nature and have to write about it in order to find out what everybody else knows already. Maybe that goes for all the people you call "bookish".'

Corinne laughed. 'I'll go along with that,' she said. 'If Grover had been a book, you'd have known that he wasn't worth the paper he was written on. Now can we have our tea?'

'While that boils,' Corinne said, filling the kettle at the kitchen sink, 'I'll show you my studio if you like.'

Becky followed her up the steep stairs. Even the bedrooms were laid out as they had been in Josh's old home. But this London house was taller; it had another floor approached by an even steeper flight of stairs.

'Studio's rather a grand word for it, actually,' Corinne said as they began to climb up. 'Really it's only a big bedroom. It doesn't have a north light either. But it faces east, which Bernard says is the next best thing.'

'He's the man you met on holiday? The one who helped you with your painting?'

'That's right. We've just had a week's painting holiday together in Derbyshire. It was lovely. I really enjoyed it. I did lots of small pictures, just bits and pieces of the landscape that appealed to me. I haven't sorted them out yet, that's why it's even untidier than usual in here,' she added, opening the door.

Becky followed her into the room. She stood for a moment, amazed. Then she began to wander about. The room was filled with familiar images. They reached out to her immediately. They spoke to her directly. She more than recognised them, she recognised the love in them, the excitement, the whole spirit of them. Everything else was blotted out of her mind; all the things they had spent the day discussing, which had seemed so important, vanished into oblivion. Even the death of Grover was forgotten.

They were everywhere, all around her, these snatches of landscape, this packhorse bridge stepping across this shallow stream, this old tree bending low over a pool, this sheep looking up suddenly alarmed for its lamb, its foot quite visibly on the point of stamping, this farmhouse crouched in a hollow, as if backing up against the hillside for protection. She recognised them all, she wanted to laugh and sing for joy. Love of them drove out all other feeling.

At first she couldn't speak, then she turned to Corinne and blurted out, 'I'd no idea. But they're wonderful, wonderful.'

Corinne looked at her, surprised. The praise seemed a bit excessive, she thought.

'They're not all that special,' she said with a laugh. 'Don't exaggerate. I mean, I've only just begun really, only had a few lessons. They can't be so very wonderful.'

'To me they are,' Becky said incontrovertibly.

She set off again around the room. The pictures were propped up on chairs, pinned on a board, stuck with Blu-Tack to the walls. Some were lying on a narrow divan bed, others were just spread around on any available flat surface. Corinne made a few odd comments, but Becky stood in front of each one, entranced, not speaking, apart from the occasional exclamation of surprise and recognition.

'The kettle must be boiling by now,' Corinne pointed out at last.

'It turns itself off, doesn't it?' Becky murmured.

'I'm thirsty, aren't you? I think it's the wine. Wine makes you thirsty. At least it does me,' she added, moving towards the door.

Becky stood in her way. 'Corinne,' she said, 'they'd be right, right for my poems.'

'What?'

'You remember. I told you. The illustrations? They were all wrong. Mostly they were too glossy, somehow too decorative. Mrs Doughtyman felt the same. We don't want pretty decorations. We want something that will stand in its own right, but be in tune too.'

She moved her hand abruptly, as if aware of the mixed metaphor, but brushing aside the unimportance of it; she who usually minded so much about such things.

'But Becky, I've never illustrated anything in my life. And I don't know anything about poetry.'

'You don't need to, that's the point. It's the whole point. Don't start with the poems, except from the point of view of the subject matter, of course. Start with what you feel about what you're painting and it'll be all right. Oh, Corinne, do believe me. I just know it will. Mrs Doughtyman will know it too. She'd only have to see *one* of those paintings to know that they were by the right person.'

'Look, Becky, calm down. I'm not being unhelpful, it's just that it's a bit unexpected. Let's go downstairs and have some tea by the fire and talk about it.'

Reluctantly, Becky followed her out of the room.

'We've got to look at the practical aspects,' Corinne said as they sat by the fire with mugs of tea. 'I'd obviously have to read the poems, but you say they're with Doughtymans—'

'That's no problem at all,' Becky told her impatiently. 'Of course I've got copies. I can send them to you tomorrow morning.'

'It's all right, Becky, I'm not trying to make difficulties.'

'Sorry. It's just that I'm so sure you can do it and—'

'Secondly,' Corinne went on, ignoring her, 'as I've told you, I've never illustrated anything. I've no idea what sort of paper to use or even what to draw with, or if it's penwork and if so what kind and—'

'Mrs Doughtyman would tell you all that. You can talk to her on the phone or go and see her. Really it's no problem. The point is that the style, the feel is right. The technical things can easily be sorted out. Actually, you know, the ones you've done already are nearly enough. They'd do just as they are. But if you could do about four or five others, you know, showing drystone walls and . . . but you'd see what I mean in the poems. Oh Corinne, I just know that it's right for you to do them, I tell you I'm sure about it.'

'All right, all right. But then I'd want to go and see the places which had moved you to write the poems. You'd have to give me some idea of where to go. I'd have to go and stay in the Dales for a few days, wouldn't I?'

'You can afford it,' Becky said, 'can't you, Corinne? And you've nothing to do here that would stop you, have you? You could easily go, couldn't you?'

Corinne looked at her. She couldn't get over this. She had thought she'd got to know Becky: gentle, rather apologetic, unassertive Becky. She found it almost impossible to believe that this determined woman, who knew exactly what she wanted and seemed prepared to fight and bully to get it, actually was Becky Portman. Slowly it dawned on her that, although Becky was one of those women who can never put herself first, she might be able to put her work first. It might be the one thing she was capable of being selfish about, if selfish was the right word, which it wasn't.

Besides, she understood it, deep down she understood it, the excitement of creating. She began to feel it stirring in her now, the need to go up there and paint, accept the challenge of this thing that Becky had asked her to do. It wasn't just the enthusiasm which was infectious, either; she caught the confidence, too: if Becky believed in her so totally then perhaps it was possible that she really could do it.

'You will send them first class, won't you?' she said.

'What?'

'Your poems, of course. First class. Tomorrow morning.'

Chapter Eleven

'And that's Gemini, my house boy, standing by his vegetable plot,' Bill said, adjusting the focus, bringing the figure more sharply into view.

'He's jolly good-looking,' Juliet remarked. 'And what a gorgeous orange skirt. I wouldn't mind having one that colour. I suppose you couldn't get me a length of material like that, could you, Bill?'

'Really, Juliet,' Matthew protested. 'There aren't any shops or markets where Bill works. It's miles away from anywhere and he's—'

Bill laughed. 'It's all right. I'll find you something, Juliet, next time I'm in Colombo or Kandy.'

'Thanks, Bill. You see, Dad, it's no trouble. Don't bother posting it,' she added. 'Just wait till you're coming back again.'

'I'll deliver it in person,' Bill assured her. 'And this is the view from my veranda,' he resumed. 'You can just make out another bungalow being built over on the left there.'

It was stuffy in the darkened room this summer evening. Not the best of weather for staying indoors looking at slides, Becky had thought, but it was the only chance they had of seeing them. Bill was leaving first thing tomorrow morning. She had dreaded, too, if she was honest with herself, seeing these reminders of the Sri Lankan holiday, but in fact it had turned out to be more soporific than anything else. Her eyes were leaden as she tried to concentrate on the succession of tropical images that lit up the screen. Her mind kept wandering off to Corinne's pictures.

They had arrived that morning, or rather the copies had, for Corinne had wisely not entrusted the originals to the post. Even

227

so, Becky had recognised immediately that they were right. Mrs Doughtyman would think so too, she knew it. She was glad now that she had seen the attempts of the previous artists; it had made her appreciate even more what skill Corinne had. How well she had caught that watery brightness of the sun slanting through the light mist of an early morning. How she had set down that uncompromising look of an old stone cottage that stared out at the world, solid, four-square and durable, as if it had grown out of the earth beneath it. And, most miraculous of all, she had sent one which would perfectly illustrate the poem Becky had not yet managed to write: out of a cleft rock a tree was growing, an old thorn, gnarled and riven and bending to the wind. It spoke of survival.

She wanted to get back to work on the poem whose image had never left her. Why did certain ideas, she wondered now, come unheralded yet with such a strong feeling of recognition, of excitement, of certainty that there was a poem in them, while other ideas visited and left, leaving no mark, no pricking of the conscience, no whispering that there was a poem which she ought to be seeking out? It was a mystery, for even with the certainty came great wariness as she gently probed and tested with her mind the validity of the image, like someone taking a tentative step on the ice to see if it will hold.

For it was her own clumsiness that she most feared. As if she was holding in her cupped hands a fluttering moth, she knew it was herself who might hurt it, this thing which she was trying to preserve, this elusive thing which she had recognised and wanted to keep unchanged, there at the heart of the poem, undamaged and undistorted. Somehow she must find a way of giving it permanence but still keeping it as it was when she had first glimpsed it, first felt the touch of its wing.

She thought impatiently of tomorrow morning, when everyone would get back to work after this long weekend of half-term. Bill would be off early, taking Juliet with him to drop off at the station. Then Matthew and Ben would go over to school and she would go into her study. The morning would be hers, she would count the hours like precious jewels to be gloated over, she who so recently had thought of her life as something to be plodded through somehow or other. Restless and excited at the prospect of getting back to work, she could now hardly wait for tomorrow to come.

The other conflicts would start up again, she realised, but she would deal with them, she knew it, with her new-found confidence. She would ward off the guilt which always assailed her when some sudden crisis – and with the young everything seemed to be a crisis – demanded attention. She would manage. Besides, they were all trying so hard to help. She could imagine the expression on Ben's face as he just managed to stop himself pointing out that his lost football boots were urgently needed *now* whereas she could do her writing any old time. Oh no, Ben, your boots are ineffably permanent, but an idea once lost is not merely mislaid, it is gone for ever. So just go and look for them yourself.

'I haven't seen these last slides myself yet,' Bill was saying. 'I've only just had them developed.'

'That's not a very flattering one of you, Mummy,' Juliet remarked. 'Whatever were you doing?'

Becky made herself take an interest. 'I'm scrambling up a rock at the foot of the mountain,' she said, 'evidently blissfully unaware that Bill's behind me with a camera.'

Bill laughed. 'I'm sorry, Becky,' he said. 'It wasn't intentional, honestly. I was trying to get a shot looking up at Cobra Hood Rock from the bottom.'

'And mostly it's my bottom,' Becky said. 'I'll forgive you but only if you put the next slide in straight away.'

'There. That's better? We're half-way up, having a rest.'

'Gosh, he's fat, the one who's talking to Dad,' Ben said. 'Who is he?'

'A man called Grover,' Bill said, and his voice was sombre. 'He was killed not long afterwards. I expect your parents told you?'

'Oh, yes, him,' Ben said. 'I remember.'

'Gosh, it really is steep,' Juliet commented. 'I hadn't realised it was as steep as that. Did you really climb up that cliff face, Mummy?'

'Yes, but there were steps of a sort and guides to help.'

Her voice was quiet. Suddenly she didn't want to see any more. There is something unnatural, uncanny, about seeing photographs of people taken just before they die. She wanted to warn him.

'And that's Grover's wife, next to your mother,' Bill went on. 'Have you heard how she's getting on, Becky?'

'Yes, I went to see her about six weeks ago,' Becky said. 'She seems to have adjusted very well. She's moved into London.'

'Good, that's the way,' Bill approved. 'Nice woman, Corinne. And there we are at the top.'

'It doesn't look nearly as steep as it did from lower down,' Ben remarked.

'No, it's very hard to get a true impression. I did film a bit with the cine-camera, trying to zoom down, but I don't know how well it's worked. I haven't projected it yet.'

'Got it with you?'

'Yes, it's here, Ben, but we'd need to set up the other projector.'

'We could do that easily, couldn't we, Dad?'

Matthew didn't reply.

'Well, we'll see,' Bill said. 'And there we are sitting on the throne.'

'Cor, what a size.'

'It held us all with plenty of room to spare. Remember, Becky?'

'I remember,' she said.

'And him, the fat one at the end. Did he just fall off the mountain?'

'We don't know exactly what happened,' Bill said. 'He must have momentarily lost his balance, poor devil.'

In the darkness Juliet glared at her brother. Why couldn't the stupid boy remember that when he had told them about that man being killed their father had asked them not to go on about it? Poor Mummy had been so ill and the winter holiday was supposed to do her good and it had ended with this horrible accident. Why don't you *think*, silly brat, she demanded in her head, casting another futile warning glance at Ben across the darkened room.

Bill sighed. 'It was a dreadful business,' he said. 'To be honest I didn't care for the man myself, but that's not the sort of thing you'd wish on your worst enemy.'

'Was it an accident, do you think? Maybe one of those guides pushed him. I mean, they might have been terrorists in disguise,' Ben suggested with relish.

'No, I don't think that,' Bill said brusquely. 'You know, back here you're given such a wrong impression of the Sri Lankans. They're not at all like that. They're peaceful and—'

'Oh come off it, Bill. They blew up trains and—'

'Oh, do shut up,' Juliet interrupted, 'about all this death and killing . . .'

'But it's interesting, death is,' her brother told her. 'And it comes to all of us in the end,' he added cheerfully.

It was incontrovertible; Bill put in another slide.

'But,' Ben persisted, 'they did do things like that, I mean try to hurt tourists, didn't they, as part of the campaign? I remember reading about it. Juliet and I were quite interested when Mum and Dad were out there, weren't we, Juliet?'

'I don't remember. Anyway, it's in the past.'

'But you must remember. We were a bit scared they might get bumped off.'

'I've told you to shut up about it.'

'All right, keep your hair on. So you're sure it was just an accident, Bill?'

'Quite. I don't believe anyone would push someone in cold blood.'

'But in a great rage you might,' Ben said thoughtfully. 'I've got a friend called Sam Bullock. I could just kill him sometimes.'

'No, Ben,' Bill told him. 'You might *feel* like killing him, but you couldn't actually *do* it. Well, that's that lot,' he added, removing the last of the slides. 'Do you really want the cine?'

'I don't think so,' Matthew said. 'You must be very tired, Bill, and you've got an early start. We don't want to wear you out before you even get to head office. We're very grateful to you for talking to the boys last week and showing us these fascinating slides this evening,' he added, sounding, Becky noticed to her surprise, like somebody giving a not particularly animated vote of thanks.

'Perhaps something to drink?' he concluded.

'Oh, I'm not tired,' Bill assured him. 'I always like showing off Sri Lanka. But yes, a cup of coffee wouldn't come amiss.'

'I'll help Mummy get it ready while you and Ben see to the projector,' Juliet volunteered as she followed her mother out of the room, hissing at her brother as she passed, 'and just shut up about the accident, stupid. Don't you remember what Dad said?'

'What?' her brother demanded loudly.

'Oh, never mind.'

It was a long film that they watched as they consumed coffee and biscuits. Bill had made it in sections from the time of his arrival on the island. He had edited it, he explained, but clearly didn't like to waste too much footage. Acres of pale green sugar-cane waved across the screen, miles of roads wound endlessly up mountainsides in hair-pin bends, waterfalls cascaded abundantly, and there seemed to be forests of dense foliage in which Bill had sat patiently photographing animals which proved to be so well camouflaged that they were invisible on the finished film.

'And there we are on top of Sigiriya,' he was saying. 'That's a shot taken from the edge, looking down over the old pleasure gardens.'

'It still doesn't look very steep,' Ben objected, disappointed.

'No, it's better if you can keep the camera stationary and have something moving across your line of vision, but I couldn't do that. I remember, after we left the throne, trying to get a general impression. You can see—'

She could see. She saw that Corinne was walking away in the opposite direction from Grover. She saw that the guides were gathered together in the distance, none of them lurking near Grover. And since Bill was taking the film, neither could he have been anywhere near Grover, who was quite a distant figure, way over on the far left, followed only by Matthew.

'I didn't take much,' Bill was saying. 'I remember now. I stopped when I realised there'd been an accident.'

Matthew had got up suddenly.

'Oh, sit down,' Ben said. 'You're blocking the screen.'

Matthew didn't move.

'The rest of the film,' Bill said, 'was taken in Farawaya just a couple of weeks ago.'

If Matthew hadn't stood up like that, she would never have guessed. By such involuntary actions, Becky thought, as they took down the screen and projectors, do we give ourselves away. He was avoiding looking at her, they circled each other as they cleared away the coffee-cups, tidied the sitting room, and bade the others goodnight.

Theirs was a big bedroom running the depth of the house. Facing east and west it had absorbed the full sun of the day. Both windows were wide open, but still it was sultry, the atmosphere heavy.

'Well?' she said, turning to face him.

'Well?'

'It's no good, Matthew, I know. I saw it in your face. It's no good trying to fob me off.'

'It should have been my burden, never yours,' he said bitterly. 'And it would have been if it hadn't been for that damned film.'

'But why, *why*?'

He had begun to pace the room. Then he stopped and turned to her.

'Out of love for you, I suppose,' he said.

'No!' she almost shrieked the word. 'I *won't* accept the guilt of it.'

'I don't mean that. God knows I don't want you to have any extra burden, any guilt at all. I wanted you never to know. You need never have known.'

'But *why*? Not jealousy?'

'No, no.'

'You've just got to explain, Matthew, you must see that. I need to understand *why*.'

He took off his spectacles, rendering his face instantly naked, vulnerable. He sat down in one of the two wing chairs by the window, his head in his hands. He looked up at her.

'I was never jealous, Becky, you know that. I was, in a strange sort of way, happy for you. I thought you were getting the happiness you deserved, undoing the wrong I'd done you. Certainly I wouldn't have tried to stand in your way. You know that, Becky.'

'Yes, I know.'

She stood by him for a moment, then went and sat in the other chair.

'It was all because of the baby bursar,' he said.

The pet name rang strangely in the context of what he was saying, inappropriate, facetious.

'She'd got the switches wrong; she'd left the phone in the bursar's office on as well as switching through to our house.'

He paused.

'You had a call that evening, Becky. I was just leaving the office when I heard it ring. Everyone else had gone so I went back and picked it up. It must have been at exactly the same moment as you did. I heard what he said, Becky, I heard you gasp. I shall never forget that sound. I can't describe it. Just audible pain. I seemed to hear a knife being thrust into your heart. When it happens to someone you love it's, it's . . .' he stopped. He stared at her, shook his head, then brought his fist down hard into his open palm. 'It's not to be borne,' he ended savagely.

He was reliving his outrage, and there was on his face an expression she had never seen before, had not imagined possible on the face of her gentle, peace-loving, tolerant, pacifist husband. As if it could not be envisaged there, it turned it into a stranger's face.

'I came back here, as you know. Oh, Becky, the agony you were in. I can't tell you what it was like to witness it and not be able to help.'

He got up suddenly and began to pace the room. Then he sat down again and, speaking more calmly now and matter-of-factly, went on, 'Do you remember, Becky, the time when Juliet was in hospital when she was a baby and there was that poor child, a little boy, with third-degree burns, in care? And do you remember how we saw the mother always sitting by his bed and the child looking up with huge eyes full of pain, silently longing for comfort? And we thought of the agony of that mother who knew if she so much as touched ever so gently that raw skin she would cause searing pain? Yet everything in her must have longed to cuddle and comfort her son. And she had to hold back, just watch, like a voyeur.'

'Yes, I remember it very well.'

'That's how I felt, Becky, as I watched your agony and could do nothing. I knew that if I tried even to touch you, I would remind you of his touch. In the most direct and cruel way it would remind you. I'd have been tormenting you, the one I most wanted to comfort. I knew you were lying awake at night, desolate in your misery. I had known that desolation when I thought you were leaving me, so I understood. I wouldn't have done once, but I did now.'

A moth flew in the window. It brushed against his face, but he did not feel it.

'I ached to comfort you, but I knew it would only make it worse. Mine were the wrong arms, mine were the wrong lips. I hated myself for being the wrong person.'

He got up and began to walk about the bedroom. He stopped by her chair.

'I did try once, I tried, just to hold you as you had once held me, for comfort. But I knew you were having to force yourself to bear my comfort. I knew you wanted to turn away from me but didn't want to hurt me. Yes, despite the agony you were in, you were afraid of inflicting even a little hurt.'

'I remember,' she whispered.

Oh yes, she remembered. She remembered lying night after night, her arms crossed over her breasts so that her fingers dug into her shoulders, holding herself tightly, rocking herself. Tears might have brought relief, but she could only cry silently for fear of disturbing Matthew, so that her throat grew raw as the sobs strained and tore it.

She remembered trying to fight back: I am middle-aged, she had reasoned with herself; I know, as the young cannot know, that things pass, time heals, we do have it in us to survive, somehow or other, all of us. One day I shall be able to bear the idea of going to London again knowing Josh will not be waiting. The day will come when I shall no longer rake the face of strangers with my eyes, hoping that one of them might be Josh.

But it hadn't worked; again and again in sleep and in waking dreams she ran to the telephone expecting Josh's tender voice and heard again the hard and treacherous words. Or else she dreamed that he was standing in a doorway and seeing her stricken face said, 'Becky, you didn't believe it, did you? How could you ever be so untrusting? Haven't I told you again and again that my love is *for ever*? How can I convince you?' And he had sounded so hurt and reproachful that she was horrified at how she had wronged him. The relief of blaming herself instead of him swept through her and she ran across to him, clung to him. 'Silly old thing,' she heard him say as his arms went round her. 'As if I'd ever hurt you.' Then she woke up.

So each day she had to try to accept his treachery anew. But she could not grasp it. It was as if she was stranded in that moment of disbelief. And since that one central thing was incomprehensible, the world became an unreal place for her. I have no grip on it, she remembered thinking, I can't manage its ways. If people you love and trust can betray you without warning, then nothing is safe. So she had slipped into the blackness.

Oh yes, she remembered the terror of that great void, the total confusion there, as if the very centre of her being could not hold together. She remembered her thoughts getting more scattered and irrational, until in the end she was just asking herself childishly over and over again, why do such things happen, why did I let Josh con me into trusting him? And why, oh why, now that I know him for what he is, can I not cease to love him?

'I remember,' she said again to Matthew now.

'Oh, Becky,' he exclaimed suddenly, 'it's a dreadful thing to know you can't help the one you love when they're in such need of comfort. I knew I'd only add to your pain with my wretched, useless attempts to help. Yet I longed to help you, bring a little human warmth. But I knew that sort of comfort would come better from anyone but me. But there was only me.'

It was very quiet now. There was no sound except from the beating of the moth's wings as it thudded against the lamp on the mantelpiece.

'And I thought,' Matthew went on, 'I thought surely to God he'll feel some compassion. It's inhuman. He must want to give some little comfort, try to heal the wound he's inflicted. He must. I was sure of it. I watched the post as keenly as you did, my love, I listened for the telephone every bit as much. I suppose people would think it strange for a husband to want his wife to hear from her lover, but it isn't strange if he loves her and can't bear to see her suffer.'

'I understand.'

'Yes,' Matthew's voice was bitter now. 'There was only one person in the world who could help you. And he wouldn't. He deliberately chose not to. At the beginning, Becky, I really didn't feel much about him; it was as if your pain blocked out everything else. Then, as the days passed and the children came back and the term started and I saw you struggling, then I did begin to hate him. I used to watch you as you chatted politely, pale and composed and dead-eyed, and I thought, he's killed her, he's killed the real her. He might as well have taken a pick-axe to her while he was about it.'

He turned and looked at her directly in the eyes. 'And I knew he didn't deserve to live. I suddenly felt this great anger, overwhelming, I understood what drives men to kill, to seek vengeance, what drives them to war. I'd never understood it before, it had seemed incomprehensible to me that anyone should ever think that force solves anything.' He shrugged. 'Well, I suppose I still knew it doesn't *solve* anything, but I also knew the source of that feeling for the first time in my life.

'I watched you in those weeks before you went into hospital, watched you struggling against the blackness. God, how you fought, how you struggled. It was like watching a drowning kitten struggling. As I watched I thought, damn him, damn him, damn him. What sort of oafish brute can do this to anyone so gentle? Why should she suffer this death of the spirit while bastards like him inherit the earth?

'I remember a moment when you were sitting waiting to go into hospital, sitting on the bed with your suitcase packed alongside you, still uncomplaining, all the fires out, inanimate somehow as the few belongings that you were taking into hospital with you. Maybe that was the moment I realised how much I hated him. Then all those ghastly weeks, every time I visited you, I'd tell myself that the world would be a better place without him, a safer place, a sweeter place.'

For a moment they sat in silence, a silence broken only by the sound of the moth which was voyaging now between the bedside light and the standard lamp by the window, beating itself now against one, now against the other.

'Women should learn to hate,' Matthew said suddenly. 'It's better than turning all that anguish inwards.'

'You mean you learned it?'

'No, I don't think I could hate like that on my own account. I don't love myself enough, I suppose.'

She saw that he was dreadfully tired.

'Matthew,' she said. 'Shall we leave it for tonight? It's two o'clock. And you've so much to do tomorrow, so many people to see.'

'No,' he said with weary determination. 'You have the right to know it all. And now is the time to tell you.'

He hesitated. 'But the next bit is hard,' he added.

'Go on.'

'Forgive me, Becky. When you were away I was tidying up some things for you and I found his letters. No, don't say anything. I didn't read them all, but I did read some. I am sorry. I know it's shameful, but I wanted to understand and I thought I might read something that would help me to understand, so that I could help you when you came out.'

'It doesn't matter,' she said wearily. 'None of it was true anyway.'

She had burned them, those pages of lies. And with them she had committed to the flames her life-long belief that people don't change.

'And of course it didn't help me to help you. It only made me realise how impossible it all was. All those vows and protestations. How could I ever tell you that I loved you? Wouldn't all loving words be hateful to you now? He'd debased the language, hadn't he? There were no words left for me. I knew it would only be inflicting more pain to tell you that I loved you.'

'It's all right. You showed it in everything you did.'

He shrugged, as if dismissing the idea that his love was worth anything. But it was true, she thought, remembering how he watched over her, helped her back into the daylight. They had been kind, of course, in that place, that hospital where she had been taken at the end of the summer term. They had drugged her, they numbed the pain, not just the pain, everything. She had felt nothing, neither grief nor joy nor any interest in anyone. When Matthew brought news of Ben and Juliet, he might as well have been talking of the children of strangers, for all she cared.

Even when she had come back in the autumn, come back here, wearily convalescent, she had still been observing everything rather than feeling it, observing it furthermore through a curtain of mist. She could see that Matthew had made everything as welcoming as possible, and that Juliet and Ben were treating her like a special guest; she could see that they were all anxious not to worry her, fearful of hurting her, falling over themselves to be helpful. She seemed to have to pretend to be their mother, feign interest, fight lethargy, peer through the mist at them.

It had lifted; slowly every day the mist had cleared a little. The outlines of things had grown sharper. It was as if, when Josh had turned out all the lights, she had been left in a great darkness, but now, one by one, they were lighting little lamps and candles, her children were, and Matthew and her friends. Some gave just a tiny glow in the distance, but together they slowly relit her world and she was warmed by them. It wasn't a brilliant light any more, but it was enough to live by.

She had known, by the time they had set off to stay with Bill in Sri Lanka, that she was as restored as she ever would be, and she realised that it was Matthew who had made it so.

Yet the same kind and solicitous Matthew was saying now, 'While you were away, I had time to work things out. Time to plan.'

'Plan what?' she asked stupidly, because she couldn't believe it.

'To track him down,' Matthew said simply. 'If you love someone you need to know where they are. And if you hate someone you want to know their whereabouts too.'

Still she couldn't believe it. She realised she had not yet grasped the truth, the reality of what he had done.

'It wasn't just chance then? Matthew, I can't believe that you *arranged* to be in Sri Lanka—'

'Oh no. That was pure chance. I set myself to find out as much about him as I could. It wasn't difficult. Nobody suspects a schoolmaster inquiring about big companies. There are all sorts of genuine reasons why he should. And I read anything that might be useful in the financial pages. That's how I read about the takeover of Bill's firm, you remember.'

She smiled for the first time. 'I remember,' she said, 'being very surprised that you knew about it.'

'I'd no plan,' Matthew reflected and there was a detachment in his voice now, almost as if he was examining the conduct of a stranger. 'I just wanted to keep him in my sights. Like a man with a gun, you know. He'd had power over you, Becky, and he'd dreadfully abused it. Now I had a sense of power over him because he didn't know that I had him in my sights.'

'But you can't have known that he was coming out to see Bill?'

'Oh, no, no. That was pure luck. I wanted to accept Bill's invitation because I thought the change would do you good, but I never for one moment thought that Grover would come out there. You remember, Bill just said some director was coming out? He didn't even tell us his name.'

'Oh, I remember that. I remember it all. The shock when they both arrived, everything. Then I seemed able to accept it. I thought, it's all right, I can manage this, it's in the past. I did truly feel that, Matthew.'

'Well, I didn't. I saw it as my opportunity, my one and only chance. I had to take it.'

He went and stood by the window, staring out into the warm night. Becky watched him. It was very still, not the faintest breath of wind stirred the curtains. The only movement in the room was the swift shadow of the moth against the lampshade as it circled the bulb beneath.

'He liked me, you know, Becky. Well, maybe that's the wrong word. I expect he thought of me as an impecunious schoolmaster not worth much, a harmless but pleasant enough guy, not to be taken seriously, but certainly better to talk to than Bill. Clearly the two of them were like chalk and cheese. And I think they'd had a pretty big disagreement about something as well.'

'So Corinne said.'

'Did she?'

He didn't seem particularly interested in what Corinne had said, anxious only to finish his story. He spoke as if driven forward by the compulsion of it.

'So he turned to me as the only other chap he could talk to. We were together quite a bit on that excursion.'

'Yes, I noticed that. I thought you were just trying to help me by not letting us have to be alone together, him and me.'

'Well, there was that too. So you see when I followed him on top of Sigiriya and then caught up with him when we were both out of sight of the rest of you, he turned to me as anyone might turn to a friend they trusted. He held out his camera. I think he was just going to ask me to take a photograph of him while he stood on a ledge. It was quite a wide ledge, there was no danger, but on a photo it would look impressive, to be standing there with apparently just a chasm immediately behind.'

He stopped talking and turned to her. 'Then he looked at me. It must have been written in my face, Becky, what I intended to do. I saw his expression change. It seemed to last a very long time, that second in which he knew. There was nothing he could do. He just waited. We looked at each other and there was on his face a look of total disbelief, utter bewilderment, as if he was saying, why should this man whom I trust do this thing to me? I recognised that expression. You had that look on your face after he rang you. And I thought, now at last he knows what it's like to be on the receiving end of treachery.'

She felt suddenly dizzy. She got up, went over to the window and breathed deeply. She tried to think of anything, anything to restore some kind of normality.

'At least it was quick,' she said at last, 'the way he died.'

'Who knows how long it lasts, that second between life and death?' Matthew asked. 'Perhaps that same bewilderment and disbelief lasts for all eternity. I hope so,' he added with quiet savagery.

Could this really be Matthew speaking, Becky wondered with disbelief. Yet it all made sense, that Grover should be a victim of the treachery he had always somehow admired, fall prey to the killer instinct he prided himself on possessing, feel in his own back the knife of the man he trusted.

Still she couldn't believe Matthew's part in it all: that he should have been the agent, the angel of vengeance. That was what didn't make sense. She began walking about the room, touching everyday things, familiar things, trying to touch reality. She let her hand run along the arm of the chair, feel the roughness of the bedspread, the silkiness of the shade of the standard lamp, beneath which the moth was lying dead.

'Then after you'd done what you did, you just walked back and joined us?'

'Yes, I strolled about a bit.'

'But you showed no sign. Nothing. I suppose that's why I can't believe it. How didn't I notice anything? I do notice things. I realised straight away tonight. I just knew.'

'You knew tonight because I was anxious. And you felt my anxiety, you guessed. But, you see, on Sigiriya I knew nobody had seen, you were way out of sight, so of course I'd no reason to feel anything. There was nothing to worry about,' he added casually.

Nothing to worry about, when you've just killed a man? On this occasion, she thought suddenly, murder to Matthew, like adultery to Grover, simply didn't seem to matter as long as it was committed abroad and nobody found out.

'But there was no need,' she said. 'Oh, Matthew, there was no need. I was better, I was over it—'

'It was nothing to do with that. It was simple justice. Because a victim forgives a criminal it doesn't mean he shouldn't be punished.'

'You risked being punished yourself,' she said. It struck her for the first time that, in entrusting her with his story, he had entrusted her with his life. Grover would never have put such a weapon into anyone's hands. Ah well, perhaps Matthew was a better judge of whom to trust than she had been.

The sky was beginning to lighten. From the silver birch tree outside their window came the first sounds of the dawn chorus.

'Tell me one thing, Becky,' Matthew said. 'Did he know, when he did what he did on the telephone, that you had once before been subject to depression, had managed to get over it, but only just?'

'Yes. We exchanged medical histories,' she said.

'So he knew what he was risking?'

'Yes, he knew. But I expect that, once he'd decided to dispose of me, it wouldn't matter to him any more if he damaged me or not,' she added, remembering what Corinne had said.

'There's only one disadvantage to murder,' Matthew said bitterly. 'And that is that you can't do it to the same person twice.'

Chapter Twelve

Bill had left, taking Juliet to the station with him, Matthew and Ben had gone over to school. Becky steeled herself to ring Corinne and tell her that it was all off.

She couldn't work with her now, she knew that. She had realised it last night, or rather this morning. For there had been no night. They hadn't gone to bed, she and Matthew; they had drunk coffee, they had had showers, and then they had roused the household for an early breakfast. And, as she did all these things, it was borne in on her that it was quite unthinkable to work with Corinne now, to accept the trust and friendship of this woman whom Matthew had widowed.

She remembered how she had cried out, rejecting the guilt of it when Matthew had first told her. Yes, that had been her instinctive reaction. But when she had thought about it she realised that she *was* guilty, it was all her fault. If she hadn't met Grover, hadn't loved Grover, Matthew would never have done this thing. Unwittingly she had caused his death, had contributed to the widowing of Corinne.

Wearily she finished clearing the kitchen after they had all gone, and made her way to the study. How different from what she had been planning just a few short hours ago, she thought as she stood in the doorway. She could see the pages of her poem still spread out on her desk, and there too were Corinne's drawings. She remembered how she had longed to get back to work, how she had counted the hours. It seemed like a different person in a different world, a world full of hope and energy. She was tired now. She laid her head down on the desk; tired, tired, tired, she thought. Oh, to be in Enderby, to be alone there, to be walking the hills, to feel the rising love of it, the reassurance, the strength of it. Just not to be here.

The telephone rang. She stared at it, not wanting to answer, but unable to bear the noise of it. She picked it up.

'Hello,' Corinne said. 'I thought you were never going to ring, so I rang you.'

'Oh, Corinne, I'm sorry.'

'That's all right. Don't sound so tragic. I know you've got family and stuff to get off. It's easier for me.'

'It's not that . . .'

'Well?'

'Oh, Corinne, I'm sorry. I can't go ahead with this, with the book . . .'

There was silence, then a very quiet and subdued Corinne asked, 'What are you trying to tell me?'

'That we can't work together. I'm sorry if I misled you—'

'You don't like them after all, do you, now that you've had a chance to look at them again?' There was an awful pain in Corinne's voice.

'No, no, it's not like that.'

'You said you loved them. You said they were just what you needed.'

'I know, and I meant it.'

'Why did you say all those things about them? I don't understand.'

The raw edge of pain in Corinne's usually cheerful voice was unbearable to hear. I'm treating her as Grover did me, Becky thought.

'Listen, Corinne, I swear to you it has nothing to do with the pictures or the poems. There's quite a different reason.'

Still it sounded like treachery. She knew, better than anyone, how much the pictures mattered to Corinne; she was betraying her, undermining her. But she couldn't tell her the truth; it wasn't hers to tell. That too would be a betrayal.

'I can't explain,' she went on, hating the sound of her own voice. 'I would love to work with you, truly I would, but it's impossible. It has to do with the past. Please believe that.'

There was silence. Oh, it seemed like a silence of understanding. She prayed that Corinne had understood.

There was a sudden explosion of rage from the other end of the line. 'You are exasperating,' Corinne told her furiously. 'Bloody hell. The past is the past. And *you* were the one who told me to use the future properly and forget the past and—'

'I know, I know. But you see it has to do with Grover—'

'You still think I pushed him? Is that it?'

'Oh no, no.'

'Even if I had it wouldn't have made any difference to our work. But I didn't, actually.'

'No, it's not that. It's just that we're linked by him—'

'Listen, Becky, just you listen to me,' Corinne interrupted. 'I don't think of myself as Grover's widow any more. I'm just me. Do me a favour and stop thinking of yourself as his ex-mistress. I don't think of you like that. You're Becky Portman and I'm the illustrator of your poems. And that matters. It matters a damned sight more than if you went to bed with my dead husband.'

Becky hesitated. If only she could tell Corinne. No, loyalty forbade it. Yet there it lay, like a shadow between them.

'Are you still there?' Corinne demanded to know.

'Yes.'

'Good. I wish I could think of some way of convincing you. Look, Becky, if I'd died first, do you think Grover would have gone about thinking of himself as my widower?'

One doesn't say that, Becky thought. You say a woman is a man's widow but you never say a man is a woman's widower. They are not equivalent words. She hadn't thought of that before. She thought about it now; words always had a wonderful power to distract her mind. And clarify it, too, of course.

'It's true,' she said, 'I'd never realised. You say a woman is John Smith's widow, but you wouldn't say a man was Mary Smith's widower.'

'Who is Mary Smith?' Corinne asked, baffled.

Becky laughed. She went on laughing.

'Are you all right?' Corinne asked. 'What's so funny?'

'You are,' Becky said. 'But right with it. You're right. I was wrong about the past. It doesn't matter. Oh, Corinne, you're right.'

'Of course I'm right. It's something I learned when Grover died. I realised that I'd always thought of myself as his wife, then his widow. It's wrong, we shouldn't think like that. Don't think of yourself just as existing in relationship to some man, dead or alive, Becky. You exist in your own right. You're strong in your own right.'

It was like a burden being lifted, the relief of it. And dead or alive, Corinne had said. It wasn't just about Grover; it was about Matthew too. What he had done had been his own choice. He didn't have to do it, whatever had happened before. Besides, hadn't he gone to work this morning, quite composed? The routine of his work would take over, he put this thing into the past, so why should she let it hang over her future? Her life was her own; she mustn't let it be spoiled by something done by a man who happened to be her husband. She'd got it all wrong.

'We'd better ring Mrs Doughtyman,' Corinne was saying. 'And tell her to expect us on Thursday.'

'I did that. I rang her last week and arranged that we'd both be there at half-past two. I was going to ring her to cancel it.'

'Well, you needn't bother now, need you? Shall we meet first? You could come here, but it's probably quicker if I meet you at Paddington. We could have a snack and check everything before we go to see her.'

Train to Paddington, Becky thought, and no Josh waiting. Oh, no.

'Oh yes, Corinne,' she said. 'That would be fine. I'll look out for you at the barrier.'

When she had put the telephone down, she went straight back to her desk. The tiredness had miraculously vanished. I don't need to creep back to Enderby, she thought, to strengthen myself. It's in me, part of me now, there all the time: a central core which once I thought could not hold. She felt the excitement of it, like the premonition of a poem, and the sense of certainty that it would work out although she didn't know how until she had written it.

She looked again at Corinne's drawing of the tree, which happened to be on the top of the pile. It was amazing how Corinne had caught the gnarled look of it, the grim look, the determined look. You could feel the roots taking the strain as the wind tore at its branches, sense that they would not give, embedded as they were in rock. And there was something else, not in the picture, something which she had until now forgotten: that in the spring the bare and spiky branches were suddenly, astonishingly, radiant with blossom.

A selection of quality fiction
from Headline